Is he alive, or is he dead?
Freight train running all thru my head . . .

I started to write those words. I stopped, raised my eyes slowly from the paper, and stared at the dark wood paneling. The air was moving, almost whispering behind me, only not making any noise. It brought with it this sudden, incredible urge to look behind me.

I stared and stared at the game-closet door, which was open just a crack. The wind banged around outside, and in the basement it started to sound like moaning. The moan got really intense, and the game-closet door sucked almost closed and then pulled out to two inches from shut again. I watched that door moving by itself a few times, and all of a sudden I knew it wasn't moving by itself. I knew somebody had the handle from the inside. Somebody who had been watching me a few seconds earlier. I stood up, silently gripping my guitar by the neck, with my eyes staring at that door like they could fry a hole through it. As soon as I stood up, the moving stopped. The door stayed about an inch from closed as I crept slowly toward it. I stopped about ten feet from it, wondering what to do next. I thought of rushing it, and the vision that Ryan had talked about shot through my head: a couple of bloody sneakers swinging out and hitting me in the eyes from where Chris's body hung from the ceiling light. I quietly walked to the door, got my hand around the knob, and pulled very slowly. . . .

The Body of Christopher Creed

Also by Carol Plum-Ucci

THE
Body OF
Christopher
Creed

Carol Plum-Ucci

HARCOURT, INC.
Orlando Austin New York San Diego London

Copyright © 2000 by Carol Plum-Ucci
Author interview copyright © 2008 by Carol Plum-Ucci
Reader's guide copyright © 2008 by Houghton Mifflin Harcourt
Publishing Company

All rights reserved. No part of this publication may be reproduced
or transmitted in any form or by any means, electronic or mechanical,
including photocopy, recording, or any information storage and retrieval
system, without permission in writing from the publisher.

Requests for permission to make copies of any part of the work should
be submitted online at www.harcourt.com/contact or mailed to the following
address: Permissions Department, Houghton Mifflin Harcourt Publishing
Company, 6277 Sea Harbor Drive, Orlando, Florida 32887-6777.

www.HarcourtBooks.com

First Harcourt paperback edition 2008

The Library of Congress has cataloged the hardcover edition as follows:
Plum-Ucci, Carol, 1957–
The body of Christopher Creed/Carol Plum-Ucci.
p. cm.
Summary: Torey Adams, a high school junior with a seemingly perfect life,
struggles with doubts and questions surrounding the mysterious disappearance
of the class outcast.
[1. Missing persons—Fiction. 2. Peer pressure—Fiction. 3. Emotional problems—
Fiction. 4. High schools—Fiction. 5. Schools—Fiction.] I. Title.
PZ7.P7323Bo 2000
[Fic]—dc21   99-44212
ISBN 978-0-15-202388-1
ISBN 978-0-15-206386-3 pb

Text set in Sabon MT
Designed by Lori McThomas Buley

H G F E D C B A

Printed in the United States of America

*This is a work of fiction. All the names, characters, places, organizations, and events
portrayed in this book are products of the author's imagination. Any resemblance to
any organization, event, or actual person, living or dead, is unintentional.*

To Ellen . . .
& Sara, Colleen, Merc, Nathan,
Krystle (rest in peace), Amber, Joey,
Dave, Ricky, Jon, Brandon, and all
the other teenagers who have so
richly blessed my life . . .

The Body of Christopher Creed

One

I had hoped that a new start away from Steepleton would make my junior year seem like a hundred years ago, rather than just one.

Granted, senior year is not a great year to be switching schools, especially if you played football, baseball, had a decent blues band going in your basement, and had known the same kids since forever. I kept telling myself at first, *Hey, going to boarding school will be like leaving for college a year early. It's cool.* But that's a hard argument to hold on to when you're looking at people whose average age is fifteen, and when we're still living under a 10:00 P.M. weekend curfew in the dorm. At first it was a weird change. But staying in Steepleton after all that had happened would have been weirder.

Mostly Rothborne has been good. It wasn't more than a couple months before I could actually concentrate in class and get decent grades again. I could spot guys from the dorm as I walked into the dining hall, and I could pull up a seat next to them and goof around. I asked a girl to the movies once, and she said yes. Nobody stares at me here. Nobody is suspicious of me. That part is gone.

I'm not saying that life has been perfect. There's the roommate thing. Cartright is pretty cool—he's a crew maniac who also loves pranks, embellishing his own girl stories, and shooting the bull late at night with me. But he's got his own set of ideas—like when to finally nod off and put out the light. And if you have nightmares, flashbacks, and other sleep screwups, it's not easy lying awake in the dark.

While I had many days of cracking into campus trees from zero sleep during the fall, this spring I've only had a couple. In some ways I'm just your basic guy again. I do have a ponytail, and most guys around here have nubs, which is more the style, if there is a style these days. Around Easter I took to adding little goofy things to it. A seagull feather, a clamshell on a suede leash, a rabbit's foot. Some girl asked me last week if I was running a dead-animal farm. I felt my face turn all red, but deep inside I was kind of happy about that remark. She was the first person at Rothborne to take my meaning. Well, sort of. I like animals and all, but I'm not obsessed with animals.

I don't let myself get too crazy when people start asking questions, like, "So why'd you come as a senior?" or, "You could pass for a model if you'd cut that hair, so why don't you?" It's always the girls who ask the stuff. Most guys are content to accept you just because you're cool and don't make waves.

But about a week ago this guy down the hall from me, Leo, barged into my room when I had the door shut. People sort of avoid Leo, though it's kind of hard to explain why. He's a tall guy with brown hair who looks like everybody else. He likes to hang out in the union and shoot the bull. He's just a little "sideways," if I had to describe him. He always talks about girls, but he stares at guys.

He came into my room without knocking, and I clicked out of my screen without even looking to see who was there. I should have known it was him, because most people would knock if your door was totally shut, but Leo never cared.

"You wanna go to dinner, Torey?" I could feel him looking, though I was watching my screen, scared to death my latest letter would fly back up there, just because I didn't want him to see it, and then my secrets of Steepleton would get air-waved to the entire student body. Only Cartright knew bits and pieces.

"No, I'm . . . doing something. Thanks."

He wandered in and landed on Cartright's bed, and his look turned into that stare that some guys don't like.

"Nobody wants to go to dinner," he said, picking up Cartright's naked-lady alarm clock, which Cartright insists helps him concentrate on his physics.

"Go by yourself," I said, faking a stretch to counter my thumping heart. "Or ask Burke or Melefanti. They'd eat five times a day, if they could."

I wanted to flip a game up on the screen but was scared of my spastic streak. I knew that letter would come flying back if I touched anything.

"You play that guitar pretty good." He jerked his head toward my Ovation.

"Thanks."

Bunch of kids got to ogling about my guitar playing this spring, when I finally started playing for other people again. That shocked me, because my friends in Steepleton had been used to it and didn't usually make a big deal. My music teacher here asked to record a couple songs I wrote. At first I thought he was being nice, but then I would hear the stuff other kids in my music class wrote and I would think, *Puke, that's so . . . doofus and* normal.

3

But my songs were too wrapped up in Steepleton. I wasn't ready for it if someone happened to see through all my symbolism.

I could feel Leo staring.

"Somebody said you used to play football," he said.

"Yeah."

"You don't look like a football player. What'd you do to lose all that weight? Get sick?"

I wondered who told him about football. Sometimes Cartright said I mumbled in my sleep. Maybe I had made football commands in my sleep.

"Yeah, I got sick," I mumbled. "Something like that."

"I hear your dad owns a huge engineering firm and your mom's a lawyer."

He watched me, and I tried not to squirm. If I let on that he'd miffed me, I would at least have to let fly with the fact that everyday questions miffed me. But I was starting to realize that I was sort of an unusual case. Lots of kids had lived with only one parent, and if they did have both, usually it was just one who had the great job.

"Your house is, like, three hundred years old, right?" he asked.

"Right. I think Melefanti's in his room . . ."

He didn't take the hint, and I watched him turn Cartright's clock over and over in his hands. Cartright would kill Leo if he saw him handling his naked-lady clock. Leo put it down and stood up, moved toward the window. He lifted my guitar case, spinning it this way and that.

I could feel an ache shoot into my knuckles, remembering . . . *Set of nostrils, huge grin, dual streams of blood closing the space between them, grin collapsing over red teeth.* This aging memory that somehow crept up on me

4

every couple months still hadn't lost its zip. In one sense Cartright was a great roommate for an only child like me, because he didn't normally touch my stuff. But somebody around here was bound to pick up one of my guitars without asking.

"You can play it if you want," I said, but my voice cracked.

I saw the case slowly sink down until it sat on one of his sneakers. He was smiling, watching me big-time.

"You're just saying that. You look like you don't want anybody touching this guitar. Why not?"

People didn't like Leo. I guessed he pried into some guys like this, and stared, and it got them thinking he was gay. Not that gayness had to be a hot issue around here. There were two other gay guys in our dorm. But they were, like, Hey, *I'm* gay, *so, like,* deal *with it.* So there wasn't much to deal with. But you could sense that Leo was struggling with something, and it made you struggle, too.

His watching me—it did something to my insides. I wanted to get up and hug him, something. I didn't. I just watched him back, wondering about myself, these twitches. *Maybe you're gay, Torey. Maybe you're gay, and Leo is gay, and that's what's bothering you.*

I couldn't think if I'd ever had a gay thought before. But all of a sudden it was me staring at him, and he was looking away. He slowly put the guitar case down where he'd found it, and stared at the wallpaper on my screen.

"What were you doing before I came in here?"

"You ask a lot of questions," I muttered, gripping the mouse in my lap. "Do people ever tell you that?"

"Yeah. All the time."

"So why do you ask so many questions, then?"

5

I watched him shrug, staring at my screen like there was something infatuating about it.

"People used to say I was weird," he said. "I used to care. But I don't anymore. People shouldn't care, people shouldn't use words like *weird* once you hit junior year. Everyone's weird. That's the way I look at it."

I watched him. Something about being weird had made me switch schools. His words got ahold of something inside of me, and all of a sudden I wasn't so terrified of him. He came toward me, and I didn't move, didn't think about what he was going to do. But he didn't touch me, and when he didn't, I gathered it was a good thing. Somehow I knew down deep inside what was up.

He reminded me a lot of Chris Creed. I hadn't said more than two words to Chris Creed since I punched him out in sixth grade. But when a kid sits behind you every day since kindergarten, sits across from you in Sunday school, belongs to your pool, annoys you in Cub Scouts, and throws a thousand balls over your head in Little League, you don't have to like him in order to love him. Sometimes I thought I would give anything to hear from Creed again. It was Chris's and Leo's similarities that were making me tingle, not anything about sex.

But this tingle, it was making me wish I could rip out my memory bank just so I could connect with people, without the stupid thoughts weaving my stomach into a hellhole, like someone out here would actually ask me some insane question, *So, you fell on a guy's decaying body in the woods?*

It's not Chris standing here, it's Leo, I told myself, but in a real sense he *was* Creed. He was an out-there type of guy who could make you uncomfortable, make you want to avoid him. He was hitting ALT+ESC, so he could see for himself what I was up to.

I hit the OFF button before I had a chance to try out my spastic streak in an ALT+ESC fight with him. He just looked at me again, like there wasn't the slightest little thing wrong with what he had just done.

"Leo, let me explain something to you," I heard myself say. "When you go into a room, you knock first. If you start asking people questions and they start tilting back in their chairs, it means they don't want to talk about it. It means if you look at something on their computer screens, they're likely to knock your brains out with a baseball bat."

"Jesus . . ." He stared at me for all he was worth. "I just wanted to see what you were up to, that's all."

"Don't give me this I'm-so-innocent routine," I muttered. "You know you bug people. You've probably been beaten on your whole life. And you've probably been letting yourself off the hook lately by saying that once you got to be a junior it wouldn't matter. Well, you're a *senior,* Leo. It does matter. You're in my personal space, so get out of it. Get out of my room. And next time you come in, knock first, got it?"

He backed up, looking all astonished and giving me a few more *Jesus Christ*s. I didn't let my eyes wander off of him, though it was hard. I had to keep telling myself that Dr. Fahdi would have said that it's okay, it's healthy, it's good for me. I told myself that people like Leo need you to get tough, or they don't get it. Once the door was shut and he was gone, I told myself the truth, which was that I had been talking to Leo but seeing Creed. And Leo wasn't nearly as bad. I had just treated another person like shit.

Torey, you leave home to escape some stupid thing that makes zero sense. Jesus Christ, are you ever going to get over this? My fingers were still shaking as I hit the ON

7

button and watched the computer go through its steps until the "document recovered" bar flashed on the screen. I relaxed some and looked over the letter, making sure none of the characters had been wiped out.

> *Dear Alex Healy,*
> *There was a kid in my town named Chris Creed. I wrote the attachment about his disappearance. If the name Chris Creed doesn't mean anything to you, then forget I even bothered you. You can hit "delete" right now. Or if you're into reading stories about people's lives, I don't have anything to hide and you might get into it. It's about everyone you know.*

I dragged my eyes out of the middle of the letter and moved the mouse slowly up to the message window and clicked on "attach document." I saw it there—Creed.doc— and the mouse crept down to highlight the file I had not looked at in a year.

Are you ready to go back, Torey? Two years ago you were happy and innocent and oh-so-fucking normal. Are you ready to find the point where you got crushed, look it in the eye, and understand?

"Creed.doc" was still highlighted. Writing it was supposed to bring me some quote-unquote *healing,* at least that's what Dr. Fahdi had said. Maybe it did; who knows? I got a load off my chest. But I was looking for other things, more important things, like the peace you get when things make sense and life seems fair. I never got that peace. Some nights I would remember and write and remember and write, and I was sure I was just being Dr. Frankenstein, trying to re-create a dead human. The dead never come back like they were. Some nights I got convinced I was creating a monster.

I took it in for Dr. Fahdi when I was finished, and I remember him holding all those pages and pretending his arm was weighed down—or maybe it actually was weighed down. And I remember he said to me, "That's an amazing amount of writing for a young man your age, Torey." And I said, "Yeah, well, I got a load off my chest." It wasn't like I had a whole lot of other stuff to do.

But you finish something like that, and the truth strikes you. I knew then that laying out the truth for a shrink wasn't enough. I had to get out of Steepleton. You can't find your life, or your peace, in the middle of a bezillion eyes staring at you.

Creed.doc had been sent across the Internet about eighty times, but the last time I actually looked at the file was when I ran it through the spell-checker before handing it over to Dr. Fahdi. Maybe I hadn't needed to look at it since. Maybe I used to remember every single word. Maybe, finally, I was starting to forget.

I arrowed up and shut the window. The letter bobbed around in front of me, all hazy and floating.

Alex Healy, what I'm hoping is that the name Chris Creed does mean something to you. That probably means that, somehow, I have struck gold.

There's nothing unusual about a runaway these days. There's also not much original about a suicide or a murder. The weirdest fact about Chris Creed's disappearance was that he was just plain gone. There was no trail of blood, not even a drop of blood. No piece of clothing on the side of the road. No runaway bus-ticket stub. No money missing from his bank account. No empty bottle that had been filled with pills the day before he disappeared. No missing razor blades. No nothing. The only thing we knew was that Chris Creed was not abducted

9

compulsively by a stranger—because there was a note, which was written at least twenty-four hours before he turned up missing.

Steepleton could have dealt with a runaway, a suicide, an abduction, or even a murder. Other towns survive them. But there are two things our town couldn't cope with, the first being a very strange mess that occurs when the weirdest kid in town suddenly disappears. He's gone, but his weirdness seems to linger. It grabs at the most normal and happy kids, like some sort of sick joke. And then it's those *people who are acting weird.* The other thing the town can't face up to is the black hole itself— the thing that comes out of nowhere and eats a kid alive and doesn't leave a hair from his head.

You can't have a funeral, because there's no body and no evidence that he actually died. But to push for some big-time Unsolved Mysteries *hunt,* a town has to feel sorry for how they mistreated the weird guy who's gone. To feel genuinely sorry, you have to be honest. And Steepleton needs its lies like a toad needs bugs.

To hear some people tell it, I saw Creed dead. I saw him dead, and it made me crazy. There are other people who add to that version of the story—that I *actually* helped kill him. They say I can't face what I saw, or what I did, *depending on who's telling the story.* They would all say I'm on this giant denial trip if they ever guessed I was trying to find him. Or they'd say that I'm trying to prove my innocence with a search that I know won't lead anywhere. I am *looking* for Creed, and I admit my bolts were not screwed in so tight for a while there. But I've never told myself any lies about it. And I'm sure Chris Creed is alive.

I guess it's up to you to decide whether I'm nuts or normal, and since this is just the Internet, I don't give a rip what strangers think. It's bad enough to put up with what some of my neighbors think. Steepleton is like most other small towns out there, I guess. Small-town people live up each other's butts, and some people will tell stories about who stinks the worst. I wonder if small towns are America's final kick in the ass insofar as prejudice and judgment are concerned. There are black families in Steepleton, a Japanese family, a couple Saudis, one family of rich Pakistanis. It's not a racial thing like my mom coped with, growing up there. But it's there, part of the little-town mentality, that thing that makes people want to sniff out neighbors who are weird or less fortunate, and talk about those people's bad luck to establish their own goodness. There are also some people who are very sympathetic about what happened to me, and they have been pretty cool.

So when I left, it wasn't entirely to get away from small-town smell-my-butts. I left to get away from death and the fear of ghosts. Small towns grow out of the woods, and the woods are dark and scary. I did see death, and I have seen a ghost. But neither of them was Creed. I will swear to that until I die, though there will always be those feebs who don't believe me. It's their problem, not mine.

Alex Healy, if you are who I think you are, everything I have said in this letter and everything you're going to read in this story will make perfect sense. If it makes no sense, then just write me off as another Internet loony who's suffering from post-traumatic stress disorder. That part has been medically established.

Three people will bear up to the truth in this attachment. My mother—not that a mom counts for much while standing in her kid's defense. There's a girl, too, who's got a reputation as being, well, not so upright.

11

And then there's the town's chief of police, an African American who walked the beat in Atlantic City for four-teen years before becoming chief in Steepleton. His name is Douglas Rye, and he became chief about two weeks after Chris Creed disappeared. He read this story and will vouch for every word.

I dropped the window down again, took a breath of cool air, and hit "attach." I stared at the name Creed.doc. It was like the door to a tomb. All I had to do was hit "restore," double click, and the stone could get rolled away. Rereading it away from Steepleton might do a lot for me, but it wasn't as important as finding Chris Creed. I decided, *Attach now, read later. You will find your peace when you find Creed out there somewhere.*

But I knew *later* was no further off than when I hit "send." I was ready to go back to death in the woods. It had taken me a year of being away, but I felt my sympathy rising for myself at sixteen, back when I hadn't written much more than a book report and a few dumb songs. I had to see what I was like back then.

Alex Healy, I swear the following account contains no lies. It is one-hundred-percent accurate. People can love their lies, tell their lies, believe their own lies until hell pays a visit. But this whole story is true. That's the point of it.

> *Victor "Torey" Adams,*
> *Formerly Mr. All-American Football Kicker,*
> *Blond Geeky Haircut for Little League*
> *and All That, Formerly of Steepleton,*
> *Southern New Jersey*

Two

Being that Sunday is the first day of the week, I guess Sunday was a fitting day for my life to start to crash. I guess in some people's minds Sunday is an unusual day for bad luck because it's a religious day, and people's lives should get better on a religious day, or at least remain equalized until Monday. I guess those people's lives change on a Tuesday or a Friday or something.

I like to think of it as starting on a Sunday. And that has always made me think it had something to do with God, though I still can't say what, for sure. I have my ideas.

There are plenty of people out there who would probably ask, "How can you imagine God in a foul bunch of happenings, you pig?" I wouldn't like to answer that, except to say that I don't imagine He was up there asleep.

I ended up in the front pew at church—me and my best friend, Alex Arrington. It was a small church, but most of the people in Steepleton went there and made their kids go there. We'd each had the standard argument with our parents—that while we had nothing against God, we didn't learn anything, because church was too boring, and they should not be forcing us to go now that we were juniors. I don't know how Alex's parents combated him. But my dad said he stood by his answer from when I had argued, "Now that I'm a sophomore" and "Now that I'm a freshman." I don't remember those arguments. But arguing with our families about any religious matter always seemed kind of purposeless.

Around Steepleton people could quote scripture, and what do you say back to that? *So, who says the Bible is true?* I wouldn't even push it that far. But I would think, *If the Bible is so magical that people around here quote it all the time, how come it can't perform the magic that would keep church from being boring?* Whatever. We always waited until the last minute to go in. And since nobody likes to sit up front in a church, if you came in last, you were stuck in the front pew.

I looked down the row past Alex to Ryan Bowen and the Kyle twins, Eddie and Pat. Sitting still for an hour was pretty much an endurance test for those three, probably more so than football practice. They're too crazy to sit still, and I don't think they know how to use their thoughts for entertainment value. I don't think those three ever had a thought that went much deeper than, *What's to eat?*

Reverend Harmon started with the morning announcements, but my brain was already hooked into the stained-glass window beyond Pat Kyle's head.

The stained glass had been there as long as I could remember, but recently it had started bugging me. I had heard somewhere not long ago that Christ was crucified naked. But in this stained glass, and in every other crucifixion picture I had ever seen, Christ was wearing this little cloth, like a loincloth. It was as if the story had been added to, so as not to disgust people too much. I just got to thinking about that, I don't know why. I wondered if it was a

14

good thing to change a story because the truth was too disgusting. I even asked Reverend Harmon when he came over one night to visit my dad. He said that the truth was less important, in this case, than the impact the truth would have on people.

I remember it gave me a twitch when he said that. I'm not sure why, I mean, it was bad enough to see Jesus hanging there, without Him being naked. But it struck me that the Church is always saying you shouldn't lie, and here was one. Pastor Harmon makes dumb puns all the time, and he said to me, "Torey, it's not a lie. It's a *cover-up*."

Alex's church bulletin caught my eye. He was writing on it: *You're staring at my ear.*

He handed me his pen, and I wrote on mine, *Above your ear.*

He glanced over the Kyle twins' heads, at the air, at the stained-glass window, at the ceiling, and he sighed.

He wrote next, *What are you thinking about, O abnormal one?*

After a minute I decided on, *Band. Who's coming over to strum'n'drum?*

My friends had some clue I was abnormal, though they didn't know the full extent of it. They knew I could stare off into space sometimes and not be hearing them until they shoved me. But they didn't know I could have long conversations with myself about whether Christ should be wearing a loincloth or not. I handed Alex back the pen, thinking I was a fine one to talk about the Church lying.

He jerked his head three times down the row, to mean Ryan, Pat, and Eddie. Ryan was the drummer in our group. Pat and Eddie doubled on synthesizer and lead guitar, whichever we needed, and Alex played bass. I was better at acoustic guitar but could switch off to lead. We were almost good enough to have gigs, but not quite.

"We had, uh . . . something has happened," Reverend Harmon said over our heads, and I guessed he was finished with the announcements. My eyes floated up off my sneakers as he went on. "Some of you know already that the son of Ron and Sylvia Creed—Christopher Creed—disappeared from school on Thursday and hasn't been seen since."

I felt myself, like, float and drop for a second. There had been some talk in school Friday morning—because a cop car had showed up outside the main entrance, and two police officers were seen going in with Mr. and Mrs. Creed. No announcements had been made over the loudspeaker, and gossip came down from who-knows-where-it-started that Chris had run away. It was just kids talking, along the lines of *"Where did that twerp get the nerve to take off?" "With his el-strict-o parents, who would have thought he had the guts?" "If I were him I would have run away from this school ten years ago, man. Nobody ever. cut him a break."*

Reverend Harmon went on: "The Creeds have asked to say a word to all of you this morning, and I certainly think that's appropriate . . . very appropriate."

I heard the clicking of high heels on the tile floor. It was loud. But Mrs. Creed always had that loud, here-I-come sort of stepping. I saw out of the corner of my eye that Mr. Creed was with her, but his rubber soles hardly made any noise. He was a silent-but-deadly type of grown-up you would no sooner speak to than kick. He was stiff and stern, almost like an old man caught in a middle-aged guy's body. Mrs. Creed did all the talking, usually. He did all the frowning.

Even that day, she came up to the podium while he stood behind her. She cleared her throat a time or two.

"First we'd like to thank all of you who helped search the woods and the creek area yesterday," Mrs. Creed said in

16

this quieter-than-usual voice. "We thank you for . . . putting our worst fears to rest. We still believe our Christopher is out there . . . somewhere . . .

Meaning he wasn't *dead*. I tried to look at her, but it was hard. By Friday afternoon this rumor had leaked out that he might have committed suicide, not run away. Probably a lot of kids thought that was really sad, but you heard loudly from the ones who thought it was a riot. At football practice guys were placing bets on how he might have done it. It ran the range of taking an overdose of cafeteria food to swallowing a bunch of plastic explosives he made with his chemistry set. Someone said he had sex with Mary Carol Banes, who could stand to lose about four hundred pounds, and systematically crushed himself. Stupid stuff. It's like there were too many one-liners about it, and I wondered if I was the only one who kept wanting to flinch. I had this thought as I came out of the locker room that night: *This kid who's been around since kindergarten is, like, missing, and it's this matter of principle that we have to laugh? What is up?*

"We really appreciate all you've done, but we still need your help. If anyone knows of any reason why . . . Christopher would run away . . ." Mrs. Creed paused. The silence was followed by this huge shifting of bodies in the pews. I guess it was because even Mrs. Creed was circling around the circumstances, which were more than weird.

Chris had supposedly been in the library on Thursday, using the Internet. After school, when the principal, Mr. Ames, was downloading his e-mail, he got a note signed *Chris Creed*. At first they thought it was a runaway note, but by Friday they were saying it could be a suicide note. The note had been very unclear. The grown-ups got together and searched the woods on Saturday, but nobody could find so much as a hair from Chris Creed's head. So, Mr. and

17

Mrs. Creed were hanging on to the term *runaway* with hope.

I got the feeling, seeing the grown-ups squirm, that they wanted to believe the Creeds. In Steepleton parents constantly hagged on their kids about how expensive it is to live here, and how parents make sacrifices so their kids can go to a school where they aren't exposed to violence and terrible stuff. In Steepleton you could ride your bike to the Wawa—our only convenience store—and leave it out front without a padlock. You could always meet your girlfriend after dark because there wasn't any reason for a mom or dad to say that a girl couldn't walk around outside after dark. Even the boons, the really bad kids, went back to the boondocks after school and kind of stopped existing to us until school the next day. Kids from Steepleton played sports, joined clubs, applied to out-of-state colleges, got cars for graduation. There wasn't much to commit suicide over . . . if you were looking at surface stuff like that.

But even Steepleton had its weird kids, and Chris had been one of them. I think the worst thing about him was his undying combo of big mouth and huge grin. He seemed to forget from one day to the next who he had pissed off. He'd come bounding up to the same kids who had told him yesterday to get lost like he was their best friend. Like his entire track record as an annoying person didn't exist. In my whole life I had never met another person like Creed.

"We . . . certainly don't have any reason to believe that Chris would run away." Mr. Creed had taken his wife by the shoulders and spoken over her left ear. "But that thought is, *er*, a preferable alternative to anything more pressing, and, *er*, sinister . . ."

His mouth was dry or pasty so that every syllable had this *m'yam-m'yam-m'yam* sound behind it. I watched his mouth, feeling kind of grossed out yet hypnotized.

18

". . . though any decision Chris made was always grounded, quite normal, not a radical type of this, *er*, nature."

"That's right." Mrs. Creed nodded.

Reverend Harmon put his arms around the Creeds' shoulders and bowed his head to pray. I was supposed to have my head bowed, but I forgot, studying Mr. and Mrs. Creed with their bowed heads.

I was thinking, *This hard-stepping mom and this pasty-mouthed father are as clueless as two aliens. Chris Creed is about as "grounded" and "normal" as a chimpanzee. How could people live their whole lives with their kid and not know this?*

By the time high school rolled around, most of us had grown out of beating kids up because they were obnoxious, and we hadn't beat on Chris in a year or so. But we had a new group of kids to deal with when we got to the bigger school.

The boons are the kids who come to our school from a certain area in the Pine Barrens on the Mullica River, which we call the boondocks. I'm sure there are lots of boon-docky places in the continental United States, each with its own version of boons. In our boondocks, the kids are generally the pickup truck, long hair, muscle shirt, and motor-bike crew that we just try to look through in the halls.

The boons weren't above busting somebody up still, if the kid was weird and had a big mouth. One really scary boon—an enormous dude named Bo Richardson—had pushed Chris off the top bleacher in the gym the year before and set him on crutches for a few weeks. Those boons could be scary, but we still blamed Chris as much as we blamed them. He was as weird as they were charged up.

Reverend Harmon went right from the prayer into the Apostles' Creed, and the voices behind me started with the usual droning echo.

I believe in God, the father Almighty,
Maker of heaven and earth . . .
And in Him, Jesus Christ, His only son, our Lord . . .

I might have gotten stuck on the crucifixion, but I had never given any thought to the Apostles' Creed or why we said this thing week after week. It was just something "normal" that we said. And the normalcy of it got me looking at the Creeds like they were normal people again, and if they could watch their kid for fifteen years and see him as normal, I guessed it didn't matter. It's just the way things are. Things don't have to be sane when they're normal.

Three

Alex and Ryan came from church with me, and we hung out in my basement, waiting for the Kyles to show up for practice. My dad had stopped at Wawa and gotten a bunch of "shorties"—that's a six-inch hoagie—and we were mowing down on them in silence. Ryan sat at his drum set. He would take a huge bite off the hoagie, put it down on my amp, pick up his drumsticks, and go *ba-ba-dee-ba-ba-dee-bay-bo-bam-boo-sssssstttt,* ending with the cymbal.

It grated on my nerves. With one huge mouthful, he got up, then crouched and tiptoed toward the game closet. He grabbed the knob and jumped back as the door flew open. He stared at the games and then turned to us, swallowing food.

"Uh. He's not in there." He cracked up and then looked miffed as I rolled my eyes. Ryan's dad was chief of police. Sometimes I wondered if he hadn't heard too much gore from his dad, which left him kind of heartless.

"Dudes," he went on, "aren't you scared he's going to, like, show up hanging by the neck on your property? Or you're going to open the laundry chute and watch him spill out, all bloody from a bullet through his brain? He did it *somewhere*. *Somebody's* going to find the spoil—"

"My dad says something about very sensitive people committing suicide in water," Alex put in. His dad was a shrink. "You watch. Next spring sometime, somebody's going to whip back the tarp on their swimming pool, clear away the brown water, and see Creed with a cinder block roped around his chest. His eyeballs, like, totally rotted through."

"I think he jumped off the dam, and that's why nobody can find the body. It hasn't bloated up, risen to the surface yet," Ryan said enthusiastically. He made some laugh that went, "*hck . . . hck . . . hck.*"

Half of me wanted to laugh because it made the whole thing seem less mind-blowing. But the other half couldn't get rid of this thought that a kid I knew might have slashed his wrists or hung himself. It was making me want to call my girlfriend, Leandra, and tune these dudes out. Leandra went to a holy roller church, which could be a pain, because she could go off about things like the devil being real and stuff that could make you twitch. But I knew in this case she'd go on about kids who died, going up to heaven, and how Creed was probably very happy—if he had died.

I kept getting this picture in my head of Creed in the sixth grade, the one time I truly whaled on him. I had only hit about three kids in my whole life, so I remembered it. He stared at me right after. Then blood came gushing from both his nostrils, like two spigots. I kept reliving those seconds between him looking so unglued and that blood gushing. I kept wondering if he felt pain. I wondered if I'd left him wishing he were dead.

"I've got it!" Ryan leaned forward enthusiastically. "He hung himself in the woods. And all those searchers were so busy looking on the ground that they never bothered to look *up*. Oh my god. His Converses were probably dangling, like, six inches above one of those searchers' heads, and they just never bothered to look *up*."

"Yo, we're eating here," I reminded them. "You guys ever hit him?"

"Yeah, once," Alex said.

"Yeah," Ryan muttered. He'd probably lost count. "I think fourth grade was the big year for me. I remember noticing in fourth grade that Creed still sucked his thumb if he wasn't thinking of where he was. We used to catch him doing that, then torture the guy until he cried. It got to be a game with some of us, to see if we could make him cry. Hey, maybe getting hit all the time that year, like, knocked his brain sideways. I think that's what started it."

"*Mm-mm*, you're wrong," Alex said, staring at his half-eaten hoagie. "I hit him in second grade. He was on people's nerves even back then. I brought my Matchbox cars into school. Remember how I had, like, two hundred of them, all in the compartmentalized boxes?"

We grinned, and I rolled my eyes remembering all those cars. Alex used to line them up in the compartments by make and model.

"I remember feeling like King Popularity that day, doling out cars to all my little race-car fans. We were going to make this huge track around the blacktop at recess. Creed kept standing there going, 'You know, there's lead poisoning in those cars. You know, what you're doing is dangerous. You know, you should really seek a more *winsome* pastime.' I remember he used that word. *Winsome*. God. We got, like, five minutes into this broken-record routine, and I just nailed him."

Alex shrugged like it was the only acceptable thing to do. This sort of thing was always going on around Creed.

"I hit him in sixth grade," I told them, feeling some sort of relief at finally letting fly. "I had brought my new guitar

23

to school. After gym I walked into class, and he was standing on a desk doing this Elvis routine with it. I saw the desk starting to rock under his sneakers. I took the guitar, calmly put it in the case, turned around, and just pounded him."

I looked from Ryan to Alex—mowing down on the hoagies around these stupid snickers—and I felt a little pissed off.

"You know, maybe we could talk without laughing about it?" I suggested. "I think we tortured the guy enough when he was alive. *If* he's actually dead."

"Dude, you're like a walking conscience." Ryan cackled. "Don't be so glum. Maybe he just . . . ran away. Truth is, can you even see Creed doing something like sticking a gun to his head? Or knocking a stool out from under himself? He was obnoxious but such a wimp. It makes for a much more boring story, but maybe he just ran off. But *damn*. Wouldn't you just love to know what that note said?"

"Of course," Alex and I both mumbled. Everyone and their brother was dying to know what all Chris had written, so that you couldn't tell whether it was a runaway note or a suicide note.

Ryan got to laughing harder. "Who but Creed would send a suicide *e-mail*? A suicide . . . *e-mail*." He was cracking up so much, he didn't notice that Alex wasn't.

"Duh, idiots. Did you ever stop to think? If it was an e-mail, we can probably get at the thing."

As Alex plopped down in front of my terminal and turned it on, Ryan and I automatically sucked up behind him. Alex was one of those brainiacs you could almost mistake for stupid because he was also a class-clown type. He had been fooling around with the school computer since the beginning of freshman year and regularly read us our grades three days before report cards came out. I watched him click on a program called Reach Over, which he had installed for me but I had never used. He said it hooked into the library files and, since only gleeps and nerds actually spent more than fifteen minutes in the library, I could sit here at home, access the library's on-line encyclopedias, and do my papers without hauling my can in there. I could still get As without appearing socially inept, he said.

I hadn't thought much about this program because, for Christmas, I had gotten two different encyclopedias on CD-ROM. One from each grandmom.

"Does the library know you're hooked into them?" I asked.

"No way. I installed the thing with Mrs. Peacock putting books on the shelves not ten feet from me, but she wouldn't know an installation from an assassination. *Ooo.* I hear the pitter-patter of connectoids."

The modem was ringing and shrieking. Ryan had quit laughing. "Dude, you really think you can get at that note?"

"If he sent it from the library, it might still be in the library's outbox . . . *Ah* . . . Library Windows Explorer, how do you do . . ."

I recognized the sight of the Explorer and smiled with my jaw half hanging. Ryan and I watched Alex scan down to the Indora file, complaining all the while that the school should get a security system. He clicked on "out.tok" and scanned down a list of dates and times. His eyes lost their funsville look and he sighed. "There's nothing here from Thursday at all. We're sure this note was sent from the library?"

"My dad said the *library.*" Ryan nodded hard. "In fact, my mom asked him why a kid would send an e-mail like that from a public place. Creed had a humongous computer system at home. But my dad said, nope, the return address said the library."

"Anal-retentive moron, he probably sent it from a disk," Alex mumbled. "Let me check the recipient."

Even Ryan kind of gasped as Alex clicked all the way out to "Network" and moved easily down another passage that showed the last names of teachers next to these little file icons. Right at the top was Ames, the principal. Alex clicked in there, and I crunched my head into Ryan's shoulder, casting a glance up the stairs to make sure my dad wasn't coming. Not like he would have any clue what we were doing, even if he saw it with his own eyes. Here's Alex virtually marching into the principal's office, opening his file drawer, and rooting through it. Yet, if some parent came down here, all we would have to do was act normal and make up some lie. On-line stuff was awesome in my mind, though I wasn't Alex the Master.

"*Ah*. A smorgasbord of e-mails," Alex noted. "Shall we set ourselves to discover if our illustrious principal is having an on-line affair? Or something of a darker nature?"

"Dirty e-mails. From Mr. Ames. Oh my god." Ryan cackled. "Would that be the end of the universe?"

"Forget it. My dad has been playing racquetball with him twice a week for ten years," I said. "No friend of my parents is a pervert. It's physiologically impossible."

Ryan seemed to buy that. My dad owns an engineering firm, and my mother is a prosecutor for the district attorney's office. Throughout my life the words had floated around me from people in church, or other parents in Little League—I had the perfect parents. I just sort of believed it. And that makes you automatically think their friends are perfect, too. Alex's dad was a shrink, and his mom was a housewife. Ryan's dad was the local chief of police and his mom used to be a systems analyst, until Earl, Ryan's older brother, came along. Earl was always in trouble—so much trouble, he made Ryan and his sister, Renee, look like angels, which they weren't. Mrs. Bowen decided to be a full-time mom eons ago—or, in the case of the Bowen kids, a full-time enforcer.

I jumped as my printer started to haul a sheet of paper through. I looked from its blinking lights to Alex, who was grinning with electric eyes.

"I should leave Mr. Ames a reprimand for cleaning out the library file but saving his recipient's copy as a souvenir reminder of better days."

I hadn't even seen the note come up on the screen, but Alex's brain worked, like, ten times faster than mine. He reached for the paper and turned to face us.

"Dear Mr. Ames," he read, and I watched his face drop the victorious look.

"I have a problem getting along with people. I know that people wish I were dead, and at this moment in time I see no alternative but to accommodate them in this wish. I have a wish. Not that anybody cares, but if anybody cared over the years, it was you. Here is my wish. I wish that I had been born somebody else."

Alex started reading the names of a couple of kids I played football with, a couple he played basketball with, *"Mike Healy, José DeSantos, Tommy Ide, Evan Lucenti . . ."*

Then, *"Torey Adams, Alex Arrington . . ."*

My heart jumped and left my chest on fire as I heard my own name come out of this note, with Alex's. It went on to name a few other guys we hung with because of sports. But our names were in there. I listened in a haze as Alex read the rest.

"I don't understand why I get nothing and these boys get everything—athletic ability, good personalities, beautiful girlfriends. I'm sure their parents will be buying them cars next year, while I will still be riding my bicycle until my parents decide I'm old enough. Quite possibly, I'll be twenty-

five. I wish to understand life and luck and liberty. But I will never do that confined to this life, the personality defects I've been cursed with, the lack of abilities, the strain. I wish no malice on anyone. I only wish to be gone. Therefore, I AM.

"Yours respectfully, Christopher Creed."

Ryan's voice was echoing some bull. ". . . kid's about to end it, and he's still talking like he wants to impress someone with his enormous vocabulary. And, yo, he mentions you guys but doesn't mention me. Doesn't he think I'm lucky?"

"You guys, he actually spell-checked his suicide note." Alex laughed in amazement. "He might have gotten *malice* right, but he would not have gotten *accommodate*—"

"Gimme that." I snatched the sheet of paper from Alex, completely sick of all their jokes. I think my life changed as the words in that note bounced around my head. I might have felt a little weird before over something so unusual happening. But I hadn't been involved personally. Creed involved me; he used my name. He all but admitted he might kill himself because he wasn't me. And he had been so damn honest. *I have a problem getting along with people . . . I know that people wish I were dead . . .* I'm not sure how many people would have actually wanted Creed dead, but still, if he heard, *Why don't you drop dead?* once, he probably heard it a thousand times.

I wanted to be pissed at someone. I just didn't know who. Chris sounded pissed at his parents. Creed's mother was a retired naval officer who used to fly jets, before she made a drill school for her own kids as a stay-at-home mom. Mr. Creed taught archeology out at Stockton State College and had inherited a lot of money from his mom or something. They lived in a big house, like, two cul-de-sacs over, had a big car and a van, and they had bought Chris a great Pentium twenty-three-gig with Surround Sound. I guessed a great computer system like that couldn't replace friends. I kind of wanted to blame the parents. They had to be part of this creating-a-weirdo process.

But I also wondered why none of us ever picked up that Creed was so down on himself. Whatever it was that he admired me for, I figured I could have helped him. I would have, if he had just let us know he was thinking of offing himself. That made me pissed at *him*.

"Dudes, he mentioned our names." I looked at Alex, who was nudging Ryan to stifle it and show some respect.

"Calm down, Torey." Alex had quit laughing, but he gave me the time-out sign. "We're not the Pittsburgh Steelers, okay? The guy is making a mountain out of a molehill. We have a normal life, and the only thing we have that he didn't is friends."

I wanted to say that was a big deal in his mind, obviously. We could have been more chill toward the guy.

Ryan started chuckling again. I got this feeling in my gut that most people would miss the fact that Chris felt he had reason to do this. Even his own fool parents weren't being understanding toward the guy. If they really wanted to understand their kid, they would not have been standing in front of a church full of people going, *Doyee, we're here to tell you that Chris was grounded in reality.*

Ryan went on happily, "The operative question to me is, What did the guy do? I just want to know . . . Is he alive, or is he dead? If he's alive, how did that little prick find the nerve to leave home? And if he's dead . . . *where's the body?*"

I said something like, "Bite me," under my breath, but not loud enough for them to hear.

Four

On Monday the third-period honors-chemistry teacher was sick, and there was no substitute. That meant Alex and I could go to the cafeteria and stay there right through fourth-period lunch. Leandra had third-period lunch, so we could hang with her. Life was good. Until I saw Mrs. Creed.

She was in school, hanging these "missing" posters on all the bulletin boards and taping them to walls in all the corridors. We caught sight of her taping one on the wall just outside of the cafeteria. She was pressing the paper against the wall so hard it was turning her fingers purple. Then she stood up and smacked her fingers against her legs, like, to get the blood flowing again.

The poster had a picture of Chris, scanned from the freshman yearbook, plus all this information, like day last seen, on it. It also had HEIGHT: 5' 8"; WEIGHT: 135; HAIR COLOR: BLOND; EYE COLOR: BROWN.

"Hey, Torey." I heard a girl's voice and felt a slight tug on my varsity sweater. I turned, and Ali McDermott was standing behind me, grinning all friendly. Ali had been a friend of ours since kindergarten. She lived on Creed's street. Last year she started to drift a little, didn't hang out with us as much. All I knew was that she didn't show up at as many parties, and at dances she would hang with us for about ten minutes and then circle around and talk to lots of other people.

I guessed that was okay, except rumor had it that Ali was, as the saying goes, "passing through high school on her back." A lot of the guys on the football team claimed to have been with her. It gets a little harder being around a girl like that once you have a girlfriend, and I hadn't hung out with her much since the spring, when I started going out with Leandra.

"Hey," I said, "no chemistry. Cool, huh?"

"Yeah, cool."

I watched Alex wave to Renee Bowen, ahead of us, and move up to walk with her. I sighed, thinking, *There goes another band practice tonight.* Renee was Ryan's sister and Leandra's best friend. About three weeks earlier, she had started getting Alex to hang out in front of the Wawa with her at night, and he would just not show for band practice. I had gone out with Renee in eighth grade, and we stayed friends afterward, but at this point she was starting to bug me.

I sighed again and turned my thoughts to Ali. I wanted to ask her if she knew anything about Creed, but didn't want to sound like a gossip hag. I didn't remember ever hearing her say too much awful stuff about Chris, growing up, though she could roll her eyes a lot. Ali was nice like that.

"Mrs. Creed's all hanging her posters," I said, finally. No arguing that.

She just rolled her eyes, the usual.

I tried again. "Everybody's wondering what's up with him."

"You know, I really don't want to talk about it," she snapped.

I thought that was pretty saintly of her and felt embarrassed. But then I thought, *Wait a minute. I'm not running around school all, "Where's the body?" like half the fools are.*

"Ali, I'm not out looking for bad stuff to spread around about Creed. Maybe I just want to understand the thing."

She cast me a sideways glance, like maybe she was sorry. "Well, you're in the minority," she muttered. "You should hear the stuff people have been asking me. 'Has he got any poison in that chemistry set of his? D'you hear anything strange coming from his place last week? Like gunshots?' People who can't even stand me have been coming up to me all morning."

"Who can't stand you?" I asked, confused. Yeah, guys joked about her sex life. But there's a difference between saying a girl is easy and saying you hate her. Nobody said that.

"Everybody," she muttered, with her eyebrows all scrunched together.

"You're imagining it," I told her. Her parents had split up over the summer. I wondered if it was stressing her.

"I'm not imagining it." She sighed. "I'm not like you guys anymore. You all . . . have perfect lives. And when something happens, like a suffering kid turns up missing, it's like the joke of the century. Because your lives are perfect."

I guessed I would be pretty freaked if my parents split, but she didn't have to take it all out on me.

"Well, thanks a lot for clumping me in with all the buttheads," I muttered. "You're being really judgmental of me, especially considering how you hate it when you think people are being judgmental of you."

I was ready to break away from her. She grabbed me by the elbow and hurried to walk along beside me.

She sighed. "I'm just in a foul mood from playing the butt end of twenty-questions all morning. I'm sorry, okay?"

"Whatever." I looked around the cafeteria for Leandra.

Ali kept pulling my arm, and when I looked, she was searching my face. "Don't let's go in here. Let's go somewhere else. I want to tell you about Mrs. Creed."

It's the unwritten rule that if you have off the same period as your girlfriend, you find her in the cafeteria and spend the period with her. I followed Ali out again, but glanced nervously around to see who had spotted me and might tell Leandra they saw me leaving with Ali McDermott. It sounded like Ali really needed to spill.

I trailed her down the long hallway until we hit the stairwell. There was an emergency exit, and I sucked in my breath as Ali put her hand on the bar and pushed.

"Emergency alarm hasn't worked since the first week of school. Don't tell anyone, okay? This is my great escape, where no hall proctors can see."

We stepped out into the sunlight. You could see straight across the lawn to the edge of the woods. It was a calm, pretty sight, and I could see why she wanted to come out here sometimes.

I heard a match light, and when I turned, she was huffing on a cigarette.

"When did you start smoking?" I asked, surprised.

She just shrugged like she wasn't interested in talking about that. "Don't tell. I'll get kicked off cheerleading if Miss Gibson finds out."

I nodded, looking her up and down, noticing little things for the first time about how Ali was changing. She used to pull her hair up in all these girly doodads like the other cheerleaders, but now she just let it hang. It fell in little strands around her shoulders, almost straight but not quite. She was real cute still, just not all dolled up the way the other cheerleaders were. And she wore army boots with her short skirt. Lots of other girls wore hiking boots or army boots, but the cheerleaders didn't seem to wear anything clunky. She was starting to look like somebody else, like one of the techies or the artists or something. Like she didn't relate to the girls she had always hung with anymore. I watched her blow smoke in a stream like some sort of a pro and felt bad that she had obviously changed a lot, almost right under my nose, and I hadn't noticed.

"So, what's up, Ali?"

"I just feel things," she said, staring at the woods. "I don't have any proof. I don't want to tell just anybody, because they'll use it to hurt Chris. You know, spread mean things about him."

I waited, seeing her take a long drag off the cigarette. She said, "So, you can't tell anyone."

"I won't."

"I think Chris snapped. I think he flipped out from a combo of everything. School, being lonely, but mostly because of his parents."

"You . . . talked to him?" I asked.

"Yeah. I talked to him sometimes." She shrugged. "As much as you can talk to a kid who grabs on to you like a magnet if you so much as smile at him. Mostly he talked. I listened. I was afraid to say anything back very often, because one time in eighth grade I told him a bunch of garbage about my family. I don't know what came over me. He was there, out on his lawn, and I was, like, in desperate need of someone to talk to. I waved. That was all he needed. He came over, and after I dumped on him, he informs me the next day that he's all into Eastern religions. You know, reincarnation and all that stuff? He told me I was his long-lost brother from a past life."

Despite the disgusted tone, her cute little grin crept across her face. That was one thing about Ali. You could take away her hair doodads, all that cheerleader makeup, and dangle a cigarette from her mouth, and that cute little grin was still the best.

"Not his long-lost sister?" I smirked.

"No. His brother. You know, even a weirdo would settle on being your friend if you acted like a friend. Him? If you acted friendly to him, you were his long-lost brother from a past life."

I wondered what bothered Ali so much that she would dump on Creed. Her parents split up, but they both seemed okay to me. Her dad owned a restaurant, and her mom had helped out a lot. They did their share of driving Ali and her little brother to sports and school stuff. They helped out at PTA and threw Ali great birthday parties. I just figured they didn't get along. I wondered why she felt she couldn't dump on Alex or me or Renee or Ryan, whatever it was. I figured if I asked her, I would get the same ice-over as when I asked her about smoking.

"Did he tell you bad stuff about his parents?" I asked instead.

"No," she said. "I don't think he really . . . understood that it was bad. It was mostly small talk. You know, 'I'm renting a movie tonight with my dad,' or, 'My mom's taking me to the mall when I get home.' Who could stand to rent a movie with their dad? Like, what movie could you agree on with your dad? And who goes to the mall with their mom?"

She shrugged like it wasn't that big a deal, but I could see where she was going.

"My mom gives me the money so I can go with you guys," I said.

"Exactly. His family's so up his butt." She shivered. "I think that if Chris's family was, like, totally off their gourd, he would be able to see it, to say, 'Wow, these people are totally abnormal, and therefore my life is not my fault.' But

36

it never got that weird. Just chronically, slightly weird. Just enough to keep the kid off balance. Make him stress. Make him, you know, weird, but not insane."

"Hmm . . ." I tried to picture this. "You're making it sound like it's more dangerous to have a slightly weird family than a totally weird family." Interesting thought, but I didn't know if I believed it.

"It's mostly the stuff I saw. I have a great view of their windows from my bedroom." She shuffled around a little, like she wasn't comfortable with looking, but she had done it anyway. "You know how your room can get to be a complete disaster if you don't pick up for two or three days?"

"Yeah. My mom turns into a hag at that point," I admitted.

"Well, Chris's room was always neat as a pin," Ali went on. "His mom goes in there and, like, regiment-cleans it, as if she's running the Air Force in there. She folds his clothes in the drawers a certain way. Pulls out anything from under the bed. Takes things down off the closet shelf and refolds them. Dusts in the corners. I've seen her do it, like, when I'm home sick from school. What's wrong with this picture?"

I was catching on a little quicker by this point. "I would kill my mom for being in my stuff like that."

"Yeah. The kid had no privacy."

"Sounds like the type of mom who would, like, read your diary."

She nodded quickly. "I think he even had one. He used to hide some little book inside the back of this picture frame on his wall. Can you believe that? I guess he didn't feel he could stuff it in between his mattresses like most kids."

"He ever mention it to you?"

She shook her head. "He just seemed to accept every-thing . . . He never said anything about it. But I'm pretty sure it was a diary because he pulled it out a few nights a week last summer, after he was in bed. He would lie there on his side and write things down in it. Then he would put it back behind the picture frame and go to sleep."

"Sounds like a diary," I muttered, but I was thinking of something else. "How come you see all this? You sound like a Peeping Tom."

Her face got hard again, and she just said, "Let's just say I spend a lot of time in my room, okay?"

"Whatever." I watched her, wishing she would tell me about herself rather than Chris. Truth, I was getting as worried about her as I was about him. There seemed to be so much stuff she would lay hints about but not say. But she just kept on going.

"And here's another one. He was very modest. I remember a bunch of times Renee slept over in eighth grade, and when we were looking out the bedroom window, we could see him come into his bedroom in only a towel. Now, how many kids would think to lower the shade just before they let go of the towel? Would you think to do that?"

Our house was on, like, three acres, so I didn't worry about the neighbors seeing that far. But I think I would have stood over toward the corner just long enough to throw on my gym trunks. She was grinning, and I smiled.

"Well, he never forgot," she said. "It was like a ritual. He would come in, in his towel. He would lower the shade. He would put on pajamas. He would raise the shade. In eighth grade, Renee and I almost made it a Friday-night game to see if we could catch him in the buff. And how about this? You know how you can see people's silhouettes when the shade is down?"

I nodded.

"One time this year, he lowers the shade. And I see another silhouette come into the room. The silhouette puts a stack of laundry in the drawers, then gets in a conversation with him. They exchange, like, three lines each, and the silhouette leaves. He pulls the shade up ten seconds later, and he's in his pajamas."

"Ew, shit," I breathed. That one was kind of nasty. His mom walks in on him when he's buck naked, and he looks like he just accepts it. "I would have been pissed."

"Your mom would have knocked," she said.

I watched Ali, thinking she had some kind of a hawk eye. I think I would have lived across the street from Creed for years and years and never noticed anything except that he was weird.

"At any rate, I hate that woman," Ali said. "I would love to prove that I only saw the tip of some enormous iceberg. Maybe she beat him. Or worse things."

"Like what?" I asked.

The look she passed me turned my blood cold. Some annoyed are-you-stupid? and don't-ask-questions look, like the one she cast me in the hall when I first asked about Mrs. Creed. She was thinking something gross, that's all I knew.

I went on, finally. "If Mrs. Creed caused this, she doesn't understand, doesn't want to. You should have seen her in church yesterday. Appealing to the people for any reason that Chris might have run away. Like she's so innocent."

Ali laughed in disgust. "She's not that dumb. She knows she's guilty."

It struck me that Mrs. Creed must have seen the note. The cops wouldn't keep it from her. It was full of stuff about his parents being too strict, yet she gave her little speech in church on Sunday. She had looked so sincere, asking if anyone knew any reason why Chris would run away. I couldn't understand how the woman could see that note and be able to push the idea out of her head that she was at least partly responsible.

I decided to trust Ali. "I've seen the note," I said quietly.

Her eyes rose to mine. She said, "Yeah, me, too."

"Really? How did you see it?"

She pulled another cigarette out of her blouse pocket and lit it. She didn't answer me. She just stared into the woods, looking sad. She hung with all sorts of different people these days, and I didn't even take a stab at who she did different things with. But I guessed maybe we weren't the only people hacking into the school's e-mail.

"Parents can be vicious, don't kid yourself," she murmured. "Just because you live in Steepleton. Just because you have the perfect life."

"Look." I squirmed around, not wanting to get on that sore subject again. "I don't have a perfect life. And whatever it is that's bothering you lately, I wish you could just tell me. Instead of taking it out on me."

She looked at me like she was sorry, maybe, but then her eyes hardened. "You wouldn't understand."

"Thanks a lot." Maybe I did have the perfect life, next to hers. I didn't have a clue. But I couldn't get past this feeling that she really wanted to tell me what had come down on her. She was leaving these bloody little hints all over the place. It was almost like she was using Mrs. Creed to show me how bad her own life could get.

She drew up half her grin again and let out an awkward laugh. "If people wouldn't take it all wrong, I'd ask you to come over some night this week. We could have a powwow and spy out the window."

"Well . . . why would people take that wrong?" I muttered. But I knew what she meant. Ali had this slut thing hanging over her head. It could look really bad because of Leandra. But I figured Ali needed me.

"I have to go talk to Leandra now," I said, staring down at my sneakers. Then I sighed. "So . . . what night?"

"Mm. Tomorrow night would be cool. Besides, my boyfriend is coming over tomorrow night. So no one will suspect you and me of doing the slut routine with my boyfriend there. My reputation's not that gross yet."

She grinned at me triumphantly, and I tried to laugh. It didn't really strike me that she said she had a boyfriend. I didn't even know she had gotten one steady person. And I was kind of shocked at her remark about her reputation, like she knew and wasn't letting it bother her.

"I'll come over after dinner," I said, and just shuffled out of there, moving back toward the cafeteria in a haze. She didn't follow me.

Five

I got into the cafeteria and spotted Alex, Renee, and Leandra waving me over. Leandra had the kind of face that lit up when she smiled, all framed with long, shiny red hair. She could spin heads. I smiled back. Alex and Renee looked mad.

"Did you forget what you have in your pocket?" Alex demanded as I plopped down beside Leandra. "Where have you been?"

My hand went to my sweater pocket, and I felt a piece of paper folded in there. The note from Creed. We had decided we were going to show it to Leandra and Renee. I guessed Alex figured this was the most important thing in the universe.

"Your favorite breakfast." Leandra handed me a bag of french fries, bouncing a little in her seat. She was always thinking up nice things to do like that.

"Thanks." I took the fries gladly and decided to let fly with the truth, because some gossip hag would probably tell one of them they saw us. "Ali. She's having a problem. She just needed to dump."

"Boy problems?" Renee said with a grin, and I thought that was mean. It must have shown in my face, because she said, "I'm sorry for her, okay? I know her folks are going through a divorce and all, but nobody told her to handle her life the way she's handling her life."

"Yeah. Not our problem." I shrugged.

She came back at me with equal sarcasm. "Once in a while, if you didn't see everybody's side in everything, it would be okay, Victor. I promise."

Victor is my real name, and Renee is the only person who ever called me that, and only when I was pissing her off.

"I don't see everybody's side in everything," I argued. "Didn't I agree with you on everything you said about Nathan Leeds last week, at this very table?"

"I just broke up with Nathan Leeds three weeks ago." She smirked. "To not agree with a girl about someone she's just broken up with is totally heartless. Besides, all I said was that he was a dip-shitz, dork-faced liar who cheated on me, smells, and will never break a thousand on his SAT. What's not to agree with?"

"Whatever. Remind me never to get on your bad side." I laughed. Just a few weeks earlier Nathan Leeds had been her swoonbag love machine. She just got this twitch that she wanted Alex instead. I thought of mentioning to Renee that Alex needed to come to band practice more often but decided I didn't feel like tangling with her.

I spread the note out on the table. Then Leandra and Renee were whispering, their lips moving, like they were trying to absorb every word. I watched Leandra's long reddish hair shine as it fell over one shoulder and dangled almost to her lap. She kind of gasped and looked at me for a moment as my own name came out of her mouth. She had reached the part where he said he was jealous of me. I laced my fingers through hers, knowing she would understand

44

how that hit me. If he had anything to be jealous about really, it was her, I thought.

When we walked down the halls together, people would stare at Leandra, and then at me like I was the luckiest person in the world. And people really liked her, even if she wasn't a huge brain like Renee. I think Renee had read the letter twice by the time Leandra got to the bottom.

"Funny . . ." Leandra murmured finally. "It sure looks like he was thinking about suicide. But it never actually says he's going to commit suicide."

I looked at how Creed had put it: *I only wish to be gone. Therefore, I AM.*

"But look at this." Renee pointed to the earlier part of the note, before our names were listed. *I know that people wish I were dead, and at this moment in time I see no alternative but to accommodate them in this wish.*

"That's suicide," Renee said flatly. "That's definitely suicide."

"Yeah, but where *is* he?" Alex asked nervously, looking over his shoulder to see if anyone might put their eyes on this note. He turned back and almost whispered, "Where's the *body*?"

"I don't know," Renee mumbled. "But he was still trying to get attention, like always. Look at the things he's saying . . . *life and luck and liberty?*" She curled her lip in disgust. "What a crock. I'm surprised he saw himself with so much truth. He always wore that grin from hell. I would have bet he grinned when he slept."

"He probably did," Alex said with a smirk. "I always figured he never was able to face up to how bad his life really was. *Denial,* my dad calls it. He lived in a state of chronic denial."

Even if you were yelling at Creed, that grin stayed plastered from ear to ear. It was like he refused to believe you were yelling. He wouldn't stop grinning until somebody hit him. Then he went totally depressive. I had seen him in a heap on the floor, wailing, after one of the boons hit him. I thought *denial* was an okay word.

"Are we positive he wrote this?" Leandra stared at the paper, looking confused.

Alex shrugged. "Mr. Ames gets the note, and *boom*, the kid is missing. Who else would have written it?"

Leandra's accent came on very thick when she was thinking too hard to cover it up, and it was thick right then. "It does sound just like him. But like y'all just said, Chris never saw the truth about himself. It almost sounds like . . . the way somebody *else* would describe his life."

"You're saying that somebody else killed him and wrote the note to make it look like a suicide," Renee said, to clear us up. She spat it out like she was reciting a weather report. She folded her arms across her chest coolly and looked around the cafeteria. "So, who's your suspect? I'd say there're a few in here."

I thought that was vicious but watched as Leandra rolled her eyes sideways in a suspicious way. We followed them and then looked back at the center of the table. A group of boons was sitting where she had just looked. Bo Richardson was right in the middle of them.

"Bo Richardson?" The words came out of Alex's mouth like he were a ventriloquist. The only time his lips moved was on the *B*. He did a whole line of ventriloquism, grinning like a jack-o'-lantern. "I don't vant to look like I'n saying his nane, cuz he's at the next tavle."

Bo Richardson was a big tough boon, with enormous brown eyes that made him look insane. If he caught you staring at him, he would mouth off at you sometimes, depending on his mood.

He bragged into the gossip channels that he had slashed more than a thousand tires last year, though we figured it was probably about twenty, because he was also known for lying—exaggerating his conquests. Also, he would fight people, which is why he showed up in the principal's office a lot.

"Well, yeah," Leandra breathed while we all just sat there dumbfounded. "Maybe one of those guys could have done it."

"They could use some scrubbing up." Alex smirked.

A couple of them—but Shawn Mathers especially—really did have bad skin. And they dressed way different than us. Our clothes were kind of loose, and theirs were all skintight, like they had to show off their muscles. All these little differences used to seem so important, but now I wanted to figure out this note. I could see I wasn't about to get a word in edgewise by the way Alex was leaning forward and putting his hands up, like *stop*.

"No, no, forget the personal hygiene. That's nothing compared to . . . the cars."

The girls laughed. That kept Alex rolling. "*Ooo*. Gold fender, blue rusted door, engine of a bus. Tell me, why do they love to make noise? Do they actually think that a souped-up old car with no muffler is, like, *sexy* or something?"

"They think of 'no muffler' the way we think of a Lexus," Leandra giggled, then smacked her hand up to her mouth. She sighed. "Y'all're a bad influence on me. See how I'm gossiping? Every morning I make a deal with myself that I'm not going to talk evil about people. Somehow I never get past third period."

I laughed because it was true. Leandra's heart was in the right place, but her mouth could take off like it had a life of its own sometimes. By third period, she was just getting started some days.

"Don't get Pentecostal on us before noon." Renee kicked her under the table.

"Ouch!" Leandra muttered, moving her legs away. "Don't be making fun of me."

"What are you supposed to say about Bo Richardson?" Renee demanded. "That he's, like, Captain Deodorant with his crew of Zest Boys?"

Leandra had to pull her lips out into her palm to keep them from spreading outward. Alex let out a shameless blast. He wasn't Pentecostal.

"How'd we get on this subject?" I asked. "We were talking about what happened to Creed, and all of a sudden it's who drives a souped-up old bomb car."

"I thought we were talking about a murder," Alex said, "and Leandra was telling us who she thought did it."

"Wait, wait, reality check." I had thought of something. "Tell me what boon could write that note? *I wish to understand life and luck and liberty . . . defects I've been cursed with—*"

Renee smirked. "Maybe it was Bo and Shawn Mathers and Dallas Everett. Three boon brains equal one normal brain."

"*God,* remind me never to get on your bad side," I said again, shivering.

Some thought passed through my head that I wished I had stayed outside with Ali. I mean, it's not like I'm some saint who had never ripped on the boons. I'd had my share of fun. I came into school the first day of freshman year, took one look at them, and thought, *What planet did these people drop from?* But now this kid was in the black hole and none of my friends seemed to care.

Even Leandra, I thought. She wasn't concerned about Chris, she was concerned about whether or not she was gossiping. It was still all about *her*. And they were scoping out boons and pointing the finger. I mean, they were talking about a *murder* here. And for evidence they were bringing up zits, souped-up cars, and people smelling bad.

I didn't feel like telling them I was going to Ali's. I hoped her new boyfriend was a college dude. A college dude might be old enough not to want to whack everybody verbally or make jokes about Creed. My own friends were getting on my nerves some.

Six

I got bummed out that night. This time Pat and Eddie Kyle showed up to jam, but Alex and Ryan were no-shows. Ryan was the drummer, and what's your group without a drummer? Alex was, like, the center of us, and if he didn't show, we would do nothing. He was just the bass player, and probably the worst musician, but he had all the edge, the energy. Finally the twins said they would haul it down to Wawa to see if they saw Alex or Ryan. They wanted me to come, and I probably should have.

But it was bugging me how Alex and Ryan never took anything seriously. Alex's grades just came to him in his sleep— he never had to study—and the basketball coach was always harping on him that he could start if he would just put out more effort. Ryan just always did what Alex did, no questions asked. Alex was making me think, *Well, I can start making stuff happen without him.* I was the only one who thought about writing our own stuff, so I would start there.

I went down into the basement alone with my acoustic guitar. I sat on the floor with this pencil and a pad of yellow lined paper. I had written songs before. We had even practiced one that I wrote. It was called "A Song to the Blues," and that's about all it was. It goes like this:

So long as I live in this here town
Where there ain't nothing to do but fool around
And there ain't nowhere to go 'round here but down
Might as well make that funny-soundin' sound.
It's called the blues.
Even around here it's called the blues.

I mean, does that totally suck? I was embarrassed I wrote that, especially when it started piling out of Alex's mouth, with our band jamming behind it. Alex and I had our first band fight over that song, because I was wanting to bury it somewhere and Alex was saying, "People around here will like this song, man."

I remember just staring at him, thinking, *Yeah, well, what is wrong with people around here, then?*

I sat down there in the basement, hearing the wind blow around outside. The wind was getting on my nerves, because notes floated in and out of my head but nothing was sticking as a tune.

I told myself, *Think of something you want to write about, and then the words will come, brainiac. Do you want to write about . . . Leandra? How beautiful she is? How sweet she is?*

Blue eyes . . . blue as the skies
Baby blue . . . I'm gonna roll all over you . . .

I snorted out some laugh and tossed the pencil down. Not only were they dumb words, but they were about as likely as flying off to Mars. What some people don't understand is that Steepleton is a real place, and there are a lot of little places like it out there, that's what I think. And in these little towns live girls who actually do not have sex.

I know, like from watching movies, there is a big portion of the world that thinks girls like Leandra are secret liars. They believe that even the best girls are all ready to dive into the woods with you, and that they're all a bunch of fakes, talking one thing and doing another. Well, I don't know what to say, except if Leandra was a hypocrite, she hadn't shown that side of herself in the five months we'd been going out. You might wonder why a guy would go out with a girl like that. I don't know why.

I knew I liked how people looked her up and down and then stared at me like I was the luckiest guy on earth. They didn't know we weren't having sex; it was like our big secret. But it just wasn't making for a very good song.

People were into sad songs. This Creed thing. I thought back on Mrs. Creed hanging her posters all over the school corridors. I wondered if Chris had run for his life from her, or if she had gotten too mad, clunked him over the head in some fit of domineeringness. . . .

Is he alive, or is he dead?
Freight train running all thru my head . . .

I started to write those words. I stopped, raised my eyes slowly from the paper, and stared at the dark wood paneling. The air was moving, almost whispering behind me, only not making any noise. It brought with it this sudden, incredible urge to look behind me. I listened through it, waiting to hear something more . . . a rustle of clothing, a whispering voice. . . . It's like somebody was staring at me, like from three feet behind me. It got to the point where the skin on my back was crawling. Finally I pretended I had an itch on my back, so I could jerk around without really looking like I was jerking around. For some reason it was important that I didn't look like I was jerking around.

Alex's bass guitar sat in its stand, and Ryan's drums stood behind them. The metal lettering on Eric's synthesizer sort of glowed in the dim shadow of the corner. I stared and stared at the game-closet door, which was open just a crack, like two inches. The wind banged around outside, and in the basement it started to sound like moaning. The moan got really intense, and the game-closet door sucked almost closed and then pulled out to two inches from shut again. I watched that door moving by itself a few times, and all of a sudden I knew it wasn't moving by itself. I knew somebody had the handle from the inside. Somebody who had been watching me a few seconds earlier. I stood up, silently gripping my guitar by the neck, with my eyes staring at that door like they could fry a hole through it. As soon as I stood up, the moving stopped. The door stayed about an inch from closed as I crept slowly toward it. I stopped about ten feet from it, wondering what to do next. I thought of rushing it, and the vision that Ryan had talked about shot through my head: a couple bloody sneakers swinging out and hitting me in the eyes from where Chris's body hung from the ceiling light. I quietly walked to the door, got my hand around the knob, and pulled very slowly. A black hole stared back at me.

My arm whooshed through the air, waiting for something to bite me, kick me, reach for my throat. I found the light string and pulled. A bunch of games stared back at me. The word *Sorry* stood out, off a game box half covered with dust.

I clicked off the light, closed the door, and shook off some crazy urge to look in the dark corners behind the big gas heater. I turned toward my yellow writing pad and the pencil lying on top, and I walked quickly toward them. Without looking in any direction, I picked up the pad and pencil and went up the stairs. I made sure I didn't run. But when I got to the top, I was kind of huffing, the hair on the back of my neck still standing straight up. I closed the door behind me.

I almost jumped out of my skin as my pager went off and sent jolts of vibration into my hipbone. I looked at the number. Leandra.

She always paged me, instead of calling, because she didn't want to interrupt band practice. I wished Renee would be so cool. I dialed Leandra's number.

"Hey," she breathed, without even asking if it was me, "I just got back from cheerleading practice."

"I thought your practices got done at six," I said, giving the basement door one more shove to make sure it stayed shut.

"Seven tonight. Whew, I'm starved."

I could hear her opening her refrigerator as I opened mine. I saw the orange juice container and pulled it out. I tried to shake off my willies without letting on to her that I had them.

"Why seven?" I asked casually.

"Because of Ali McDermott. She was late again. So, we had to stay after for an hour. It's the fourth time in two weeks. Girl's gonna get herself kicked off after one more time, and some of the others are really starting to rag."

I really didn't want to hear a whole crock about Ali. Leandra was like Ali in the sense of not *liking* to gossip. She said her youth group pastor used to give the kids speeches on the subject. The difference was that Leandra had to work at it, whereas Ali came by not gossiping naturally.

"So, are you still on the bottom of the pyramid?" I asked, because I really wanted a new subject.

"Yes," she snorted. "Why do I have to be so tall? I'm always in the back or on the bottom. I always have to catch people—"

"Tall is good," I tried to assure her.

"Yeah, tell that to my knees since, thanks to Ali McDermott, I had to be on the bottom for an extra twelve pyramids."

I sighed. Her mentioning Ali so soon again meant she was dying to tell me this thing.

"I've heard so much about Creed, I'm not sure I can take a load of grief about Ali," I said. "Let's talk about the band."

"Oh, it's not a load of grief," she told me. Leandra was pretty well tone-deaf and didn't really appreciate the band. "I'm not totally mad at her. I mean, if my parents split up out of the clear blue, I'm sure I'd take it hard. Who knows, I might do some wacky stuff. I just hope I wouldn't be off doing the nasty with some guy when I was supposed to be at cheerleading."

I rolled my eyes.

"When she finally did get to cheerleading, she had a bunch of leaves in her hair," Leandra went on.

"Maybe she thinks she's an Indian," I muttered.

"*And* . . . you know that little suede doodad she's been wearing around her neck? It looks exactly like those things all the boons wear. So people are saying some boon guy gave it to her, so now she's doing it with a boon."

"Maybe she likes little suede doodads," I snapped, but I wanted to kick Ali. I couldn't figure why she was bringing this kind of talk down on her head. I mean, every school has a few girls who go down like subs, and we had more besides Ali. But mostly they were bigmouths and kind of nasty looking, the kind who would do anything to get somebody to go out with them. Ali was cute, could catch anybody she wanted to, if she wanted to. It didn't make sense.

Leandra was quiet for a moment and said in a real confused voice, "Why are you standing up for her?"

"Leandra . . ." I stumbled. "I just don't think Ali was off doing the nasty in the middle of cheerleading, and adding a boon to the story just makes it sound even more retarded. People should cut her a break."

"Well, she's not cutting us much of a break," she continued. "She'd rather get us all in trouble, while being out in

the woods with one of those greasy . . . nary-a-haircut . . .
foul-smelling . . . tattoo-loving—"

"Leandra! There was no boon!" I snapped.

I heard my voice bouncing around, and became sort of
aware that even my own thinking was a little cockeyed.
We're talking about a boon off boffing one of our friends,
and I'm more concerned with the *who* than the what or the
why or the where.

There were about thirty boons in our school, maybe
seven in the junior class with us. There were a couple boon
girls in college prep, I think, but no boons were in the honors
program with me. Most of the boon guys were in vo-tech,
which meant they went to class on the other side of the
building. I realized I had never really talked to a boon.
They did look gross and kind of mean, and we'd all heard
about Bo Richardson slashing tires and pushing Chris
Creed off the top bleacher in the gym.

"I don't understand you," Leandra came back at me,
sounding hurt. "I come in here all starved, at a quarter to
eight, complaining some, and you're making it sound like
I'm some sort of gossip hag."

"No . . ." I groped, confused. But I was having a thought
that was stirring me all up. "Leandra. Have you ever
smelled a boon? I mean . . . did you ever stick your nose up
to one, breathe in through your nostrils, and, like, fall
down because the stench was so bad?"

She stayed quiet for a moment and finally spat out,
"Why would I want to be sticking my nose up to a boon?
Are you insane tonight?"

That was her answer; that's how she knew boons stank—
because I was insane tonight. She spouted off some more.

". . . *got* to be Dallas Everett, Renee decided. She got all
talking about how Shawn Mathers has so many zits you'd

have to *swim* through them. And Bo Richardson wouldn't enjoy *any* girl unless he was *raping* her at *knifepoint*. Dallas could be cute. If he didn't have all those *tattoos*—like, what's he *up* to now? *Fifteen* or so? But there's none on his *face*, so . . ."

She was on a roll tonight. I sighed pretty loud, but I don't think she heard me.

"But I think Renee's going overboard," she went on. "I mean, it could be some college guy from Stockton. I mean, they've got cars, and they're not all nailed down to school when they're not in class. Doing a college guy would make a girl sort-of-like sophisticated and above high school kids. Doing a boon would make her psychotic."

"That's really generous." I scratched my foot, though it wasn't itching.

"Torey . . ." She sighed a long one, like she was getting the drift of my tone of voice. "If something is totally bothering me, don't you want me to tell you?"

That was the thing with Leandra. She never viewed herself as a gossip hag when she got on one of these rolls. She just thought she was troubled about something and needed to vent. Usually I didn't mind, and sometimes it was actually a laugh. I didn't know what was coming over me. Maybe I had just never heard so much goo in one day before. It struck me that Leandra and I spent a lot of time on the phone doing this. Me listening to her blow a ration of grief about somebody else.

"I have to go." I told her I would call her back later, and then I figured I could tell her I fell asleep, if I wasn't up for it.

I went into my bedroom and lay there on the bed for a long time. Every time the wind moaned I would wonder if Creed's ghost was in my basement, his undying grin leering up the stairs. When the wind died down I would wonder if he was alive out there in the woods. I don't know which thought bothered me the worst. I figured if he was out there alive, walking around, he would be completely scared and cold and maybe wishing he was dead.

There had been times when his grin faded, and I remembered those times as I lay there. There were times when he crossed his own line into complete sadness. His only trigger seemed to be physical pain—like just after somebody hit him. And at that point, he would look so hurt, so depressed, so . . . *suicidal*. It struck me that he probably wasn't despairing over his shiners and bruises. He was seeing himself at that point the way other people did—as a social 'tard, an obnoxious reject.

Yeah, I decided. Creed absolutely could have written that letter.

And yeah, he could also have been murdered—I didn't totally deny that. What bugged me was how quick people were to think that he had been murdered, that he could never have written that note. It was easier to point the finger at somebody else. If Creed had written that note, we would have had to point the finger at ourselves, or at least take a good long look at our ways and agonize over questions. Like, could we have played it out differently? Could we have been nicer? Do we have a heartless streak, and can we be bastards?

Easier to blame the boons. Yeah, hell, they sure looked the part—they sure smelled and all—with all their backyard-made tattoos.

Maybe it was my time in life, or maybe it was this whole thing with Creed. But something inside of me felt totally ready to be completely nice to the rejects—people like Creed, the boons—and to be somebody who's not so drowning in surface junk.

Then again, I could be nice to boons without wishing one on Ali, I reminded myself. Her being with a boon would create a major set of problems for her. The way most kids hagged around school, she might as well get her GED and just never show up again. I told myself that for Ali's sake her boyfriend ought to be some college dude.

This load of thinking was making me way tired. I slept about ten hours that night. It was the last good night's sleep I would have in months.

Seven

I thought that sleeping so much would take away my bad mood. It didn't, really. In homeroom I decided to rip on Alex about band practice. He swore he had been home the whole night, that he had been working on this history paper we had due next week. He swore Renee wasn't with him.

"Yeah, since when do you *not* knock out a history paper ten minutes before it's due?" I asked him in disgust. "Could you at least have called?"

"Well, you could have called me," he said, like I was his mother. "Hey. Guess what? I remembered this one time I hit Creed that I totally forgot about. Can you believe I hit him twice and totally forgot about the second time?"

"If you can forget band practice you can forget anything, I guess," I muttered, but he ignored me.

"We were about twelve years old, and I was riding my bike to Ryan's and passed by that old Indian burial ground behind your house."

"Lenape Indians' burial ground. Yeah." It was in the woods out behind our property, though whether it was an actual burial ground was unproven. All we ever dug up as kids were a few arrowheads.

"I saw Creed coming out of there, and he had this piece of paper," Alex went on. "He showed it to me from, like, ten feet off, and wouldn't let me come any closer. He said it was his treasure map, and he had just buried treasure in there."

"He *buried* treasure in the Indian burial ground?" I asked. I'd heard of kids digging in there. I'd never heard of anyone burying anything in there. Leave it to Creed.

"Yeah. And he was being so obnoxious with this map. He kept waving it by the corner and going, 'I would venture to say that my treasure will be very valuable someday . . . I would venture to say that it wouldn't be wise for me to share it with you.'"

"His smart-mouth mode," I said, and shuddered. "'I would venture to say . . .'"

Alex laughed. "And 'Suffice it to say.' He always said, 'Suffice it to say.'"

"Right." I laughed, too.

"So, he's dangling this treasure map in front of me and telling me he doesn't want to tell me what he just buried." Alex laughed again. "We were, like, *twelve* years old, not *eight*. He thinks I'm gonna beg him to see this treasure map, right? What would make him think that a twelve-year-old would want to play pirates? First I grabbed the map and was going to tear it into a thousand pieces. I couldn't look at it, you know, give him the satisfaction. So I tried to tear it. But he had sent it through one of those plastic machines, so that it was inside something that felt like a place mat."

I cracked up totally, despite myself. "You mean he *laminated* his treasure map?"

"Yes. And he was all looking at me like *nanny-nanny-boo-boo* when I couldn't tear it. So I just threw it down and hit him."

I was still laughing. "Oh my god. I would keep that story under my hat. Because if not, everyone's going to be digging for Creed's treasure in a few weeks and keeping me awake all night."

Alex shook his head. "Actually, the Indian burial ground is not the main attraction. All of a sudden the Pine Barrens is. Did you hear about Mrs. Creed in the Wawa last night?"

"No," I told him. "I was sleeping early."

"You shouldn't sleep, man, you miss everything."

"That's why I was sleeping."

He wouldn't take the hint. "Ryan was down there and came to my house all freaking. He said that Mrs. Creed had been in there, like, three times, looking to guilt kids who had not helped her search the woods for Chris on Saturday. Renee and I were afraid to go down to Wawa after that."

"Oh, so you and Renee sat in your house instead of hanging at Wawa?" I blasted. "Don't give me this history-paper shit."

He got kind of quiet, like, *Ooops*.

I looked up at the clock. Five minutes until the bell. I really didn't feel like hearing this.

"Mrs. Creed talked to Mrs. Kyle one of the times she was in the Wawa last night." Alex grabbed my arm, like this was totally important in comparison to his lying in my face. "She says she and Mr. Creed really want to believe Chris ran away. But she said she had kept every dime of his paper-route money for six years. He's got three grand in the bank. She's been watching the bank account—like, going online for the balance three times a day—and not a penny of it has moved. In other words, he hasn't touched his bank account, and no money is missing from anywhere in town. No money, no bus ticket. No muscle, no surviving in the woods. Yeah, she's starting to think he's dead. She's saying somebody else wrote the note to make it look like a suicide. And what really happened is that one of the boons—probably Richardson—killed him and dumped the body. In the Pine Barrens, maybe the boondocks."

I pulled back and stared at him. "Just like Leandra was saying yesterday?"

"You got it."

I shut my eyes and tried to tell myself that there was something to enjoy in this. Even my friends were getting some kind of roller-coaster ride out of it. When your friends start talking all negative on the boons, it's one thing. But here was a mature adult. The kid's own mother.

"Well . . ." I felt confused. "Did anyone see Richardson with Chris after school on Thursday?"

"I don't know." He shrugged like that wasn't important. "All I know is that Mrs. Creed is now saying he had it in for Chris ever since he pushed Chris off the bleachers last year and busted his foot."

"Oh." I had forgotten about that point. Here I was the night before, thinking the boons were overrated in the violence department. I had to admit to myself that of all the kids who had punched out Chris, Bo's thing had to be the worst. It made for a trip to the hospital, for X rays and crutches and all that stuff. Plus, Bo carried a knife and mouthed off to people all the time. I was wondering if I should feel like a fool yet.

Alex watched me look confused, and he shrugged. "Makes perfect sense to me."

"Yeah," I muttered softly. But something about it was bothering me. The vision floated through my head of the day Bo pushed Chris and all the medics showed up and that red flashing glare of the ambulance bounced around the classroom walls. The medics had taken Chris out in one of those nonmovable neck contraptions. It was a big deal. Bo got in a lot of trouble. Especially when his only excuse was,

"The dude was all motormouthing right in my ear and wouldn't shut up!"

We used to hit Creed for the same type of stuff—in, like, sixth grade. But this was high school. It made Bo seem out of control, totally violent.

Sixth grade. It was easy to remember all that blood running from Creed's nostrils—so much so that the other details kind of got lost. Maybe I had wanted them to get lost.

The whole thing came wafting back to me like a bad smell. The teacher had come running over and collared me, and she called me selfish for caring more about a guitar than another human being. She hauled us both into the corridor, but because of Chris's bleeding nose, she dropped him at the nurse's office before taking me to the principal's office. The nurse took one look at him and said, "It could be broken. He should have an X ray." And so, as I was sitting in the principal's office, I saw the medics out the window. They took him away on a stretcher.

Richardson had sent Creed to the hospital, and the only other person in the world to do that was me. Nobody was wondering if I had killed Creed.

The bell rang, and I almost jumped out of my chair. Alex stood up beside me going, "How's La La Land, abnormal one?"

"Fine."

I probably should have reminded Alex about me in sixth grade. But I was starting to feel there wasn't too much that would get in the way of his *perfect* sense. He was my friend, my best friend, but even best friends have this line and you don't cross it. I had never thought about Alex's line before, because I had never come so close to it. But I knew it instinctively now, like I knew Alex. Some people you joke around with, you play poorly written songs with, you bust on boons with. But you don't go after their version of reality. He wouldn't hear me; it would just piss him off. That pissed *me* off.

"I can't do band practice tonight," I said.

He crossed himself like he was Catholic, as we went into the corridor. "Are you at death's door?"

"No." I shrugged kind of casually. "Ali McDermott wants me to come over."

I watched him stare, and almost added the one detail I didn't really care about, which was "to meet her boyfriend." But I decided just to let him think whatever he wanted to.

Eight

It was dark when I got to Ali's that night. I waved to her mom in the living room, and her mom waved back and smiled but didn't get up off the couch. She looked tired. I wondered if the divorce had turned out to be harder than she had expected.

Ali's little brother, Greg, was watching TV with his face, like, right up to the screen. My mom used to lecture me for doing that. Mrs. McDermott didn't seem to notice.

Ali and I went upstairs into her bedroom, and she slammed the door. I jumped a little at the loudness of it.

I started to take off my jacket, and she said, "Don't let that get too far from you. If my mom's new boyfriend comes over, we have to leave. We can go out in the yard, okay?"

"Sure," I said. Whatever she felt she needed.

She flopped onto her bed, and I could see that from her viewpoint she had a bird's-eye view into five different windows at the Creeds' house. It looked like the den, the kitchen, and a row of three upstairs bedrooms.

I pulled up onto my stomach beside her and heard the bedsprings groan. "Is your mom going to freak that I'm up here?"

She turned her head and passed me another one of those mystery smirks like she did yesterday, like, *It's cool, but I don't want to talk about it*. Leandra's mom would have pitched a fit.

Then I had another thought. "Where's this boyfriend of yours?"

"He won't mind you lying on my bed, either," she muttered, watching the Creeds'. "He knows you're coming. He's not thrilled, he doesn't trust you. But I told him you're cool and that he'll trust you if he gives you a chance."

"That's really good of you," I said, getting a little tired of all the mystery shit. "So, who is it? I take it it's somebody I know, if he doesn't trust me."

"It's somebody."

At that moment, my heart almost fell through the bed. I got this idea in my head and I don't know where it came from. *It's Creed*. It's not like I could exactly see Ali going out with Creed, but supposedly Ali went out with anybody and anything these days. I watched her, thinking there was some logic to this. Her dumping on him, talking to him probably more than anybody else . . . She said she had seen the note . . . She's running around these days with a mystery boyfriend . . . *Maybe he's sleeping in the crawl space under her house or in the attic or something.*

I decided to back off. If she was hiding Creed, it would be a complete stress to her, and I would find out soon enough.

"See the middle window upstairs?" Ali whispered.

"Yeah." There was a darker window between the two lit in the upstairs. It looked like a small lamp was on inside, while in the two other rooms, the overheads were on.

"That's Chris's room. She's not in there right now. She goes in there every night for about half an hour."

"To do what?" I imagined Mrs. Creed, like, sitting on the bed and crying or something.

"She's looking for something. She goes through his drawers, his mattress; she even pulled the whole rug up as far as the bed last night."

"What do you think she's looking for?" I asked.

"His diary, probably."

That was way interesting. I could see Mrs. Creed downstairs in the den. She was talking on the telephone, and her mouth was going a hundred miles an hour.

"She's talking to the cops," Ali muttered.

"How do you know?"

"I overheard Renee say she badgers them every ten minutes. They're trying to look at him like a runaway. They're thinking if he committed suicide—*duh*—there would be a body. There's not much they can do about a runaway. But in her mind, they should be spending their every waking breath looking for her kid. So it's probably them. It's not like she has a whole lot of girlfriends or anything."

"Maybe it's a relative," I put in, watching Mrs. Creed's mouth run on and on.

"She has two sisters. But they can't stand her, either. I found that out one night when I had to eat dinner over there in, like, fifth grade. My parents were going out, and I had to take Greg over there to eat. Mrs. Creed was at her mother's funeral, in Texas. Mr. Creed was all worried about her being at this funeral. He said that Mrs. Creed's two sisters couldn't stand her, hadn't even talked to her in years. I think if Chris turned up dead, she would call them. But not yet."

She pointed to something upstairs.

"See that picture on the wall? The one right in the center of Chris's room?" she asked.

"Yeah." There were five pictures on the wall, and four surrounded one.

"The diary, it's inside the lining of that photo." She turned a triumphant grin on me, and I looked from her to the photo, completely hypnotized. "See how it stands out about an inch farther than the others? Can you imagine having a mom so nosy that you'd have to find an ingenious place like that to hide your diary? If she had found it, I don't think she would still be in there searching."

She giggled, and I got the feeling this was some sort of game to her. She enjoyed knowing that Mrs. Creed couldn't find this thing, while she knew exactly where it was.

"You really, really don't like this woman, do you?" I asked her.

"I hate her. But then again, I hate all mothers right about now. That's really why you're here. I'd like a second opinion on whether I'm crazy or not."

"Whatever." I shrugged. The back of a head rose over the top of a TV chair in the Creeds' den, and I realized Mr. Creed was sitting there with his back to the window, reading a book. You could just make out the outline of one side of him, with the chair covering the rest.

Upstairs, Chris's youngest brother, Matthew, was sitting at a little desk in a bedroom, with his back to us. It looked like he was doing homework. From seeing him around church, I gathered he was about nine. The door opened to the other room, and Chris's other brother, Justin, came in, dressed in pajamas. He kind of flopped onto his bed on his stomach but didn't bother to turn off the light. He just lay there, staring. He looked about ten, though I wasn't sure about him, either.

You could see into their house so well in the surrounding blackness, I could see that Justin's eyes were open. He just lay there on his stomach, staring out the window.

"Now, check out some weird things," Ali whispered. "Look at Matthew's room, Chris's room, then Justin's room. Notice anything funny?"

I looked up and down the row a couple times, and then it struck me. "Same furniture. Same . . . type of desk, dresser, mirror—"

"Right down to the bedspreads." All had the same blue bedspread. Even the mirrors were the same, in the same spot. Chris had the biggest bedroom, but the two end ones were just about identical in every way. These kids didn't even have any posters on the walls. Chris's five pictures were all framed, not like something a kid would put up himself. Each of the other two rooms had three pictures on the walls, but you couldn't see what they were, only that the frames matched.

"Great place to get a sense of individuality." Ali smirked. "You've really got a shot at having your own identity in that place, huh?"

"It's sad," I muttered.

I heard the front door bang beneath us, and Ali cursed. "That's my mom's boyfriend. He's a pig."

She got up without breaking her stare at the Creeds' and tossed me my coat with a sigh. I really didn't feel like sitting on her front lawn. It was cold enough that you could see your breath outside. She grabbed her coat, and I felt like asking her, "What's the difference between staying in here and going out to the front lawn?" Either way, she was within thirty feet of the guy. I heard Ali's little brother trudging up the stairs and going into his room. His door slammed.

"See?" she told me. "He's such a pig that he can't even fool a seven-year-old."

I laughed a little. "So how come your mom goes out with him?"

She rolled her eyes, putting one arm into her coat. "She's ready for a mental institution, that's why. She's waiting for me to call the loony bin on her."

She froze with one arm in her coat. I turned around and saw Mrs. Creed at the doorway of Chris's room, and the light suddenly went as bright as the other two rooms.

"You can't miss this. Just . . . lie back down. Maybe the pig will just leave tonight."

I lay back down in my jacket, watching Mrs. Creed shout something out into the hallway. No sooner was it out of her mouth than both kids got up—Matthew out of his chair, Justin off his bed. Matthew looked to be arranging his schoolbooks and stuff, and Justin just stood there rubbing his eyes.

"Lights-out . . . Troops, march . . ." Ali muttered. "In the summer the windows are open. You can hear her clear to Atlantic City. She thinks she's cute. She's clueless that her own family wants to puke on her."

Matthew put out his light, and the room went dark. Justin reached for the light switch, but before he hit it off, he flipped the bird out into the hallway.

"Did you see that?" I let out a laugh.

"He's the only one with any spunk," Ali said. "Yeah, I really like ol' Justin. He's actually about twelve, though he looks a lot younger."

A knock at the bedroom door made me jump a little.

"How you doing, Ali-girl?" a man's voice rang out.

"I'm going out." She sounded tense.

"Oh yeah? Who's in there with you? That boyfriend of yours again?"

"No. Nobody's here. I *said* I'm going *out* . . ." She added under her breath, "Not that it's any business of yours. Christ . . . it's Albert, Mom's New 'Soulmate.'"

She turned back to the window, and this time I could see Mrs. Creed in Chris's room, scratching her chin, looking this way and that like she was sizing up every space in every corner.

"She'll find it one of these nights," Ali told me.

Mrs. Creed walked slowly over to the closet. It was the sliding-door type of thing that takes up a whole wall. There weren't many clothes hanging, but there were some sweatshirts and things on the shelf above. Mrs. Creed picked up a sweatshirt, held it by the shoulders, and let it dangle open. She shook it. Looked down the neck hole, felt each sleeve, then tossed it on the bed. She picked up a second one and did the same thing.

"Does this look like a woman on a mission?" Ali asked.

"Yeah . . ." I breathed. "It's not like she even looks sad. Just . . . determined or focused or something."

"Diabolical," Ali added, and I couldn't argue with that one.

I watched Mrs. Creed take a few books off the shelf and rattle through the pages. We sat there for about twenty minutes more, our eyes going back and forth from Mrs. Creed to Mr. Creed, who had not moved from his chair downstairs. I was starting to get a little bored, but it was hard to be completely bored, because Mrs. Creed was being such a fanatic with this search. She had the whole top half of the closet on the bed and was starting to fold things and put them away again.

At that point a strange noise from overhead caused me to look up. It sounded like somebody was moving bedroom furniture around, dragging heavy things across the floor. Ali looked up and sighed, cursing under her breath.

"Whatever noises you hear tonight, just remember, I did not cause them. I have nothing to do with them, okay?" she muttered.

"Yeah, sure." I listened some more—I mean, you couldn't help it—and I suddenly realized there was some rhythm to it. Then it struck me what it was. I thought of conversations I'd had in school with some of my friends who had actually caught their parents. Mostly they were completely grossed out. You don't want to catch your parents. But all this banging around was so loud it was ridiculous.

"He screams at the end," Ali said. "Just . . . thought I'd warn you."

Oh my god, I thought. I was, like, dying for her. "Maybe if you laid a broad hint on your mom when he's not around—"

"Oh, you don't understand." She shook her head hard. "They're doing this because he enjoys the fact that other people can hear him. It doesn't matter to him that it's two kids. Maybe that's part of it."

I just stared at her. "You're not serious."

"Oh yeah. When my mom's not around, he's asked me if I enjoy the sound effects."

I know my jaw was bobbing. I had no clue what to say to her.

"My mom, she's, like, asleep on her feet. I've said something right to her face, and she denies flat-out that they make any noise at all. She's had a lot of boyfriends over the years. That's why my dad finally left."

"Oh." I was in shock. I never had any clue that Ali's mom was cheating at all, let alone doing it with lots of men. I wondered why Ali was pulling the same tricks, if she thought her mom was so awful.

"See why I say I'm not like you?" she asked me. A match lit, and I could see her eyes looking at me from behind a cigarette. "You know anybody else in your entire life who has to endure anything like this?"

I was starting to realize why Ali felt the need to find new friends. Ryan and Renee were fun, but they were kind of naive. Stuff like this didn't happen in any of our houses. I tried not to stare at the ceiling, but I had this totally helpless feeling there was nothing I could do for her. It made sense why she wanted to go outside. Couldn't hear if from out there.

"I think—I'll bet this is abuse," I finally managed. "You could tell the police. He's not molesting you, but he's, like . . . using you. Gross."

"I can't," Ali said, shaking her head. "I could never tell this to Chief Bowen."

"Are you— You're scared it would get all over school?" I was thinking of Ryan and Renee.

She shrugged, then nodded like she wasn't really hearing me. It was hard to hear anything but that stupid banging. But one noise did come through—another door closing from downstairs. We could barely hear it, so they obviously didn't hear it.

"Oh my god," Ali said, standing up. "It's my boyfriend. How the hell am I going to explain this?"

She let out a sob, and I pulled the cigarette from her hand, scared she would drop it. I could hear heavy steps on the stairs, around the noise from the top floor. I kept thinking they would hear these footsteps and stop their racket. But they didn't. Finally the bedroom door swung open. My heart was in my throat for her. I was half expecting to see Creed. The light switch clicked on, and I think my jaw dropped onto the bed as I stared. The last person I was expecting to see was Bo Richardson.

His eyes were as big and black as usual, but out of his mouth came a mild, "Hey."

He looked all concerned at Ali but didn't even seem to notice me. I looked down and saw the tip of a knife handle sticking out of his belt. He was wearing a white T-shirt, cut off at the waist, and a huge jean jacket, and a bandanna around his neck. He looked big and kind of dangerous. I heard Ali sniff and turned to see her attempting a grin.

"Welcome to my house," she sputtered.

His eyes shot up to the noise, and then back down again. He didn't even blink. "This is the thing? The thing your mom does that you were afraid to tell me?"

She nodded, sniffing again.

I figured, him being a boon, that stuff like this went on in his neighborhood all the time. I guessed a minute later that I was way wrong. He turned and left the room, and I heard him clomping up the stairs. I shut my eyes as Ali dived her head into my lap. I could not believe this couple was up there doing the nasty, banging off the walls, and Bo Richardson was climbing the stairs like taking them on was nothing.

The banging stopped. I heard Mrs. McDermott scream and the man's voice holler.

Then Bo's voice. "Hey, shut up . . . Don't give a shit . . . I'll throw you out the window, asshole . . ."

The man said something in a lower voice and Bo broke him off. "You ain't calling the cops, you pervert. You're gonna be quiet or get the fuck out . . . And you—you got kids . . ."

Mrs. McDermott said something short I couldn't hear, then he cut her off, too.

"Wake up and smell the coffee, woman . . . Don't want to hear it . . . You got kids. Now, be thinking of your kids, or I'm calling the cops on *you*. You got it? . . . Hey, tell your troubles to Jesus, Mrs. McDermott . . . Don't want to hear one more peep out of this room. Just . . . be cool."

The door slammed. Bo's footsteps came back down the stairs, and Ali shot up out of my lap. I heaved a sigh, hearing him knock on her little brother's door.

"Greg, my bro. How are you, my man?" I heard Greg say something soft and run across the floor. Bo came back into the room with the kid on his back, piggyback-style. I sat on the corner of the bed farthest away from them, wondering

76

if I should leave. I wanted to, but I didn't want to. I watched Bo spin Greg around front so he was holding him monkey-style, wondering why I didn't have the nerve to trudge up those stairs and do what he just did. Probably because I never heard the nasty before, not outside a movie. Upstairs was so deadly quiet all of a sudden, I wanted to laugh.

Bo sat down beside Ali, sort of slap-wrestling Greg with one hand. He threw an arm around her back.

"He's a pervert, okay, Ali?" he said. "You want me to get rid of him? I'll go back up there right now if you—"

"No, there'll just be somebody else next week. One of them's gonna decide they enjoy doing something worse. That's what I keep thinking—"

"Hey. Somebody lays a hand on you two over my dead body. You got that?" He quit play-slapping Greg. "Greg, be a good man and go to bed. I need to talk to Ali, okay?"

Greg put his feet on the floor. "Last time you came over, you said this time you would take me out for baseball cards."

"Yeah, well . . . Saturday, okay? I promise, cross my heart. Baseball store is closed now."

"It's only eight," he argued.

"Go to bed, Greg," Ali begged.

He left, muttering, "Saturday. You promised."

Bo watched Ali, letting out a sigh, and then his eyes turned to me. He stared at me, and I stared back, trying a slight grin that didn't really work.

"What're you doing, Adams? Getting an education?"

I decided to be truthful. "Yeah."

He laughed and pulled the cigarette out of my hand, and I realized I'd been holding it since before Ali dived her head into my lap. He took a huge drag off it, and then Ali took it from him. Her hands were shaking still. He just stroked her back some and watched her.

"Shit, my old lady's been married four times. I got five younger brothers and two younger sisters. Five different dads." He laughed. "If you knew some of the shit I been through trying to keep my place from turning into an insanity fest . . . My old lady never pulled this one. But she'll go off to the grocery store and show up five days later. Come on, babe. Be cool. 'S okay now."

She took a deep breath and actually quit crying. There was a long silence, and he rubbed her arm and kept kissing her head. I guessed she was lucky to have him, funny as it seemed. Because none of *us* would have had the first clue what to do about her mom and Albert.

He jerked his head at me. "You tell Adams about us?"

She shook her head, blowing a stream of smoke out. "But he knew you were coming and all. He's cool."

She was saying I was cool, but I guess he could tell I was surprised by the look on my face.

I tried a shrug. I had already decided I wouldn't have a problem if Ali was with a boon. I stared back as he looked me dead in the eye for an eternity. Finally he muttered, "Yeah, I guess maybe you are cool. God knows why. But you gotta keep 'us' to yourself, okay?"

He kissed her on the side of the head one last time. "She's been going through a heap of shit around here. She don't need any more from school, okay?"

"Yeah. Fine." I watched him, thinking, *He's so old. He's so mature.* I mean, for all the stuff he got in trouble for around school, you would never think he had this big side, this side that was unselfish enough to think of Ali. I felt young in the room with them, like they could almost baby-sit me. It was a stupid thought, and to break out of the silence, I said something. "This is stupid, but I thought you might be Creed. All I knew was her boyfriend was coming, and she's been acting all mysterious and—"

78

They both cracked up, not like they were laughing at me or at Chris but like it struck them as funny.

"No, no," Ali said. "Cross my heart. I have no idea where that little bugger is. I wish I did."

"I've hit him before," Bo said. "I've hit him *hard* a couple times before. He just could get so far up your ass . . . coming up to me all, 'Bo! Guess what?' *Blah blah blah*. Like I hadn't just beat the shit out of him three weeks ago. Guy's got a memory problem."

I laughed. I knew exactly what he was talking about.

"It's not like I ever thought he'd pull a stunt like this." Bo shook his head. "But if he shows up next week? I am really, *really* gonna hit him for scaring everybody half to death."

"Shook you guys up, too, huh?" I asked, meaning him and the other boons.

He laughed, like I was stupid. "Shook us up? Them ain't the words. We're pissing ourselves in the Barrens, because— you mark my words—if Creed don't show up soon, one of us is gonna hang."

"They'll blame you?" I asked innocently, but I couldn't help remembering Leandra prattling on at the lunch table about them being killers. And Mrs. Creed had supposedly been saying that, too.

"Yeah. They'll find some way to blame one of us. I hear Mrs. Creed already started on that. She don't want to admit her part in it. Either she drove him to it or she outright did it. Look at her. She's in there trying to find the evidence that will hang her, so she can burn it before the cops find it. Then she can waste one of us. It'll probably be me."

"Don't even say that," Ali begged, and I started getting all churned up for her.

"How could they pin it on you?" I asked. "I mean, they need evidence or something."

"No, they don't." He smirked. "They'll find a way. I ain't that smart to guess on how. But I have a pretty good idea."

I watched him, waiting for him to say more. He just kept watching Ali, who looked all worried. Finally I broke my stare and looked over to see Mrs. Creed putting one last sweater on top of the shelf. The closet looked as neat as an army barracks locker.

"Guess she didn't find it, Torey," Ali said, as Mrs. Creed put out the overhead, leaving just the little lamp on. She shut the door on her way out. "God. She doesn't even look upset. Just . . . focused. She'll find it tomorrow night. Yeah. Miss Methodical. She's coming around to that wall in her military search."

"She didn't find the diary?" Bo muttered, and Ali nodded. They must have had a few conversations about this before, I gathered, by the knowing sound in his voice.

Bo started breathing sort of funny, sort of seething. The two of them were staring out the window, and I could see so much fire in their faces. Their own moms were such a problem, I didn't guess they would even bat an eye to imagine Mrs. Creed as a murderer. All of a sudden, I didn't know what to think. I never would have thought of Mrs. Creed as a murderer, but I never would have thought of Mrs. McDermott as a turbo slut. And I never would have thought of Bo Richardson as a courageous person.

Bo started yanking off his shoes. They were big work boots, and he shook the whole bed, pulling them off. Then he took off his jean jacket. I thought he was just making himself comfy.

"Piece of cake," he muttered, never taking his eyes off the Creeds' house.

"Bo, don't!" Ali tried to grab his arm, but he shook it off easily.

"Who do you want to have that diary, babe? Her? Or us?"

"Oh my god," Ali said, putting her face in her hands as he charged out the door.

Something inside of me went off. I charged over her and went flying out the door behind him. I knew I didn't want to feel like a helpless little kid for the second time that night.

Nine

I didn't know what his plan was, and I was scared he didn't have one. I didn't want him to go shuffling up the drainpipe or something, with Mrs. Creed right in the next room. I grabbed his elbow as he got to Ali's curb and said, "Hold up."

He huffed a little, and I did, too. I was also shaking, even though I had my coat on and he didn't. He didn't even have shoes on. He stood there dancing a little in his socks.

"You got a plan?" I asked him.

"No. I just got guts." He laughed but didn't take off again. He stood there on the curb, staring at the Creeds' house.

"Okay, we've got to have a plan," I said.

After I stood there in stunned silence for a minute or two, he said, "Well?"

I was clueless. "You ever do a break-in before?"

"Yeah. Lots of times."

"So, how do you do it?" I wondered why he was waiting for me to think it up, knowing I was all wet.

"Usually we wait until dark and get all drunk. And then we just try it. I probably broke into twenty places. After a while I just stopped doing it. Last year, probably."

"How come?" I asked.

"Because I always got caught." He kept laughing.

"*Always?*"

"Always. I had bad luck. Once, it was a trailer and the windows were real small. I got stuck on the way in. Cops had to wedge me out with a crowbar before they could charge me."

I looked at him with my jaw hanging. "Seems like if you tried it twenty times, you would get a little bit good at it."

He shrugged. "Maybe I didn't really want the stuff. Maybe I was just trying to raise some hell. Make some kind of a point. I don't know. All I know is I didn't want that stuff as bad as I want this diary, or whatever it is."

"Why do you want this so bad?" I hunted for something that made sense behind this insane-looking determination of his. He pulled a cigarette out of his jean jacket pocket and lit it with a lighter. He inhaled really deep, then exhaled.

"I got called into the principal's office on Thursday for cutting out at lunchtime. In my car. Proctor seen me."

He took another drag on the cigarette. It was no secret that he tried to cut out at lunchtime every day in his car. Half the time the proctor didn't even bother writing him up anymore. It wasn't worth the slip, because Bo never learned his lesson.

"Anyway, I was in there after school when Ames made the first call about Creed to the cop station. I could hear him from his inner office. He said, 'I have this e-mail here. Could be a runaway, could be a suicide. I need you to come down here.' Of course, my ears perked up. *Suicide?* This could be way interesting. Then I hear him tell Chief Bowen it was sent from the library. I stick around long enough to realize Ames is, like, hanging by his balls over this, and he ain't gonna even remember to give me no detention, okay?

Next morning, me and Ali sneak up to the library. There was nobody too interested in the terminal yet, because they still figured he just ran off. But we were jumpy, looking up that note, because we were together and didn't want to get seen, start a lot of talk. We found it pretty quick, but instead of wasting time there reading it, we moved it onto a floppy and figured we would read it at Ali's later, which we did. After school we looked at the note at Ali's house. We closed the file, and she gives me the disk, god knows why. It was just one of those things. I took it. Stuck it in my locker the other day with this other pile of shit from my car."

He flicked the cigarette and stared across to the house next to Creed's. I looked where he was looking and thought I saw a curtain flicker but didn't focus on it. This story was too interesting.

"Mrs. Creed had started in that it was some boon, and they killed her kid in the Pine Barrens," he went on. "I don't know why—probably because I messed Creed up so bad last year with that bleachers thing—but Ames broke down, hauled me into his office yesterday and asked me where I was Thursday after school. I mean, for the first half hour after school, I was sitting in his office watching him sweat bullets. He wanted to know where I was before that. I actually had gone to class for once, so that was good. Alibi. Then the cops want to know where I was *after* that. I was laughing at them, you know, '*After* that? Ames already had the good-bye note *after* that.' But since there's no body, there's no saying *when* he died. I was all, 'Shit, man, what do you think? I holed him up in my trunk, alive, then sent an e-mail from the library? Then went to get my detention slip, then went back and finished him off?' Does that make sense, Adams?"

"No." I laughed, feeling nervous. Seemed like the cops were really reaching.

"Anyway, I was afraid to tell them where I was *after* Ames's office. I told them I was alone."

"Where were you?" I asked.

"With Ali. We were out in the woods."

I thought of Leandra's little spiel about them hooking up in the woods. Bo's eyes got kind of far off and concerned, but I wouldn't say he looked all proud, like he had scored.

"I been trying to get her to tell me about what's been going on with Albert," he went on. "She never wanted to say that part. But we'd go out there walking and she'd dump a whole lot of stuff on me that had been bothering her. I figure, so what if she don't make it to cheerleading? Bunch of stuck-up PMS babes. It ain't like they're gonna do anything for her. They ain't gonna hear this kind of shit very well."

"Yeah," I agreed. Their imaginations couldn't fathom anything beyond Ali doing the nasty out there.

"Anyway, I was scared to tell Ames I was with Ali. It seemed like if he was trying to pin Creed on me, he might end up dragging her in and pinning it on her, too, if he found out I was with her. So when I said I was alone, the cops asked to search my locker. I said, 'Bite me. You can search my locker from now till doomsday, fools.' I totally forgot about the goddamn disk. Now they have the computer disk and a bunch of my other stuff. Any minute now they're gonna stick the disk in some hard drive and see what's on it. They're gonna see that Creed's suicide note was in my possession. You think they're gonna believe our story? No way, man. They're gonna think I had that note all along. I wrote it, killed him, sent it from the library to cover my ass, the whole insane thing."

I stood there dumbfounded, trying to think if I ever heard a worse bad-luck story in my life. "Basically, me and my friends did something worse than what you and Ali

86

did," I muttered. "We broke in electronically, and you just . . . put it on a disk. Holy shit."

"You seen the note?" he asked.

I nodded. "Yeah. We hacked in. It's weird, but Alex said there was no longer a copy in the library's outbox."

He laughed. "Yeah. It's on Ali's disk. So how did you bums—"

"Ames's copy. The recipient's mailbox."

He looked at me with huge eyes. "Oh my god. You guys can dream up thieving that would never cross my mind. And to think I'm the one with the reputation. Sweet Jesus."

It seemed weird that we were just more sophisticated about our thieving.

"How could they think anyone else could write that note?" I asked. "Chris is in honors. It's kind of a flowery, well-spelled note. Don't you think they'll realize that?"

I was trying to find a nice way to say that no boon could have written that note. He didn't seem too bothered by my meaning. He shrugged, dragging hard on the cigarette.

"If they knew about me and Ali, they might say Ali wrote it. She's in honors, and she's known him her whole life. See, that's another reason I don't want people knowing about Ali and me right now."

"But since she's in honors and she's known as a good kid, maybe she would make them believe you," I argued.

"She's just the girl I'm fucking right now, that's how they'll see her. It'll look bad for her, rather than good for me. Especially after she's been down with so many guys. That sort of thing don't look so good. You want to know what's the funniest thing?"

"What?"

"I ain't been with Ali. Not even one time." He must have noticed my look of total disbelief, because he laughed. "Truth. I ain't playing with you."

"Well . . . why's she with everybody but—" I stumbled.

"But not me?" He flicked the cigarette butt into the gutter and exhaled a huge blast of smoke. "I got this thirteen-year-old sister, Darla. Something's up with her—I don't know what—but she turned thirteen and I couldn't keep her off her back to save my life. I threatened her; I told her I'd beat the shit out of her next time I caught her with some boon. One day I pinned her neck to the wall. She'd been with Billy Everett, Dallas's little brother. He's already got one kid, and he's only thirteen. I said to her, 'Darla, why you so determined to make yourself a mama?' You know what she says to me? She says, 'I just like to feel crazy.' I wasn't thinking, you know. I told her, 'I'll show you crazy,' and almost knocked her head clear through the refrigerator. But later I got to thinking, what does she mean by 'I just like to feel crazy'? I don't know, man. I don't understand it. But some girls just like to be wicked on themselves. Makes them feel alive or something, to hear people laughing at them, hear these guys all passing around the gory details. When I first started hearing about Ali in the locker room and all—it was before I ever talked to her. But I remember thinking, *Damn, she sounds like Darla.*"

He pulled a fresh cigarette out of his jacket pocket and stared, like he couldn't decide whether to light it or not. Finally he stuck it behind his ear. "I could have Ali five minutes from now, don't think I couldn't. I just don't want her taking out her problems on me, using me because she's messed up. That ain't what I want from her. You know what I'm saying?"

"Yeah," I said, though my head felt empty. These were deep, dark problems, and I didn't have anything to say back. But I was getting the message about one thing. Bo Richardson had a good-guy streak that was just as wide as, probably wider than, his bad-guy streak. I didn't know too many guys who wouldn't jump on Ali if they had the chance, and why she was doing it wouldn't create the least problem for them. I bet he looked out for the younger kids at home, too, because of the way he treated Greg and sounded off at his own sister.

I sighed and watched the Creeds' house, and it was starting to strike me, the greatness of the person Mrs. Creed was trying to hang. So many people would suffer if she hung Bo. I thought of her up there in her neatly trimmed house with the matching bedrooms, screwing up two more kids. With all the people depending on Bo, she might as well just screw up the whole town. It seemed so completely unfair. I wanted to puke.

"Okay," I muttered. "We've got to get that diary. We need a plan."

"Like what?" For somebody so streetwise in some ways, Bo was incredibly stupid in others. Me think up a plan, yeah right, because I watched Alex hack into a mailbox. But then something clicked in my brain.

"Here's a plan. I saw it in an old Hitchcock movie once. This guy and his girlfriend wanted to search a killer's apartment, but the killer was in there. So the guy calls the killer on the phone. He tells him to come to this certain bar and to bring cash. The killer leaves the apartment, all scared that somebody's on to him. The girl swings across and searches the guy's apartment while he's going to the bar to be blackmailed. Of course, there was nobody at the bar when he got there. But it gave them enough time to search."

My eyes went to Richardson, who was staring at me in disbelief. "Goddamn, you *are* cool. Ali was right about you—"

I was not cool, I was pissing myself. But I knew I couldn't cope with it if I just let this thing come down on Bo.

"I'll do the break-in," he offered. "That's a higher offense if we get caught. I already got some other stuff with the cops, so it don't matter. But I promise I won't get caught this time. You make the call."

I turned slowly to go back into Ali's, wondering how he could make that promise when he'd been caught twenty other times. He grabbed me by the shoulder and shoved me in the direction of the street. "Phone booth, asshole. They can trace those calls."

"Oh yeah," I muttered, and when I grinned, the corners of my mouth were shaking. He must have noticed, because he looked sympathetic and swatted my hair absently.

"Look, just be cool. Think of what you're going to say. As soon as they leave, I'll break in. I'll be in and out so fast, those little kids won't even have time to jump out of bed."

I turned numbly and started walking the three blocks to where I knew the nearest phone booth was, and tried not to think about what we were about to do. There was no point in making myself crazy over it. I tried to focus on what I would say. How I would disguise my voice. It was hard, like trying to turn into somebody else.

The nearest pay phone was at the ball field, hooked onto the side of the refreshment stand, which was dark and deserted, and had been since summer. I didn't know the Creeds' phone number and had to dial Information for it. My fingers were shaking totally, but it was an easy number— too easy to forget. Standing there in the darkness of the wide-open field, I could hear the wind whip up, making these *whoosh!* noises that made me feel alone. The two street-lights, about a hundred yards off, looked like spotlights on a vacant stage. I could feel the hair on my arms rising, and I turned slowly away from the street lamps, searching through the blackness. That feeling I'd gotten in my basement was with me again. That feeling like somebody was watching me.

Somebody with ten thousand eyes. *Watching me, patiently watching me. It's Creed, dead but still living somehow, crawling the woods with some army of Lenapes, to get me to do his bidding. Nobody's holding him for ransom. He's holding me. He's dead . . . He wants revenge . . .*

I picked up the phone just to keep a grip on reality. Mrs. Creed needed to come out here and meet the bloody other side. I put the quarter in and said "Up yours" to my life.

A woman's voice answered the phone. I recognized her "Hello."

I made this gravelly voice and spat out a speech that sounded like and felt like somebody else. "I have some information about your son. If you want it, do *not* call the police. Just bring your husband and come to the ball field. Do it *now.*"

Reality was setting in major. I was actually talking to another person who could feel hurt, feel pain, feel terror. Maybe what I was saying could kill a kid's mom. I didn't have a clue.

I stood there gripping that phone like my fingers had turned to concrete.

"Now you listen to me," she finally hissed out. "Do you know I was a pilot in the United States Navy? Did you know I have friends in very, very high places? I will hunt you down, you coward. You will wish you had never been born. Nobody takes my Christopher. Nobody takes one of my babies and gets away with it."

He's not your *baby. He's not* your *Christopher. He's a human being.* My head banged, though I was shaking so bad my mouth wouldn't move. I wanted to reach through the phone and kill her for making me piss myself. I was— total truth—feeling warm piss run down my leg, and it was making me crazy. It came clear to me what she could do to Chris if she could make me piss my goddamn pants.

"Shut up!" I heard myself snarl through my terror. My brain jumped to that Hitchcock movie and the rest of the phone conversation with the murderer. "Bring money! Bring lots of it!"

I slammed down the phone and ran like I've never run before. In football or anything. But you can't run from your own stupidity, and as I flew into the woods, I wanted to scream at my own dumbness. I could feel all those eyes on me still, and it was like they were laughing. I tried not to think about that, to think about what went wrong with that conversation. Something was definitely not adding up, something she had said, I just couldn't think of it right then. I couldn't think of anything except ten thousand laughing eyes, and it struck me like a freight train how unfunny all this was.

"Bring money"? Torey, you didn't even give an amount. She will know you're some total moron who doesn't know shit. I took this dark trail I knew would come out behind the Wawa. I took it in less than a minute, though it was at least a quarter mile, and when the Wawa came into view I stood there huffing and shaking from head to toe. I felt cold and realized I had pissed clear through my jeans, and you could see it plain as day. *"Bring money." Jesus.*

I turned back into the darkness to walk the rest of the way home. There was nowhere else to go with wet jeans. *This is a bad dream. I didn't just make that call. She did not threaten my life. I did not piss myself.*

It was on that short walk that I realized everything that could happen. Mrs. Creed, with all her guts, would probably call the police, anyway. Or Bo would get seen by one of the little kids. Bo wasn't good with planning and might go stupidly back over to Ali's and not run off. He'd be easy to catch there. I had forgotten to wipe my fingerprints off the receiver at the ball field. That last one totally petrified me.

I walked into my house and went straight up to my room. I could feel this thing unwinding as I pulled off my jeans and threw them in the back of my closet. It was almost like I had already been caught. And even if we never got caught, I didn't see how I could walk into school and rattle on with my friends about the boons smelling bad or Creed's body being in somebody's swimming pool, like life was some goddamn joke and we had nothing to worry about. I had become a little like Ali, with the unperfect life. I had just done some sort of serious crime. I had done something the cops could be very pissed about. And here I was, the type who could never even lie without looking guilty as all hell.

Ten

I sat in the police station with my mom on one side of me and Ali on the other. I remember being glad that my dad had been working that night. You don't know how your parents are going to react to trouble if you've never been in any. My mom was totally blank as those cops took me away in the cop car. They had told me I could come down in her car, that they just wanted to question me. But I muttered, "I don't mind," because somehow the cop car seemed a better deal than having my guilt seated next to my mom in a closed-in car. I wished she would have gone ballistic, though my mom had never gone ballistic that I could remember. But I hadn't ever done anything like this before, either.

There were two other rooms in the police station, and I could hear hollering coming out of both of them.

In one Bo was saying, "You're wrong! I don't have to answer your stupid questions, and I don't have to talk to you about anything! I want a lawyer!"

Chief Bowen's voice came back at him. "I guess you've been in here often enough to know the law, Richardson. To get a lawyer at this point in the game, you have to pay for one. Don't forget who you are. A bigmouth with a record, with one foot in Egg Harbor and another foot on a banana peel—"

"Aw, kiss my ass."

"Don't you"—a thunder of chairs clattering made the building shake almost, and Chief Bowen's voice cut in at the end of it—"*ever* talk to me like that!"

Two younger officers charged out of the other room, which Mrs. Creed was in, and shot past us into the room where Bo and Chief Bowen were. Ali shot out of her seat, and I grabbed her by the back of the jeans and jerked her down beside me again. She had been crying and now added to the mess with louder sobs. I couldn't take her sobs. I shot up out of my chair toward the room with Bo, and my mother jerked me back down like I had done with Ali.

"Mom! They're beating him up!" I cried.

"No they're not. Stay calm, both of you." I looked at her sitting there tensely as the yelling and furniture clanging continued.

And from the other room, Mrs. Creed's voice blasted, "He either murdered my son or he's holding my son! If you let him go tonight, I will sue you for—"

"You're a liar!" Bo's voice thundered, and my mom reached over me and grabbed Ali, who was screeching with her head in her lap.

"How can you say they're not beating him?" I pleaded with her.

"They're yelling, mostly. They yanked him out of the chair and the chair fell over, then he kicked the chair, and then one of the other officers tripped over the chair."

"How do you know?" I asked.

"These noises are my life." She stared at the door, too calm.

"How can you let them talk to him like that?" I demanded. "They're the police! They're trashing him—"

96

"Torey." She cut me off and did not look thrilled. "I don't have time right now to give you a lesson in juvenile delinquency. Nobody is beating him, all right? There's just a language that these kids understand, and if you don't use it, you might as well speak French to them. They're just doing what cops do."

"Mom, just do what lawyers do. Please, do something for him," I mumbled, and I could feel myself starting to bawl.

"Would you care to tell me what happened tonight?" she snapped.

"We're . . . in some trouble," I stammered.

"I wasn't born yesterday," she muttered, her jaw barely moving, like she was trying not to be overheard. "This looks like some chapter from my office files. Only problem is, my son is in it. What is going on?"

"Mom . . ." I heard Bo scream out the word *liar* again as the cops hollered for him to shut up. "Mom, please trust me. You gotta help that kid in there. He's innocent."

"Innocent of what?" Her mouth didn't move again, but the tone of her voice was totally pissed.

"Mrs. Creed wants the cops to pin Chris on him. He didn't do anything. Okay? You have to believe me and help him. He's a boon, so they're being mean to him—"

She jumped a little in her chair, to let me know I had said enough.

"Do you know anything about that kid in there, Torey?" she muttered again. "I don't care if he's from Guadalajara. They're not picking on him because of where he's from but because he's got a record as long as your arm. I have personally seen that kid in court five or six times, did you know that?"

"For what?" I asked, feeling my stomach sink through the floor.

"You name it. Breaking and entering, mostly—"

"Mom. He's stupid about it. He's not cut out to be a thief. That's why he keeps getting caught—"

She jumped around again, then cleared her throat, smiling at Chief Bowen's deputy, who went back to Mrs. Creed's little room, shouting, "Mrs. Creed, Chief Bowen says you have to calm down!"

"You are being very stupid right now, young man," my mom said. "I might be a lawyer. *First,* I'm your mother. As your mother I'm telling you: This is not the type of person to whom we expect you to endear yourself, considering we are paying five thousand dollars a year in property taxes to send you to Steepleton High School."

My brain leaped to Ali's house and Bo stomping up those stairs like it was nothing. I thought of him standing on the curb with me, talking about his sister Darla and Ali. . . . He had to have so much courage just to live his life. He saved Ali. I didn't really care about the rest.

I shut my eyes tight as Chief Bowen kept nabbing at Bo. "Look, forget Egg Harbor, forget the juvenile delinquent slumber party up there. You want to go to *Jamesburg,* Richardson? You got one foot in real jail, mister. You have pushed us and pushed us for years—"

"I'm not arrested," Richardson spouted back. "You can't send me to Jamesburg. And besides, I'm telling you, I did not break into that woman's house! I don't know what happened to her dorky kid, but I'll bet you she does!"

"Richardson, when you go to the chair, I'm pulling the switch!" Mrs. Creed's voice dive-bombed the place from across the hall. I almost pissed myself again at the sound of her voice. I shut my eyes and thought, *God, do something here. Because I can't cope with this all by myself.* Ali was wailing, Mrs. Creed was screeching, and my mom was talking about her taxes.

Mom stood up. She looked too calm and too slow in this storm. She turned and looked me dead in the eye and said, "You need to do two things: Stay calm, and keep her calm."

She did not look thrilled, and she said it like it was a military order. I reached down and bodily picked Ali up from her heap on the floor, dumping her back in the chair and keeping both arms around her so she wouldn't slither down again. I kept muttering "shhhh" to Ali as my mom walked toward the door to the room where Bo and Chief Bowen were. The door was open about halfway.

"Guys," she said in a calm voice that stopped Chief Bowen, "are you going to charge this boy with something or not?"

"What're you doing here, Susan?" Chief Bowen asked. He sounded annoyed. "Oh, that's right. We've got your son out there. Mrs. Hoffsteader saw him out her bay window, standing in front of the McDermotts', having a cigarette with this outstanding citizen here."

I wasn't smoking! climbed halfway up my throat, but in a haze I realized that being accused of smoking was a fart in a windstorm. My brain flashed back to that flickering curtain at the house next door to the Creeds'. It hadn't even registered that somebody was watching us. *Stupid.* I hoped I could straighten it out later.

"Are they being charged or not?" My mother's voice was edgy.

"What's your game, Susan?" Chief Bowen asked. "Are you representing one or both or neither of these young men? I think it's against the law to represent your own son; I'll have to check that one out."

"I'm not representing anyone," she said as casually as she could. "I just want to know how I can help get a move on here. It's late. These kids have school tomorrow."

I heard Chief Bowen sigh loudly. "Bring your son in here, Susan. And the McDermott girl. I wouldn't want your son to miss his bedtime. Tiny, take Mr. Richardson out, and please keep him away from Sylvia."

Tiny was, like, a 250-pound officer. We passed him and Bo in the doorway, and it was a squeeze. Bo just stared at the floor with those insane-looking black eyes, but I could see fear in them. He was coming across like machine-gun fire to Chief Bowen, but I knew he was just as scared as I was, or more scared. I noticed he still didn't have his shoes on. He must have been caught right there in the street. I could feel my mom's fingers pushing me in the back. I had won something with her, I just wasn't sure how much.

Like my mom had predicted, there was a chair turned over. I turned it upright and sat in it. Ali edged into the chair beside me, and my mom sat beside Chief Bowen, on the other side of the table. He looked from me to Ali, back to me again.

"That kid out there is not the type of person your parents would want you associating with," he said.

It was my turn to go crazy. I slumped back in the chair, then leaned forward again, pushing Ali, who was hollering that they didn't know the first thing about him.

"You know, everybody has their own little version of reality going here!" I yelled. "And it has nothing do to with what's true or not true—"

"Torey!" my mother hollered, staring at the table. "Remain calm."

I dropped back in the chair and began rubbing Ali's back, not caring that I was sniffing.

"This is an insanity-fest," I muttered. "This is crazy. And it's not all Bo."

"You see this?" Chief Bowen picked up a huge file that was sitting in front of him. "It's twenty pages long, and it's Richardson's file. He's a thief. And a liar. And an upstart. It's obvious from this file that he's not particularly good at thieving. Lying? I would say he's an ace. Now, there was a very unusual phone call made to the Creeds tonight. If you kids know something about that—and something about the disappearance of Chris Creed—and you are protecting Mr. Richardson—"

"Bo doesn't know anything!" Ali whined. "None of us does!"

"Well, somebody made that phone call to the Creeds tonight, and I'm praying that it wasn't either of you," he said, eyeing Ali, then me. His voice got sort of friendly.

"Whoever made that phone call is in serious trouble. Somebody either knows where Chris Creed is or they've committed a harassment crime that takes the grossest form of mental cruelty. The Creeds have lost a child. Their pain and suffering are not to be understood by you. But that doesn't mean a judge wouldn't understand it. If the caller was perceived as a 'spoiled little rich kid,' that family could pay quite a bit. Don't count on having any money to go to college with. And that just covers the penalty for harassment. The caller asked for money. That's extortion. Extortion is a very serious crime, far more serious than harassment. Extortion has sent a number of kids to Jamesburg. Skip Egg Harbor; do not pass Go."

I got this hope that he was exaggerating the truth to scare us. I shot a glance at my mom. She just sat frozen in the chair like she was determined not to show any emotion. I couldn't read anything from her at all. *Extortion. Jail. No college.* I couldn't even get my brain to consider the words that were banging through my head.

"So . . ." Chief Bowen leaned into the table and spoke in a low voice. "This is critical. I need you two to tell me that the caller wasn't either of you."

The peaceful grin on his face floated in front of my eyes. Something about it was making my stomach knot up.

Ali broke in with a shaky voice. "What . . . makes you think it was *any* of us?"

He cleared his throat. "Normally in this type of situation, it's me asking the questions, not you," he said softly, jerking his eyes to the door like the other officers might hear him. "But I'm not out to make criminals out of the kids my children were raised with, all right?"

He leaned in like he was telling us some big secret and doing us a huge favor.

"I got a call from the Creeds about an hour ago. They were calling from the ball field, and said Sylvia had just taken a phone call for them to go there. The caller was supposed to give them some information about Chris and told her not to call the police. When they got to the ball field, no one was there. They called me from their car phone. I sent Tiny to check out the ball field and told them I would meet them at their house. I pulled up right behind them, and the Richardson kid was coming across the street toward your house, Ali. He was out of breath. He's not from these parts."

He sat up straight, took a deep breath, then leaned into us again.

"Now, I can't help it if the two of you have decided that he holds some sort of charm. We think it was a little suspicious that a kid with a record nine miles long is in the neighborhood just when all this is happening. He denies having broken in. He could be lying. He could have broken in. Mrs. Hoffsteader, the elderly lady who lives next door to the Creeds, came out and said she saw Torey and Bo Richardson come out of your house and stand on the curb, Ali. They were having a conversation and staring at the Creeds' house."

"Was anything missing?" my mother asked.

"Sylvia doesn't think so. We think the kid probably wanted to break in and didn't have enough time. He was either running back from the ball field or looking for a way to break in and wasn't finding it. Her other two children claim not to have seen or heard anything. So breaking and entering is not an issue. But this phone call is. So, please. Tell me it wasn't either of you."

He looked that way again. Kind of smiley. I got his message this time and almost got sick.

"What? You want us to pin it on him?" I jerked my thumb at the door.

Chief Bowen's eyes widened a little, but his little smirk didn't disappear. "I want you to tell me it wasn't *you*."

I stared at him, trying to tell myself I was dreaming this, I was reading him wrong. He wanted us to say it was Bo, even if it wasn't true, just so his kids' best friends would be off the hook. Just so he wouldn't put his friends, my mom and Mrs. McDermott, through anything. That smirky grin on his face didn't change. Something came screaming up my throat along the lines of, *You can go fuck yourself,* and my mom must have sensed it coming.

"Torey!" She stood up and her chair flew backward, making both me and Ali jump. She swallowed and looked from Chief Bowen back to me again, shaking her head. "He's not answering any questions here and now, Daryl. I'm sorry."

Chief Bowen was slightly overweight. The roll of flesh around his collar turned bright red. "Susan, please don't do this. I'm only trying to—"

"I know. I appreciate it, but . . ." She looked at me hard, like, *Keep quiet. You're too young to understand, you moron.* "Daryl, I want to speak to you in private."

Chief Bowen waved us out, staring at the table. I backed out, watching their faces the whole time. My mom wasn't looking at me. I think she was ashamed of herself or something.

Out in the hall, I saw Bo sitting in one of the chairs in the row, studying the floor. I sat down next to him, and Ali sat on the other side. She was still crying, and he wrapped his arms around her. Mrs. Creed was wailing, and the deputy stuck his head in the door and yelled at her to calm down.

Bo muttered, "You guys, you have to let me take the fall for this."

"Why?" I demanded in a whisper.

"Because. At some point they will question you, and you will never hold up. You've never been in trouble before, and I have. And besides. They're going to pin Creed on me. I'm going down, anyway—"

"It's nowhere near that bad!" I muttered. "They can't! My mom will help you—"

"Yeah, right." He laughed. After a minute he kissed Ali on the side of the head and got up. He marched in on my mom and Chief Bowen without even knocking. They both blew him a few lines of grief, but he just shut the door. I couldn't hear a word they were saying. A phone rang, and I heard Chief Bowen talking loudly. I sat there, helpless, thinking Bo was confessing or something. I was afraid to charge the door and stop him, for fear that wasn't what he was doing. I just sat there comforting Ali, thinking whatever happened, I could straighten it out with my mom later.

A few minutes later my mother came out. "Come on," she said. "I'm taking you two home."

I stood up, but Ali grabbed both sides of her chair like she was glued there. I realized my mom had said you *two* and not you *three*. My mom tried to pull her up by the arm, but Ali kept crying out that he was a sweet person, and my mom didn't even try one of those speeches on her about being stupid.

"He's not going to Jamesburg, I promise," my mom said. She crossed her heart as Ali froze, watching her suspiciously.

"So, why can't he leave with us?" She sniffed. "Are they charging him with something?"

"Juvenile delinquency." My mom put a hand on Ali's shoulder and explained quickly, before Ali could freak. "Before you came out of your house tonight, he gave the police a hard time. He shoved an officer he thought was trying to search him illegally, though the officer was just trying to steer him to the—"

"I know, I was watching out the window." Ali sniffed some more.

"At this point, they're very tired of his lack of respect. He'll have to be released to his mother or some other responsible party."

Ali let out a sick laugh when she heard his mother referred to as a "responsible party." My mother just went on.

"So, this is not serious, not directly related to Chris Creed. We don't have to worry about that tonight."

I didn't like the "tonight" part, though I thought it may have gone over Ali's head. I also remembered Bo talking about his mom going on these five-day binges, and I hoped she was around tonight.

My mom patted Ali's back, watching her in a mysterious way. "You really like that boy in there, don't you?"

Ali cast her a suspicious glance but kept gripping the arms of the chair, like she wasn't leaving Bo.

"He asked me to go by your house and pick up your little brother, and then take the two of you to our house. Bo said he's afraid of your mother's boyfriend."

I wondered, with horror, if Bo had spilled the whole story to her. Whatever—my mom was starting to look like she saw some good in him. I figured she had to be blind otherwise. They're looking to detain the kid, and the first thing he wants to say is: *Protect my girlfriend and her kid brother from her mother's pervert boyfriend.*

"Come on, I told him you were coming home with me," my mom said. "He's not being charged with anything serious right now. I promise."

My mom smiled like she was trying to be nonchalant as she helped Ali up, but I knew her, knew she was thinking that Bo deserved her help.

Ali didn't look thrilled, and she was still crying. But she came with us.

I followed them out, still not liking my mom's choice of words, ". . . not being charged with anything serious *right now*."

Eleven

Ali's mom wasn't even home. It looked like she had gone out with that Albert guy after Bo raised that stink. So picking up Greg and just leaving a note was not a major problem. It was about eleven o'clock, and Greg flung himself sleepily into the car. Ali had packed two backpacks, one for her and one for Greg.

My mom just drove on in silence. When we got back to the house, she took Greg up to the spare bed in my room, and me and Ali wandered into the kitchen. Ali looked completely dazed. Her eyes were really swollen as they swept around the kitchen.

"I haven't slept over here since, like, third grade," she said with an absent laugh. "Remember how we would string burglar traps across the bedroom door frames? God. Funny how things change. Now we're the criminals."

Her grin faded away to nothing, and I said I didn't think we were criminals. She just flopped into a chair and didn't answer me. My mom came in and sat at the table. Her tired eyes glared.

"You guys have about two seconds to start spilling it."

"Mom, the story is so long and so complicated . . ." I stumbled. I mean, what do I tell her? About Ali's mom? About Bo helping Ali and Greg with the pervert? About Mrs. Creed searching her kid's room like she was scared for herself? It was all a part.

My mom was watching Ali, and she sighed. "Look. I do understand one thing." Her jaw bobbed up and down a couple times. "You know how you kids hear about every other kid's business in school? For example, you know who goes out with whom, who's in hot water with whom, who cheated on a test, and all that? And while you know all these things, you think the teachers are oblivious to it?"

We both sort of nodded.

"Well, the grown-up world is the same way. We know which grown-ups go out with whom, who's in hot water with their neighbors, who is living differently than they used to. And you guys are sort of oblivious to it. Okay?"

Ali's eyes moved from the table to my mom, and they stared at each other for a minute.

"I just want you to know that we know more than you think, and your staying here isn't a problem," my mom said.

I didn't know what Richardson had added to the info my mom was hinting about. I knew he had added something, or Ali wouldn't be here.

"Do you want me to be able to help Bo?" my mom asked Ali.

"Yes," Ali mumbled

"Then you need to be honest. You need to tell me what you know about him, how close your relationship is, if he's in any way involved in the disappearance of—"

"He's not involved, I swear it!" Ali said. "He was with me when Chris disappeared. He doesn't want to say that right now. But *I'll* say it, if the cops start suspecting him—"

"You may have to," my mother informed her. "He told the police he was alone after school that day. Why did he lie?"

"He just . . ." Ali squirmed. "There's been this rumor that I've been going out in the woods after school and doing it with somebody. We weren't doing anything out there except walking and talking. But I have this reputation. Some people think I'm a slut. He . . ."

She trailed off awkwardly, but my mom picked up kind of quick. "He doesn't think you'd be a very credible alibi."

Ali blinked at her a few times and said, "I guess."

I waited for my mom to show some surprise about Ali's rep or give her some parenting type of look. She just stared at the edge of the table with her arms crossed.

Finally she said, "Your reputation isn't a concern. If you say you were with him, whatever you were doing, or have done in your past, is not relevant. The bigger problem is, he's already lied. Not on the record, but it still would have sounded more credible if he had told the truth from the start." I watched my mom staring, her mind working like a calculator. I guessed this was her lawyer side. I was so used to the mom side that it made me stare, too.

"So, you're saying the police suspect him?" Ali asked.

My mom shrugged. "They don't have any evidence. Not yet, but—"

"They won't have any evidence! He didn't do anything! I just said he was with me!" Ali whined.

"He was with you at the time Chris disappeared. If for some reason they come to believe that Chris is dead, there's still no body. There's no saying what time he died. It's complicated." She sighed. "How long have you known this boy? Can you think of any reason I'm unaware of that the police might connect him with this—"

"I haven't known him long, but I know him *well*," Ali insisted. She laid her head down on the table and talked in a dead voice. "I had seen him around school, but we don't usually talk to boons, so I had never talked to him. First time I ever talked to him was at the Wawa about three weeks ago. I was standing there alone, and he was, too, so we just started saying stuff. He was mad at his mom because she had just showed up after some five-day drinking binge or something. He laid it all out for me, didn't hold back. And so I found myself laying my mom out to him. Well, sort of. I told him how she always had boyfriends, and how my dad had found out and left. I didn't tell him how bad it had gotten. But still, the stuff I told him didn't shock him or anything. I never met anybody before that I felt could look at my life and not hold it against me."

My mom watched her for a minute, and I expected her to follow up with some lecture on picking your friends, but she just kept staring. "Did you ever discuss Chris Creed?"

"Not really," Ali told her with a shrug. "The main reason we got involved was because Bo was in the principal's office when Mr. Ames placed the first call to the cops."

She went through the whole story about how they put the note on the floppy disk and how it got into the hands of the police. My mom sighed loudly, rolling her eyes. I guessed the disk thing wasn't good. Ali didn't seem to notice.

"Mrs. Creed, Mrs. Creed . . ." Ali muttered. "This whole thing is her fault. She's blabbing this idea all over town that some boon killed her son, and, Mrs. Adams, I think it was her! I think she's trying to blame Bo so no one will suspect *her*."

My mom shook her head sadly, glancing from the corner of the table to Ali. "Mrs. Creed did not kill her son, Ali."

Ali looked defensive.

My mom said, "She may be trying to alleviate her guilt over the idea that her son ran away. She may be pointing the finger so she doesn't have to look at her child-rearing tactics. That's probably more likely."

"Whatever," Ali spat out. "She was all over Chris, all the time. He had no privacy, no choices of clothes, no CDs . . . He had an eight o'clock curfew in the summers. How is a kid supposed to make friends when he's got an eight o'clock curfew? What other kids would want to put up with that? What if Chris stood up to her, let's say? Like, maybe this year he said, 'Mom, I'm staying out until eleven,' or something, and she got so mad she just . . . clobbered him and hid the body?"

My mom shook her head. "Don't waste your time or energy going there. And don't worry about the disk, either. There is only one thing I really want you kids to worry about. Being honest and being fair."

"Well, people aren't being honest and fair with us," Ali started, but my mom pushed away from the table and walked to the window as if she hadn't heard.

"This isn't the first time something like this has happened in Steepleton," she said, staring out the window. I watched her face turn from that calculating-lawyer look to that caring-Mom look. "In fact, that Indian burial ground out there is supposed to contain the bones of more than Lenape Indians. Rumor had it, when I was just a little older than you, that a man named Bob Haines walked into those woods and never walked out again."

The silence only hung for about three seconds, and Ali and I both pushed back our chairs and walked up behind her. The light was bright above the sink, so you couldn't see anything out the window but pitch-black. I knew there was a road out behind our pool, beyond our fence, and on the other side was the place where, supposedly, the local Lenape Indian tribe had buried their dead. There hadn't been any Lenape Indians living here since 1692, when they moved to Oklahoma. I had seen pictures of them, in school, and the men looked fierce. They wore Mohawks and let feathers dangle from their hair, and they pierced their ears and wore heavy ornaments in them. When you're in second grade, seeing pictures of them, you would think they were savages. But supposedly they had been very nice to Henry Hudson and the other first white people. The white people introduced them to some of their own worst habits, like nipping the bottle, and the Lenapes finally decided the whites were a bad influence on them. They left without a fight, leaving nothing but arrowheads—which people still find centuries later—and their graves.

"I never heard any story about any Bob Haines, Mom," I said.

She sighed. "You wouldn't. It was something this town could never admit to. When I was in fourth grade, a teenage boy ran away from home. His name was Digger Haines. Digger was a high school football player. He got his nickname because he played defense and he could dig in and not let anybody past him. Runners would bounce off of him and land in a heap. His junior year, Digger was thrown off a motorbike down at Turkey Run. He lost his leg. Needless to say, his football days were over, as were his dreams of having a military career like his father's."

She lowered her eyes from the window for a second, then raised them up again. "Some kids started calling Digger 'gimp' and 'pirate' and other names behind his back. But things like that get around, get back to the victim. I was only in fourth grade, but I remember hearing them. I don't think anybody meant anything by them. I think they were just calling names because . . ." She ran her fingers through her hair and looked ripped up. "As long as kids could make a joke out of it, then it meant that nothing serious had happened. It couldn't happen to them, couldn't even touch them."

I thought of the jokes flying around school about Creed. I thought of Ryan and Alex joking around . . . *Man, somebody's got to find the spoil* . . . *My father says that very sensitive people commit suicide in water* . . . Some things never change.

"Digger lost his athletic look, trimmed down to almost skinny, grew his hair. You might have thought it was from the sudden lack of sports. But Digger left a note to his father saying he was going to the West Coast to 'find himself,' or something. It was during the hippie era, and I guess he decided he wanted to head out to San Francisco. There were a bunch of kids living in the Haight-Ashbury district who were opposed to any sort of violence, and after his accident he was drawn to the place. Some people say Digger's accident helped him become a more compassionate person. Some people thought he went off the deep end.

"Before the accident, his father had always wanted Digger to go into the Marine Corps, play hero in Vietnam, and sort of mirror his own life in World War II. The accident and the change in Digger were very difficult for Bob Haines to accept. All his dreams for his son had to change, and while I don't think he meant to take it out on Digger, it was hard for him to cope with his disappointment. In the note, Digger said he was having trouble getting along with his father and he couldn't take the tension any longer and he was going to Haight-Ashbury. He left, never to be seen around town again."

She stopped, and I broke my stare from the window to shoot a glance at Ali. She was watching my mom intently.

"Did anyone think that Digger died, like they think about Creed? Committed suicide or something?" I asked.

My mom shrugged. "Not right away. Digger's note made it plain that he was leaving. But Bob Haines went on a month-long trip to try to find him, bring him back to Steepleton.

113

Digger never surfaced in San Francisco or anywhere that Bob could find. Bob started to blame the kids in Steepleton for calling Digger names and driving him away. The town responded by blaming the father for being unable to cope with a son who could no longer meet his expectations. They said *he* drove Digger away. At that point, there were some rumors that Digger might be dead somewhere. Nobody knew. See, guys, this is what happens when a kid suffers a personal tragedy. Nobody wants to take responsibility. Nobody wants to admit they had a part in it. So, they spend a lot of time pointing the finger, and things just get worse and worse."

I stared through the blackness toward the Indian burial ground and felt sad. This story rang of all the things I'd been thinking about people—nobody wanted to admit they treated Chris badly, not even his own parents. Everyone was pointing the finger at everybody else.

"Did anyone ever find any trace of Digger?" I asked.

"Yes. I did." My mom grinned, still staring out the window. "He's an attorney in Detroit. When I was in law school at the University of Michigan, he was a guest speaker at one of my lectures. He was going by the name Troy Haines, which I think is his birth name. I saw that gimp and heard the last name, and I'll tell you, I was very glad to see him and to talk to him after class." She sighed. "I have his address somewhere. I should write to him . . . if he could stand to hear from somebody from Steepleton. He was glad to see me at the time. But that was before his father . . ." She trailed off.

I never even remembered hearing the name Haines around here. "What happened to Mr. Haines?"

My mom tore her eyes from the window and turned and stared at the floor. "People think that after years of being called a bad parent, he was tired. One day his house was dark and stayed dark. Some people say he simply left without even telling anyone good-bye. Others say he was seen wandering into the Indian burial ground with his old World War II pistol in his belt. Supposedly he found one of those little burial caves, crawled in, and pulled the trigger."

We had heard of the caves in the woods but never found any. Some were mapped out by the geology department at Stockton, but it had never been prime on our list to find them. There were three huge rocks in the center of the burial ground, and Alex and I used to climb on them and play King of the Hill. Sometimes we used to get into the old legends and dig around for bones. We never found any bones. We stopped digging once we decided we didn't want some Lenape Indian ghost crawling out from under the bed at night, with his Mohawk all decorated, seeking revenge. I hadn't thought about it in years.

Ali shivered a little, watching my mom. "Well, what do you think happened to him?"

A sad smile crept over my mom's face. "I'm not afraid of ghosts anymore. Not after facing life's realities every day at work. But whatever happened to Bob Haines, I know this town destroyed him. They blamed him, because it was easier than admitting they were partly responsible. I think the Indian burial ground story was somebody's imagination, a few people having one last *ha-ha* to tack on to an already tragic story. I hope he moved to Los Angeles and became an art dealer or something. But . . . that's why I say it's very important to leave Sylvia and Ron Creed alone. They'll end up rotting away like Bob Haines, or . . . something worse. They aren't perfect. But they didn't kill their son, kids."

I cast one final glance over my shoulder at the window as we moved slowly back to the table. Ali got way quiet and dropped down in the chair beside me.

"I should be able to clear Bo's problems up tomorrow morning," Mom said. "Right now you need to tell me if he actually broke into the Creeds', and if he actually made that phone call."

"No," we both said slowly. I looked at Ali, and she looked at me.

"He . . . did want to break in," Ali stuttered, getting all red. "Bo wanted to search Chris's bedroom for something to counteract the fact that he had the disk. We felt there might be evidence inside that would prove Mrs. Creed was responsible for Chris's disappearance. I watched him actually shimmy up a drainpipe and check Chris's window. When it was locked, he crawled up and over the roof. He came around the side of the house about a minute later. He didn't have any time to break in. And believe me, he would have told me at the police station." Ali looked almost disappointed. I don't think she quite believed my mom about Mrs. Creed.

"And the phone call? Did he make it beforehand?" my mom asked.

"No," Ali and I both mumbled. It was on the tip of my tongue to confess, if for no other reason than to prove Bo didn't do it.

My mom spoke up quickly. "I know this is going to sound incredible to you, but if either of you made that phone call, I'm going to ask you not to tell me just yet. I'm not talking to you as a parent right now; I'm talking to you as a lawyer. I'll be a parent again once I help the kid out. For now I would be better off just knowing that he didn't make the call."

My mom wasn't stupid. I think she knew I made the call. Maybe she wanted to face the police without feeling like she had something to hide. And then she'd kill me later.

Ali watched her for a minute with some look like my mom was a superlady. "You can really help him, Mrs. Adams?"

She nodded, but not enthusiastically. "That disk could look extremely incriminating. But my thought is to let sleeping dogs lie. Any day now I would expect something to break here. Either Sylvia will accept the fact that her son ran away or maybe Chris will come home. And even if he doesn't, it's not likely that Bo Richardson could be arrested for murdering him."

"You're sure?" Ali asked again.

"Very sure." She shrugged. "To arrest somebody for a homicide, one needs evidence that there was a homicide. Under normal circumstances there has to be a confession if there's no body. He's obviously not going to confess to something he didn't do. And right now there's no body."

Something made my eyes jump to that window again as a chill came over me. I don't know what caused it. The window was just black. Black as pitch. I stared at it, maybe because the disappearance of Creed seemed so black. It's hard to think that the disappearance of the town weirdo could cause a chain reaction of bad happenings like the ones we were going through. It had brought out some intense side of me that was driving a wedge between me and my fun-loving friends. It was worsening Bo Richardson's already difficult life. It was making my mom have to choose between being a lawyer and being a mom. It was making Mrs. Creed so hateful that she would waste another kid's life, a kid with disadvantages in the first place. This weird kid leaves, but the weirdness stays. It starts coming out of everybody else. I felt like Chris's ghost was in us, trying to speak. Trying to make us feel what he felt, trying to make us understand.

I could hear my mom's voice telling us we needed sleep and to go to bed, or we would never get up for school. I didn't quit looking into the darkness, though.

"I almost forgot . . ." I heard her reach into her handbag for something. "Just before I left Bo, he said to give this to you. He said you'll need your book for class tomorrow."

She tossed a composition book on the table, the kind with the black-and-white-speckled hardcover. I could see Ali's name scribbled on the outside.

"Thanks," Ali said.

Something cracked in her voice and made me look. Her face appeared completely casual, except the corners of her mouth were shaking as she opened the front cover. I could see her name printed clearly on the cover, but it wasn't her handwriting inside.

Her eyes met mine, and I had to look away really quick to keep from falling off my chair. Yeah, I guessed Bo *was* an ace liar. He got Creed's diary to us via my own attorney-mom, and I knew I would never get over that fact as long as I lived. I also would never get over how you can become invisible and do magic if you want something bad enough.

My next hope was that Creed's words were in there: *My mother has threatened to kill me, and I'm afraid she will.*

Twelve

I lay in bed thinking I could crawl on the ceiling. There was no way I could sleep, not with that diary in Ali's paws in the guest room. I heard the big door downstairs close and my dad's briefcase hit the floor with a thud. I knew my parents would be upstairs in half an hour. I would just have to wait it out. I cast a glance over at Greg, in the other bed, who was curled up in a little ball, making him look even smaller than he was. I wondered what I would have felt like as a seven-year-old with a mother acting like a turbo slut and a moved-out father.

One day earlier I might not have been able to imagine it. But having been there made it easier to put myself in Greg's and Ali's shoes. I figured Greg would be okay for a couple years, but by nine or ten, kids stop being sweet. If something didn't change, he would start to respond to it. He would have his thoughts: *There's nobody to really look out for me . . . I better act tough or somebody will think that I'm scared . . . I better cut up a lot so people will laugh, and so long as people laugh, the world is still a big joke . . . I better pick on lots of other kids so that everyone sees their problems, and then they'll miss mine ...*

It struck me that I was describing Bo Richardson's life. I had been thinking about how I would be if I were Greg at nine or ten, and I had just described the worst kid in school. If I were Greg, I would become like Bo. If I had Bo's life, I would be Bo. Probably worse. That was a real awakening thought.

I tried to decide what Ryan and Renee would get out of it if someone forced them to live in Creed's house or Bo's house or Ali's house. If the average Steepleton kids had to walk a mile in one of their shoes, would that make them more understanding? I had this weird feeling that it wouldn't change a lot of my friends. It might scare them or piss them off, but it wouldn't make them understand.

That made me feel all alone and kind of strange, like I didn't know who I was all of a sudden. I had always been just "normal," Torey Adams, that kid who wedged his way onto the football team despite the fact that he can't throw or block. *Well, hell, he can kick, so we'll let him on.* The kid who played guitar well enough for being in high school, but who wrote dumb-ass songs that didn't mean anything. The only thing that ever made me stand out, I thought, was Leandra Konefski—the most beautiful girl in these parts.

Some fear grabbed hold of me—like if I changed too much I would lose Leandra. I had the feeling my new understanding of Steepleton was going to cause a few fights, and it made me nervous.

I came out of my thoughts, realizing that the house was quiet and my mom and dad must have gone to bed. I listened for floor creaking and was sort of aware of having heard some but didn't hear any at the moment. I shot out of the bed, stuck my head into the hall. There was no glow to indicate that a downstairs light was still on.

I stepped close to the wall to keep from making squeaks as I crossed our three-hundred-year-old floors. I pushed open the door to Ali's room slowly and faced an eerie orange glow. She had taken a towel and draped it over the lamp to keep it from shining very bright. She was on the bed in a sweat suit, with the diary hiding her face. She laid it flat and looked at me.

I tiptoed over to the side of the bed and pointed to the wall, as if to say, *Squash over*. She squashed, and I sat down slowly so we didn't make a lot of creaks.

She eyed the ceiling nervously, and I whispered, "If they get out of bed, you'll hear the floor creaking really loud. What's he saying?"

I gripped one side of the diary and pulled it over so that half was in front of each of us.

"His handwriting is terrible," she whispered. "I've only gotten through four pages. It starts last summer. He hasn't said anything about either parent yet. But guess what? You won't believe this. He had a girlfriend."

"No way."

She nodded. "Her name is Isabella."

I looked to where she pointed on a page. His handwriting was mostly scribble, but I could see the name Isabella in a line that I eventually made out to be: *Isabella told me she loved me today, and I promised her that I would come back tomorrow.*

"Who is she?" I asked. "There's no one named Isabella in Steepleton."

"She lives in Margate. Chris's uncle owns a coffee shop in Margate, on the boardwalk, and according to this, his parents let him give up his paper route to be a busboy over there. This Isabella is a waitress."

"Wow . . ." I breathed. Creed having a girlfriend was like Uncle Wiggly going out with Miss America. "I wonder if she's weird, too."

"He said she's beautiful," Ali muttered. She turned back a couple of pages and pointed to the top entry, under the date of June 27.

I read the first lines, which went: *I'm going to describe Isabella, so that even when I'm not with her, I always have a full description of her with me.*

Her dark hair dances like an angry sea. Her cheeks glow like soft white lanterns. She is as tall as thunder and as lean as lightning. . . .

I let out a breathy laugh under the weight of this goo. He described Isabella from the top of her dancing hair to the tips of her rosy red toenails. It took up, like, a page and a half. Then he went into how shy and reserved she was, so *not* like the girls from Steepleton, and how it had taken her three days to get up her nerve to talk to him.

I realized when she finally came over to the table I was busing that she probably wouldn't have the nerve to say what was on her mind. I was quite right. When I asked her, "Would you like to walk the boardwalk with me during break?" she looked at me with pure thanks that I had said it and saved her the risk.

As we walked, the sun beat down on us, and it was pure heaven. She was telling me about her family, how her big sister was so unlike her, but I could hardly hear. I could hardly believe this goddess had agreed to walk with me.

I read on and on. Creed was totally smarmy about her, and it went slow. Three pages later, they were still walking on the boardwalk. But a part of me wanted to give this girl a trophy.

"How come one of us couldn't have been nice to him?" I wondered out loud. If this girl could put up with him, I guessed we could have, too.

"Sometimes people need a fresh start," Ali said after a minute. "People have these geeky reputations, but they get

122

with somebody new, somebody who doesn't know about them, and they can change almost their whole behavior."

"Yeah," I agreed. I remembered that last summer Alex had met a girl on the beach in Brigantine. She didn't know that he was class clown and supercomputer brain, and in front of her, he didn't really act like it. I kept reading.

I wanted to kiss her so badly, but I couldn't find the courage. I knew if I waited, the right moment would come. Tomorrow, the next day, or the next. I knew this much, Isabella and I would do a lot more walking and talking. She could talk forever, and I wouldn't care what she said. It all sounded like music, and the words were irrelevant. As we returned, my loins were bursting . . .

I threw my head back on the pillow and cracked up.

"Shh!" Ali whispered. "We're not going to laugh at him, okay?"

How could you not laugh at a kid saying *loins*. Ali was going overboard with the diplomat routine. I remembered other words Creed could pull out of his head, *winsome, tyrannized, cathartic . . .*

"I can't help it." I laughed again. "Ali, it's like he lived on another planet."

She sighed. "It's his parents. You know, he learned all those words from his father, and his mother kept him so under lock and key."

"What if . . ." I got this thought. "What if this girl dumped him, or his mother refused to let him see her anymore? And that threw him into a state of depression, and that's what made him flip?"

"I know your mom is convinced about it, but I'm still thinking Mrs. Creed did it. For Bo's sake, I sure hope this diary says something—"

I wanted to check out my own theory. I jerked the book away from her and turned to the end.

The last entry was dated September 10, the day after school started. The entry looked like a list.

1. *I have excellent skin.*
2. *I have a nice arch to my eyebrows.*
3. *My teeth are straight.*
4. *I am not fat.*
5. *I can read music.*
6. *My mom makes great food, and I have enough to eat.*
7. *I can pop wheelies on the concrete at ninety-percent pop.*
8. *I have $3,000 in the bank, which I can claim someday.*
9. *I have six, no seven, friends on the Internet.*
10. *Isabella and I are one.*

My eyes returned to the sixth thing. It didn't sound like he was pissed at his mom.

"Ali, he is *so* weird. What kind of a list is—"

Ali pointed at the number 10 thing and mumbled, "Whoa. I wonder if they did the nasty . . ."

I tried to imagine Creed losing his virginity before I did. Another Uncle Wiggly–type of thought.

"Guess she didn't break up with him," Ali murmured. "At least not by September."

"I don't know . . ." Staring at this silly list, I realized that some of the things Creed was saying about himself were basically true. It almost seemed like an exercise in trying to brainwash yourself into believing good stuff about yourself. I wondered if he had done that in his head the whole time he was growing up. *I'm good at this, I'm wonderful at that* . . . And maybe he brainwashed himself into believing that stuff, instead of believing he had just been beaten up the day before. It was a weird thought, but that was one weird list.

"You know what?" Ali whispered, running her finger down this list. "He was never ugly. Did you ever realize that?"

I muttered something about guys not looking at other guys' appearances, but she smirked and said that I could be a real guy without being blind. I knew what she meant.

"People are blind," she said. "All they see is a person's reputation."

"Well, this girl obviously saw more," I said.

"I'm going to read this all night if I have to," Ali whispered. "There's got to be something in here to prove Mrs. Creed's guilty—and therefore Bo is *not*."

I looked at the clock and saw to my amazement it was three-thirty in the morning. I got up to leave but froze, sitting straight up. The early part of the night had been such a brain hag that nothing had been really clear to me. But now that I was this relaxed and tired, the truth hit me.

"Get some sleep. Don't waste your time, because you won't find anything," I muttered. "Mrs. Creed spoke to me. Over the telephone at the ball field. I just thought of it now. Oh my god."

I realized something about this Hitchcock movie that I had stolen the phone-call idea from. When the murderer received his mystery phone call, he immediately asked if it was *blackmail*. He knew he was guilty and assumed the call was for blackmail money. Mrs. Creed asked if this was a *kidnapping*. If she had killed her own kid, she would have assumed it was blackmail and probably would have blurted out the same type of thing. Her knee-jerk reaction would not have been to give me that speech about how nobody takes her baby.

"Maybe she drove him to it, I don't know . . ." I stumbled. "She didn't outright kill him. You're not going to find anything in there to help prove that. Because it didn't happen. So get some sleep."

The shocks of the night caught up with me full force, and I thought I could roll off the bed and fall asleep on the floor. I mumbled, "Sleep tight," as I left, but Ali didn't answer me. She just stared wide-eyed at the diary, in the eerie glow of that orange light.

Thirteen

I knew we were in for it the next morning, about two seconds after I climbed on the school bus. Alex, Ryan, and Renee were staring at me all pop-eyed. I wanted so bad to not deal with them. But I had to make some attempt to act normal. I plopped down beside Ryan, in front of Alex and Renee. Ali sat down in front of me.

Ryan was looking me up and down like I was purple. Alex's and Renee's faces crept around so they were practically licking my ears on either side.

"Hear you had a bit of a run-in last night, bro," Alex said.

"We overheard my dad telling my mom that he almost had to book you last night. That's sweet, Torey, real sweet." Renee smirked, and I rubbed my eyes, which after three hours of sleep felt like bowling balls in the sockets.

"Ali, how come you're getting on the bus on our street?" Ryan asked.

Ali was running her mouth to this girl sitting beside her, a quiet girl in some of our honors classes. I knew she was doing it so she wouldn't have to explain herself to the audience behind her. Their eyes came back to me.

"We . . . uhm . . ." I stuttered. "Mrs. Creed has been bugging Ali. We wanted to spy out her window and see if Mrs. Creed did anything weird over there . . . you know."

I guessed they didn't. *Ker-BLAM*, the power question came barreling out of Alex: "What were you doing with Bo Richardson?"

"Well, he was there. And, well . . ." I watched the back of Ali's head, almost hypnotized by it.

"My dad said Mrs. Creed thinks he killed Chris." Renee's eyes burned on me.

I saw Ali's shoulders freeze up. I felt like food for three hungry snakes. I'd known the night before that all this new stuff could make me feel sort of "out there" compared to my friends, but I hadn't known it would happen so fast. I just felt through my gut and blurted out what I felt.

"You guys, this whole thing has gotten way serious. It's too serious, I don't want to yap about it, I don't want to joke about it. I don't want to talk about it."

They made all the I'm-insulted groans, but I didn't let myself get sucked down as they filled the air with comments.

"You think we're gossips, thanks a lot—"

Ryan went, "Torey, bro. We're just glad you're not bones this morning, man. Bo Richardson? Whatever happened, we assured our dad that he forced you into it. Pulled that . . . that *stiletto* he carries around on you, or something—"

I stared at the back of Ali's hair. It would kill Ali if I didn't do something.

I got up, walked toward the front of the bus, and plopped down beside Lyle Corsica, who was known as a science geek. There were no other empty seats near him, so there was no way they would follow me. I started a conversation with Lyle, like Ali had started with that quiet girl. I didn't care that they were gawking, probably wondering why I could run my mouth to Lyle Corsica, about I-don't-even-remember-what, but I couldn't talk to them. I kept telling myself I didn't care. I figured I would start to believe it by the time we got to school.

I didn't see any sign of Bo in the cafeteria and hoped he wasn't still at the cop station—as in, his old lady was out drinking again and never showed up to sign him out. My mom said she had to stop there anyway and would make sure he'd been picked up, before she dropped Greg off at school.

Since I didn't really feel like talking to anybody, I just went to homeroom early and fell asleep with my head on my desk. I woke up because someone was nudging me, and when I opened my eyes, the room was half filled with kids. I shot my head up as Alex quit nudging me from behind. Our names, Adams and Arrington, meant I sat in front of him. There was no getting away this time.

"You didn't even hear the bell?" Alex asked me.

"No." I rubbed my eyes and shivered. I couldn't believe I slept through a bell.

"You look like you're on crack."

"Well, I'm not," I snapped. "I only had next-to-zero sleep."

"Look. Whatever's going on with you, Torey, I'm not the enemy."

My eyes moved past all these kids who were finding their seats, pushing each other and fooling around. Lyle Corsica was sitting just about in the middle, looking up from an Algebra II book. He was watching Justin Briggs and Mike Carroll, two jocks, arm wrestle in the front row. He looked back and forth from Briggs to Carroll sort of cautiously. *He's wishing he could jump into Carroll's set of muscles and walk around in them. He's wishing he was somebody else. He's wondering why his old man had to pass on chicken legs to him, while Carroll's old man is a tennis pro.*

I had never given Lyle Corsica a real thought before, and all of a sudden I felt like I could look into his head and see his thoughts. See pain there. I realized Alex had his hand cupped to my ear and was whispering in it. Lyle's head turned, and his eyes caught mine this time. *Adams and Arrington whispering. Nobody's ever whispered anything to me. Nobody thinks I'm that important.*

I grinned at him. I had been running my mouth to him on the bus about the weather, the puddles, the snow coming, all this stuff. He should have thought I was insane. Now, here he was looking at me all admiring because some bro was giving me some secret lowdown. I wondered if being a geek made you a better, less judgmental person.

"Where in the hell did you pick up Bo Richardson? I can't see why we should *protect* you if you won't even let us in on what you were doing!"

I jerked my ear away from Alex and turned to stare at his concerned face.

"Protect me from *what*?" I asked.

He looked all around the room in amazement. Flocks of kids were all doing their usual homeroom things—talking, laughing, finishing up the homework they didn't do before. But they had fangs like snakes that came out when something rubbed them wrong. I knew it. I'd been part of it. They could bite. They could ruin my life, turn me and Ali into a sideshow.

"You want all these people looking at you and thinking you're a candidate for Future Convicts of America?" Alex asked, right on cue.

"No." I had two years to finish in this high school. Two years is a long time.

Leandra stuck her head in the door and waved at me. She looked all cute in her jeans and this little tiny sweater.

"Your chem teacher's still out! I'll see you third-period lunch. I'll buy you french fries, your favorite breakfast!" she said in that Southern accent that drove me nuts.

She left, and I felt Alex's eyeballs burning a hole in my cheek. "We're your *friends*," he reminded me, in that same voice as a teacher. . . . *You're going to* fail *if you're not careful.*

I wanted to tell him parts of it. But I knew I'd be screwing up his version of reality by telling him Bo Richardson was a nice guy. And if I told him Bo was going out with Ali? Forget it. He'd tell Renee, and it would be all over school. *Guess who McDermott's doing it with now, oh by the way?*

I just got up and wandered out into the hall, forgetting to take the hall pass. I was trying to think up what great lie I could tell the nurse so she would send me home. I leaned against the lockers, thinking how twenty-four hours had turned my whole life into one lie after another. I heard my name in some whisper and looked behind me. Ali was out in the hall, waving the pass from her homeroom so I would follow her. She moved quickly toward the emergency exit, and I followed her.

She shut the door behind us and stared at me. "You loo terrible," she said.

I sighed. "This is like some stage show, Ali. I'm lying ass off every time I turn around. My folks, my friends; about to lie to the nurse. It's like being an actor, only never get offstage. It's complicated. I want to cut out of k

She lit a cigarette and blew out a trail of smoke. want to go home?"

"Yeah," I muttered. "Go back to sleep, so at som I can think again."

"Torey, I'm really sorry." She looked sad all of a "I shouldn't have brought you into all this. You'r out for it. Do you see what I mean about your pe

I didn't say anything. I couldn't think.

"Look," she said, dragging on the cigarette, and I could see her fingers shaking, "whatever you have to do, just do it. If you don't want to talk to us anymore, it's okay. If you have to lie about us, just do it—"

"I don't want to do that, Ali," I snapped. I looked out into the woods and sighed. "Creed . . . he's got a real talent for creating problems. Even when he's *gone*."

"Yeah." She laughed sadly. She stared off into the woods, too. It was a calm, sort of gray day with no wind. I could sense her scanning the trees. Like maybe Creed would just materialize and walk out of them or something.

"I have the diary in my locker," she mumbled. "I went into the girls' bathroom this morning, sat in a stall, and read some more. Kept me from having to be in the cafeteria, you know?"

I nodded, watching the woods alongside her.

"Toward the end, he went to a psychic with that Isabella."

"Really?" I looked at Ali. That didn't seem like something a sheltered kid like Creed would do.

Ali nodded. "She was a relative of Isabella's or something. The psychic told them she saw death in the woods. The death of one of them, I guess."

I felt the skin on my arms starting to crawl as I stared out toward the woods again. I was thinking, *We can be pretty sure it wasn't* her *death. She's from Margate, by the ocean, and there aren't any woods in Margate.*

For some reason I thought of Alex and me playing in that burial ground when we were about seven, and walking these woods. We used to walk through there telling stories about the ghosts of dead Lenape Indians. I would get an image in my head of an Indian ghost with a Mohawk and stone earrings and all those feathers. This Indian ghost was always half crouched with a bow and arrow poised in his arms, staring at me like I was an animal and he was hunting.

One time, when I was seven, something materialized about twenty feet in front of me. It looked exactly like this image I had conjured up in my head—crouching Indian, staring, ready to shoot an arrow through my heart. I screamed and pointed, but as fast as the Indian materialized, it disappeared again. I got so freaked that Alex half dragged me by the hair back to tell his dad, the shrink. Alex hadn't seen it.

Dr. Arrington told me that by virtue of the fact that the Indian looked exactly like something I had long been imagining, it had to be my imagination. He somehow managed to calm me down. He was a grown-up and a very confident doctor. Alex and I ended up playing in those woods a lot as kids, and I didn't constantly look over my shoulder. I never did see that Indian again.

But now I was remembering it and feeling like I could see a dead Chris Creed just materialize and walk out of the woods. I watched between the trees, watched for a skinny blond kid to appear and stare back at me. For the first time ever, I thought maybe Dr. Arrington was wrong. Maybe I had some special gift to see things like that. Maybe I saw the Indian exactly like I had been imagining him because the dead Indian somehow "put" the image in my mind before I ever "saw" it. I shivered. Felt like I was losing it.

A sensation came up behind me—breath on my neck. I stood there frozen, knowing somebody was standing there staring into the back of my neck. Just like before, in the basement. I didn't want to jerk around like an idiot this time. But I finally knew it was real because Ali jumped around.

She flew behind me, and when I turned around, she was kissing Bo really big.

I let out a sigh of relief and started to say hey, but they were busy kissing. I figured I would just go pass off my lie to the nurse. I started to move past them, but Richardson grabbed my arm. He gripped me like that until he finished kissing Ali and turned his black-eyed stare to me.

"Your old lady, man. She's a rip. She walked into the lockup this morning and had Chief Bowen's 'nads in her handbag, like, ten minutes later." He laughed. "Goddamn. Next time I get caught breaking and entering, I'll know who to call."

It was a relief to hear a loud voice. I grinned, shaking off my spooks. "So she had to get you out?"

"Yeah. My old lady wasn't home. I lay down in a cell and crashed out."

"Lucky thing she decided to come by," I said, looking him up and down. He was wearing sneakers and smelled like a shower. His hair was still kind of wet. Last night he was brought to the cop station in his socks. "How'd you get other clothes?"

"Your old lady took me home before dropping me off here. She likes me, I think."

She's just doing her job, I thought, but didn't want to say that. "So . . . I guess you broke into the Creeds'."

"No. I didn't break in. You won't believe what happened. You know ol' Justin? Chris's younger brother?" He shook his head like a dog, like he couldn't get over something. "He came to the back window just as I jumped onto the ground. He heard me. I seen him and figured, *Oh, shit. Well, you have not because you ask not.* So I asked him. I said, 'Justin, how's about loaning me your brother's diary and not telling your old lady, huh?' He's got Chris's grin, but goddamn, it don't look the same on him. Looks evil. I think it *is* evil. He disappears up the stairs like lightning and comes back about ten seconds later. *Guess* what he's holding?"

Bo was laughing in hoots, but I could only stand there with my jaw dangling. I couldn't get over this. "You mean, he got it out of Chris's picture frame?"

"No. I mean, he had gotten the diary out of the room sometime before. He must have known about it somehow and was scared his mom would get it. He had been switching hiding places—"

"Why would he give it to you?" I asked.

"Because of his old lady! He says to me, 'Take it, get it away from my mom. Just don't forget to give it back to me somehow.'"

Ali made this victory laugh. "Damn, he's got guts."

"There's this pen in it, right? Already I'm hearing cop cars, but I'm thinking they're behind me—they think I'm jumping the fence to run out the next cul-de-sac. Instead of pushing the diary into the bush, where it could get rained on, I just whip out Creed's pen and write Ali's name on it."

"What made you think to do that?" Ali breathed.

"It just came to me." He shrugged like it was nothing. "I been lying for years. Then I wanted to get the book off of me and out of the cop station bad enough—I ain't never lied that perfect before, God Almighty. Hey. I was sorry to do a lie around your old lady, man, she is really juice. But I didn't know what else to do. If they found it on me, that was my life's end. There's no way I would spill on Justin, get the kid in deep shit with his old lady. So . . ." He knocked Ali's chin with his finger. "You're not all pissed at me for telling Torey's old lady about Albert the Wonder Schlong, are you? Where'd you sleep last night?"

"At Torey's. Greg did, too." She looked kind of worried. "What did you say about my mom? Is she in trouble?"

He shrugged, looking worried himself. "I don't know. You can't think about that, okay? Mrs. Adams is gonna talk to your mom."

Ali rolled her eyes and looked panic-stricken. Bo grabbed her by the shoulders. "Look, I see this happening a lot on

135

my side of town, and it sucks. Parents get all drunk and disorderly, do all these insane things, and the kids protect them like it's their duty. Maybe she'll face the music if she has to. You ain't her Jesus, okay?"

Ali tried to nod, but all of a sudden it's like I was reading *her* thoughts, too. *Where will we go? Where will my stuff be? Will we have to live in my dad's one-bedroom apartment in another state? Will everybody find out about my mom?*

I rubbed the back of her neck, and Bo lit a cigarette and handed it off to her. That seemed to make her feel better. She exhaled and stared at the trees again. She told Bo most of the stuff we had read in the diary, including the psychic she read about in the girls' room.

"The psychic told him she saw that he would die in the woods?" Bo asked.

Ali nodded with a shudder. "Something like that."

He just shook his head. "I'm thinking we should find her. Or at least we should find that babe he was going out with and talk to her."

I watched him stare across to the woods. He muttered, "I'm worried the body will show up. If there's a body, it can look like a murder. If he hung himself or shot himself or did something to himself that somebody else could have done to him, Mrs. Creed is going to howl murder until the sun is scared to come out. Maybe the girl knows something. Or maybe she's hiding him and we can all relax."

I told myself I would have thought of that, except that I was really exhausted. The bell rang.

Bo flicked the cigarette into the dirt and glared at me. "Listen, Adams. Whatever you do, don't come up to me in school. Don't even look my way, okay? Ali don't need that right now. If something happens—like you hear something from your old lady, or something awful comes down—just come out here. Inside, you don't know me from Adam. Got it?"

I got it, but I didn't like it. I figured, *Why should I be scared of all those morons passing judgment on me?* But I remembered how I felt in homeroom, and I also knew how Ali would feel. She had enough to cope with.

"I'm going home, anyway," I told them. I didn't feel like being forced into any of these retarded lying games.

Ali shrugged, kind of wide-eyed, and said, "Thanks, Torey. Thanks for everything."

I said, "You're welcome," but my voice kind of cracked.

Fourteen

I got in the car with my dad and faked sleep so he wouldn't ask me stuff. I'm sure my mother had told him that something came down the night before, but the nurse told him my story—that I puked in the john—which gave me an advantage. He wouldn't nag at me if he thought I was sick, but I could feel discomfort wafting off him like a horrible smell.

I felt the bump of our driveway and opened one eye.

"Your mother's not in her office, so if you need her, call her on her cell phone," Dad told me, and I nodded. "She'll be late. She's doing something for that Richardson boy after she gets out of court."

I turned and looked at him. He was staring into the steering wheel, gripping it until his knuckles were white. He hadn't said it mean. He just looked like he was agonizing. I wanted to tell him I was sorry about getting hauled into the cop station. But I didn't want to admit to anything. I decided on something in the middle.

"Bo Richardson's not all bad, Dad. He's got a good streak that . . . runs really deep. It's just not . . . wide." Whatever. I was tired.

139

"Your mother said things like that." He let out one of his confused sighs. I grabbed my book bag, and as I opened the door, he let fly with another complete shocker. Up until this point, I had been ready to throw myself onto my bed and sleep. But what Dad said next changed my mind.

He said, "Your mother told me being charged with murder is not the Richardson boy's worry at the moment. Apparently the police told him they confiscated the phone receiver at the ball field to have it fingerprinted. Before they went to the trouble, he confessed to making that phone call. That call could cost him dearly."

I slammed the car door and headed for the house in a complete haze. I didn't even say good-bye. I figured that silence was the biggest lie I'd told so far.

I paced around the house. Bo hadn't even mentioned anything when we were standing outside with Ali. He knew I would go nuts on him. But I should have known he wouldn't let me hang. Now I could only sit around or pace until Ali came over and we figured out what to do about this. *Especially considering that phone call was your idea, Torey, you idiot.*

I went clomping down to the basement and picked up my acoustic guitar and headed back up the stairs. The basement was spooky. I hadn't spent more than three minutes down there since that night I thought I was feeling Creed's ghost. I passed the kitchen window and decided it was too spooky to be in the kitchen, too. I didn't want to sit in there playing guitar near that window, where you could see the Indian burial ground.

I finally lay down on the living-room rug and stared at the ceiling, playing a bunch of scales and runs in that awkward position. I didn't care, the sound of my guitar made me calmer, somehow. Guitars are like "woobees." They're your security blanket. I lay there playing scales, trying to think about nothing at all.

Clearing my head of the morning, I remembered something that happened the year before, which I hadn't thought about since it happened. The memory just came back to me. I'd had my guitar in the cafeteria, and I was fooling with it for my friends at the table. I got into playing this one thing I had heard on the radio not long before. That was like a gift for me, *hearing* music. *Reading* music was not my gift, it was a pain in my ass. It was too much hard work. But since I could hear something on the radio and, like, see chords in my head, that made reading music seem even more worthless. At any rate, I played this thing I'd picked up on the radio. When I finished I looked up and there were about thirty kids standing around watching me.

They kind of applauded, and I felt dumb being caught off guard like that. My friends were used to me and didn't applaud—they usually just rocked and looked happy. But this weird thing caught my eye that made me forget about myself. These kids standing around weren't all from my neighborhood. Some were boons, some were from the middle-class neighborhoods like Leandra's, and some were from Steepleton. A couple were techies; one was a science nerd. I remember looking at all of them and feeling good about this guitar. It could bring people together, and it didn't matter where you were from.

The part I'd totally forgotten about was Bo Richardson. He had been standing there, too. As we were leaving the cafeteria he shoved me in the shoulder and said, "'S a nice box, man. You let me play it sometime?"

It's not like I was scared of him in that massive group of moving kids, but I remembered the time Creed picked up my guitar in sixth grade. I was funny about people touching my guitars, even Alex and Ryan.

I said to him, "You know how to be careful?"

He looked at me for a minute and then laughed. He said, "You know how not to be an asshole?" and he took off.

I didn't give it a thought at the time because he was always calling somebody an asshole, and I was no different. It didn't occur to me at that moment to think, *Bo Richardson plays guitar, too,* or, *He'd probably get a major thrill out of playing an Ovation because most people would, and I should share and just be cool.* All I thought was, *Sure, screw you, you're calling me asshole, well, what do you expect from that fool.*

I shut my eyes and felt them kind of filling up. That's something the guitar could make me do once in a while. I'd play something really sad, and it would fill up my eyes, God knows why, except the music got me.

I sniffed and said out loud, "You know, it's a shame you can't write songs that aren't complete crap. You might be worth something, fool." But I was just telling myself some minor truth to try to get the bigger truth out of my head. Which was, there are all sorts of kids out there with bad luck. And I can't even consider them long enough to let them play my stupid guitar.

I almost jumped out of my skin as the phone rang. I grabbed for it in a haze, thinking it might be Ali. It was Leandra.

"Are you all right?" she asked me. "Somebody said you were throwing up. Y'all didn't look too good this morning."

"Yeah, I'm . . . just laying low for now," I muttered.

"Are you crying?"

"No," I said quickly, but she kind of set me off into my craziness. "Leandra, where are you?"

"In the cafeteria. At the pay phone—"

"Leandra," I begged, "do you see Ali anywhere in there?"

I heard a long silence. Then, "No. She's not in here."

I sighed, and she went off, "Torey, what is up with you today? Alex says he knows all this stuff he can't tell. He seems really mad at you. Renee and Ryan are, too. Everyone says you're being really frigid, and Ryan and Renee said their dad hauled you into the station last night and you won't tell them a thing—"

"Leandra, this is really important. If you see Ali, can you tell her to call me? And then don't tell anyone I asked you that?"

The silence was long enough for me to realize I was sounding like a total bastard. I was refusing to tell my girlfriend something and then telling her to get a message to another girl. Deep thinker of the universe, I was too busy panicking to think.

"Torey, what is going on between you and Ali?" she demanded.

"Nothing! Nothing at all!"

"Torey, you cut out of school without even saying goodbye to me—after you've been at a cop station and you've been seen with Bo Richardson, Mr. Dirtbag. And then you can't tell me anything, but you send me off chasing after some turbo slut for you? What do you take me for?"

She was sniffing up tears. I was in shock. How could the truth in life be so opposite from what it looked like sometimes? I couldn't go past that.

It was pissing me off. I said, "Leandra, maybe, just maybe, Bo Richardson is *not* a dirtbag. And just maybe Ali is *not* a turbo slut. Did that ever occur to you?"

"Not from all you're telling me! I only hear what *other* people tell me!"

I don't know what came over me, but I flew out with, "So why do you waste your time running down to the Pentecostal church every Sunday if you come around on Monday calling people dirtbag and turbo slut?"

I heard her gasp, but I was pissed and continued, "What, you think someday you're gonna tell Jesus, 'Well, I called people dirtbag and turbo slut, but that's okay, folks! I was a virgin!'"

"You're crazy! You're . . . insane." She hung up.

I clicked off the phone and laid it down next to my guitar. She was right. I was insane. And I totally didn't care. I walked down to the basement and just sat there in the middle of the floor, hoping Creed's ghost would materialize and come mess with me, haunt me, push me over the line to where I would see things. I must have sat down there for an hour. I didn't see a blessed thing.

Fifteen

Ali walked all the way to our house after school, because she didn't want to get on my school bus and start more talk. She had on her army boots, which turned out not to be real leather. They were soaked through and sort of ruined, and she had these enormous bleeding blisters on her feet. While she sat on the bathtub ledge and soaked them, she told me that Bo had been charged with juvenile delinquency again, this time for making that phone call. I didn't think juvenile delinquency was such a big deal, then she explained to me that it is the only thing a minor can be charged with, even if he commits a murder. So, it could get bad. Depending on how Mr. and Mrs. Creed and the cops played it out, he could do up to six months in Jamesburg for the extortion part.

I swore to her that I would tell the truth, and that just made her wig further. She swore that if I confessed, she would call me a liar and confess to making the call herself. I didn't know what to do. We went into the family room, arguing about it.

Then the phone rang, and Ali was so wound up, she jumped ten feet in the air, then picked up without thinking. It was Leandra.

"Is that Ali McDermott?" she demanded when Ali passed the phone off to me in total panic. I didn't say no, but I didn't say yes. It was along the lines of, "Leandra . . . please . . ." I just watched Ali's eyes rolling back in her head almost, because this was too much.

Leandra hollered through a sniff, "I guess I know who's been making Ali late for cheerleading practice every day!"

It wasn't like I could say it was Bo Richardson and not me. I said, "Leandra, that's bullshit!"

She just said, "Well, Ali's not here at cheerleading, and you're not at football practice, so—"

"I came home sick!" I defended myself.

"You went home guilty, that's what! No wonder you can't look your friends in the eye!" And she hung up.

I got my football practice in, anyway, because I had to tackle Ali in the front yard to keep her from running off. I lay on her chest and shushed her while she screamed, "I can't stay here! I can't stay here!"

After fifteen shushes, she cried a bunch, and I was afraid to get off of her until she stopped, for fear she'd take off into the woods. We lay like that for an eternity.

When she was finally just sniffing, she turned her head from keeping her face halfway in the grass and looked at me. "Torey?" she asked. "Do you . . . think I'm a slut?"

I rolled off her on that note. I hadn't been wanting to think of her in terms of sex, but it's hard not to think that way when you're lying on some girl. I sat on the grass, staring at it, trying to catch a full breath.

"No," I said finally. "I think you're confused and . . . pissed off."

She eased up some and sighed. "I don't know what I am. My mom has so many boyfriends, I wonder if it's genetic."

I didn't have a clue. I finally said, "If it were genetic—I mean, if it were something like you just get incredibly horny all the time—then it wouldn't make sense. I mean, it seems like your mom could have taken out horniness on your dad."

"It's got nothing to do with being horny," she told me. "God. I don't think I've ever been horny."

I always thought horny and sex went together like hungry and food.

"So, then . . . what's up?" I pretended to be all interested in a blade of grass.

"I don't know. For one thing, I really love to piss off my dad. As flirty as my mom is? He's, like, the opposite. He's sort of pristine."

"So . . . he knows?"

She looked at me like I was crazy. "No way! It would kill him. I want to piss him off for leaving me and Greg to cope with Mom. I don't want to send him into cardiac arrest or something."

"So . . . what's the point?" I couldn't see how she planned to make him mad if he never even knew.

She sighed. "I guess it's just the point that *if* he knew. It makes me feel like laughing sometimes. It's like . . . the only way in my life I've ever been mean to somebody."

"Ali . . ." I trailed off, thinking she was being a lot meaner to herself.

"Yeah, I know it's hard to understand," she admitted. "It's hard for me to understand, and I'm not even perfect like you."

"Christ's sake, Ali." I didn't feel like starting up on that again. My life wasn't perfect anymore, so she was going to start in on my character. No way. "You don't have a clue how weird I am. Nobody does. I'll lie on my bed for hours just thinking."

"Well, I don't think that's so weird," she said with a shrug.

"I do," I argued. "I mean, I'm not sleeping, I'm not moving. I'm just lying there, thinking. And it's about stuff that nobody else would care about."

"Like what?"

I shrugged, recalling the morning last week I woke up at six and lay in bed until seven.

"What it would feel like to be drawn and quartered between four horses," I confessed. I had seen some old movie on late-night, where this fifteenth-century guy had been tied between four horses. At the same time, the riders all took off galloping in four different directions. I had to lie there figuring the thing, from six until seven, where he got separated—at the waist or the legs or the arms—and how long he could have stayed conscious.

"God, that's terrible," Ali breathed. I guessed she knew what drawn and quartered meant.

I kept going. "And especially since all this came down with Creed? I just feel different from everybody else all of a sudden. Nobody else seems to think about *how* he is. Did you ever notice that? Everybody wants to know *where* he is, but I haven't heard one person wonder about *how* he is. Unless they're saying that he's dead. I feel like the only one—and then I figure it must be me; I must be weird. I feel like a secret weirdo. Like it's this giant secret, and one day somebody's going to realize and spew it all over the cafeteria in megavolume. 'Everybody take a long look at Torey Adams! He's weird! And we just never realized it!' And the truth will be out."

I could feel her turn, but I was too embarrassed to look at her. I wished I hadn't said all that.

Finally she said, "Torey, everyone around here has a secret. You know that girl I was talking to on the bus this morning? That brainy one that's so quiet and gets all those straight As? Her mom is an alcoholic. The girl keeps her head chronically in a schoolbook because it's not as weird as the real world. You know Mike Healy from football? During the off-season his dad makes him swim behind a rowboat while he keeps track of Mike's time. If Mike doesn't do good enough, his dad hangs the stopwatch in front of the TV in Mike's bedroom so he'll swim better the next day."

That's sick, I thought. I wondered how she knew that stuff. Before I had a chance to ask her, she went on. "You know Lyle Corsica? You think he doesn't have friends because he's skinny and small. Well, Mark Fein is skinny and small, but he's a catcher on the baseball team and everybody thinks he's okay. Lyle Corsica doesn't have friends because he still wets the bed. And he's afraid to get too close to people because somebody will find out. Everybody feels weird, Torey—"

"Whoa!" I stopped her. I was seeing how deep her bank of secrets went. I had thought it was just Creed and Bo that she kept quiet about. "How do you know all this?" I asked her.

She was pulling grass out by the tips, but there was getting to be a whole clump of ground there. I grabbed her hand to stop it.

"Because . . ." She sighed. "My mom slept with all their dads. And they told her, and she told me."

She collapsed backwards on the grass and stared sadly at the sky. I collapsed backwards, too.

Bo called after dinner, and I let Ali take my cordless phone into her room. I went down to see what was on TV. I had to pass my mom's office, and she was in there, writing at her desk.

My mom has been writing with a feather pen since I can remember, and as a little kid I used to sit on her couch and watch that feather waggle as the pen flew across the paper.

Once I asked her why she didn't e-mail Grandma, or something more practical. She gave me some spiel about how writing letters to Grandma had become her tradition, and that traditions gave you a feeling of sanity and security, even if they weren't practical. I felt like everything was changing in the world, except my mother and that stupid pen.

"You feeling better?" she asked without looking up.

"Yeah. Some." I watched the feather bob, kind of hypnotized by it.

"Ali's mom went to the spa in Florida." I caught a click in her voice, like she was intentionally trying not to sound too concerned. "It's about two miles up the road from where Ali's grandmother lives. About ten miles from *your* grandma. She'll be there for two weeks. I told her that Ali and Greg could stay with us. I hope that's all right with you. None of us really wants . . . Ali staying alone."

I wondered what that meant. I wondered if she'd found out about Ali's sex tricks. Maybe Mrs. McDermott knew and spilled the beans to my mom. I wasn't about to ask.

"It's fine." I shrugged but wondered how I could stand having some little kid in my room all that time. For Ali, I could do it. "What's a spa? Like a health club?"

"Actually, Mrs. McDermott and her mother call it the spa. But there's a drug and alcohol rehabilitation unit in there, and that's where Mrs. McDermott is."

I glanced at her and watched that pen move again. "Mrs. McDermott is addicted to drugs? I guess that's good . . . I thought she was just crazy."

My mom let out a slight laugh. "I've been with the DA's office a long time now. Ninety percent of the time, inappropriate behavior and crimes are linked to two things: drugs and alcohol."

I guessed that made good sense. "So, what did you say to her today?"

She squirmed uncomfortably. "Not a whole lot. Some people know when the game is up. Some people *want* the game to be up, and they're just waiting for someone to step in and blow the whistle."

I stared at the wood floor until the slits became double slits somehow. "Everybody in town has a skeleton in the closet."

"True," she said.

I was just repeating Ali, but I was surprised how quickly Mom agreed with me.

I watched her and toyed around with telling her that I had made the phone call, not Bo. I knew I had to get Bo off the hook, but I got scared Ali would start in like she'd promised and say that she had made the phone call. I had disguised my voice when Mrs. Creed answered—half snarl, half whisper—and I wasn't sure you could tell it was a guy. I got to the point where I was ready to blurt it out to my mom, when I heard a noise behind me. Ali was standing there looking kind of awkward. This wasn't the time.

I sighed, feeling hungry all of a sudden. My dad had made chili for dinner, and all those spices gave it the appeal of a pile of thumbtacks. I had basically pushed it around in the bowl. "Can I walk down to Wawa for some of that macaroni and cheese?"

My mom reached around for her handbag and pulled out a five. "Ali, do you want anything?"

Ali shook her head as I stood there looking at the five, feeling a little strange. I didn't want to take money from my mom, not while I was lying about that phone call and Ali and I were lying about the diary—all these lies. But I took it, anyway.

I felt Mom watching me as Ali and I put on our jackets and headed out the door.

Sixteen

"You have ESP," Ali said as we walked down the road. "That's where Bo called me from. I just have to see him. I don't know how I'm going to do this for two weeks, but I'm afraid to ask your mom, you know, if he can come over."

"Yeah, I don't know what she would say." I tried to think about it. "I don't think she's as prejudiced as a lot of people around here. But after just confessing to making that phone call—*God, why did he do that?* . . . I wonder if she believes him. At any rate, I don't know if she wants him all hanging out in the basement with us yet."

We got to Wawa, and Bo was out there pacing and huffing on a cigarette. No other kids were there, but he pushed us around to the side of the building, anyway.

"Listen to me. You're not doing six months in Jamesburg for that phone call," I told him.

"You got a better idea?" he asked. "Do *you* want to do six months in Jamesburg?"

"No." But I couldn't take the thought of how many people depended on him: Ali, Greg, his brothers and sisters.

"Look, six months is the max. I won't get the max," he reasoned. "I ain't never been actually sent up before. Fortunately, all those robberies I pulled? I never got caught with anything in my hands, and I always got caught before I could leave the property."

He laughed like that was something hysterical. "So I never been charged with robbery, only breaking and entering. That ain't worth the taxpayers' money. Besides, if we find Creed, his old lady will be so happy she'll, like, wet herself and forget I'm such a bad guy. Let me see the diary," he mumbled, and Ali pulled it out of her jacket.

I got so caught up in that thought, I actually let the phonecall thing go for the moment.

Ali opened the diary to a page where she had a matchbook stuffed in it, and held it open to him. She pointed to a line. "What do you think it says?" she asked him.

He looked, and I looked beside him, where she pointed. She took the cigarette from Bo, and I could hear her inhale to her toes.

"Stupid things," she muttered. "I've got to be addicted to them. I felt like I was going crazy, hearing you smoke over that phone."

Bo pointed to a word that followed the word *Isabella*.

"Karzan? Tarzan? What do you think it is, Adams?"

It must be the girl's last name, I figured, staring at the letters. Creed's handwriting was awful.

Bo cursed in frustration, and I said, "Wait. Let's back up and read a little bit. Maybe it'll just back into our heads after we've looked at his handwriting long enough."

I went along as best I could. *"We sat down on the beach and stared into the evening . . . stars,"* I read aloud. It looked like *stirs. "I lay down thinking that she would lie down, too, but she was too shy."* I sighed in disgust, and Bo cracked up.

"Come on, Adams. Two virgins rolling around under the stars. That's sweet, you know?" He was trying to be serious but was laughing a little.

I tried to be serious. *"I finally reached for a strand of her . . . long bland hair*—blond hair"—I cleared my throat—*"and pulled her backwards. She was very shy and did not want to at first, but after a moment she did. I kissed her lips, and before I knew it my hand was cupping her breast—"*

Bo nudged me, half knocking me off my feet for laughing. I quit laughing but had to find my place again. *"Her breast. And I said to her, 'Isabella Karzden, I love you . . .'* Karzden. It's Isabella Karzden." I spelled it and handed the book back to Ali quickly. That was a death-defying feat in not laughing anymore.

Ali threw down the cigarette and said, "Wait here." She disappeared around the corner and came back a few minutes later with the Wawa phone book. "Manager said I have to bring it right back, so hurry."

She flipped open the pages to the *K*s, and we looked down them. There were four Karzdens in Margate. No Isabellas. None of us had a pen, so Bo and Ali each memorized one number, and I memorized two. After Ali returned the phone book, we tried three of the numbers, which turned out to be the wrong people. We ran out of change. I went inside to get more by buying my macaroni and cheese. I didn't really feel like eating it at this point, but I needed dimes and quarters. As I was standing there, lo and behold, Alex and Renee came in.

I waved at them, trying to act casual. Alex came up behind me in line, and Renee went to the candy aisle.

"Hey," Alex said.

"Hey. Wha's up?"

I could feel him staring at me. "You left school sick today, so I figured we had no band tonight."

"Right," I said. For once it was *me* totally forgetting.

"I don't suppose it's any coincidence that you're in here and Ali McDermott is outside."

He didn't mention Bo, and I hoped that meant that Bo had seen them coming and cut out into the darkness.

"No," I said honestly. "Her mom is in Florida for two weeks, and she's staying at my house. Her little brother, too. Our moms worked it out, or something."

I could see his eyebrows shoot up with a look of apology wafting off his face.

"Oh," he said. "Well . . . do you think it would be nice to explain that to your girlfriend? I heard you blew her head off on the phone today. She was a mess. You could have told her what was up."

"She accused me without giving me a chance." I started in but didn't want to blame the whole thing on Leandra, either. It sounded wimpy.

Renee had come up beside Alex, with a bunch of candy in her hands, and she said, "Why in the hell does Ali have to stay with you? She could have stayed with me. You're a guy."

"So?" I asked for lack of something better. She had big ears, hearing all that.

"It just doesn't *look* very good, that's all. How do you think Leandra feels?"

It didn't *feel* very good, thinking I had to run my life around this relationship that was starting to seem kind of annoying and small.

"You know what? I just don't think I can be with Leandra right now, you guys. I'm going to tell her tomorrow, so don't butt in and tell her first, okay?" I just blurted it out, but after I did I felt some great relief. I couldn't believe it. Last night, lying in bed, I was all afraid of losing her. Now I was saying I would break it off.

"What is up?" Renee asked. She started in with how they were my friends.

"If you're really my friends, you'll just have to hang back from me right now. I can't explain."

They were pissed. The manager was waiting at the register, and Renee burst past me, pushing me hard in the shoulder. I wanted to grab a clump of her hair and pull it out. She paid and stalked away.

"She's precious," I muttered to Alex.

"Yeah, well, you always said you never wanted to get on her shit list." He grinned, all smug. "You're on it. Leandra's her friend."

"Yeah, well, so am I. Maybe you guys could grow up, thank you." I flipped the five onto the counter and watched the manager reach into the drawer. "I need quarters and dimes for the phone booth, please."

"*Oooo,* that's grown-up," Alex said. "What're you guys calling, nine-hundred numbers?"

"Bite me," I said under my breath, took the change, and walked out.

Outside, Renee was big-time in Ali's face. Bo was nowhere I could see.

". . . could have stayed with me and Ryan. You have to butt in on Leandra's turf? Are you stupid?"

"No, and it's none of your business!" Ali came back.

"Leandra's my business, she's my friend—"

"Oh, get a life," Ali said, backing away from her. "It shouldn't matter to you where I stay."

"Your stupid sex life makes it a problem where you stay!" Renee hollered. "I didn't cause your legendary rep, Ali! You caused it! If people think you're a slut, that's because you practically begged them to! My dad told me about your mother. Well, guess what? You're no better."

Ali balled up her fist, and before I knew what was happening, Renee went flying into me, all screaming. Ali screamed next, surprised at her own punch, I guess. I grabbed Renee, and Alex was hollering, "Ladies! Hold up!"

Renee elbowed me in the gut, and I thought my whole chest had caved in.

"Renee, Jesus!" I yelled, trying to keep from slinging her into the wall.

"Maybe you don't know her mom is a major slut, Torey."

I grabbed her by the hair to keep her off Ali. That got Alex bear-hugging me from behind, which wasn't helping my aching gut.

Renee spat out, "Well, I know about her mom! My dad told me!"

An enormous hand reached from behind the wall and gripped Renee's wrist, keeping her from swinging. As Bo came walking out, Renee walked backward and he continued walking forward. He finally slung down her wrist.

He said, "God, you look funny when you're scared, Bowen. You don't get scared too often, I guess. Not with that big fat mouth of yours always flapping along in front of you."

"I'm not scared of you, you 'tard," she croaked.

He jumped forward at her, hollering, *"Rahhh!"* or something. She screeched.

I started laughing under my breath. It was funny, watching her piss herself, considering she just sent my gut halfway to hell with that elbow job.

"Why you so scared, Bowen? Let's see. Is it because I'm a boon? Or is it because you think I'm a murderer? What, you think I did Creed? And I'm coming to do you next? *Raaahh!*"

She screamed again and worked her way over to Alex, who said, "Maybe we should all just . . . make like a tree and leaf."

"My dad's a cop." Renee breathed nervously. "Don't fuck with me."

She looked so ridiculously scared, and it was pissing me off that she could assume Bo might kill someone without even knowing him. She could be just as vicious as he could sometimes, and no one was accusing her. Bo was laughing.

"Oh! Oh yeah, right, Renee! I killed him! I—" He looked at me with these huge laughing eyes. "How did we do it, Adams? I forget."

I wanted to frame her face to remember the day Renee Bowen got scared. Who knows, maybe I still had the Digger Haines story in my head.

"We took a gun and shot him?" I asked. I felt guilty right away. I didn't really want to make fun of them. I only wanted Renee to know what it felt like to be on the receiving end.

"Oh, that's right! I forgot! I took a gun and shot him and left him for dead in the woods," Bo said. "And as for your dad, it's way funny that he should be calling Mrs. McDermott a slut. What does that make your dad?"

Ali grabbed his arm and croaked his name out with wide eyes. She had looked ready to croak since she'd hit Renee. That was so out of form for her. But now her eyes looked ready to roll back in her head.

"What are you babbling about, Richardson?" Renee muttered.

Bo ignored Ali for the moment. "I mean . . . *your dad was screwing her all last year!*"

Ali let out a bloodcurdling screech and covered her face with her hands. She started sobbing and shouted, "Why did you have to tell her that! I'm never telling you anything ever again, I swear to God—"

She started to take off toward the woods, and Bo ran after her. I couldn't hear what he was saying to her, but I could hear her sobbing, "That was *stupid*! Why do you have to be so *stupid* sometimes."

I turned and looked at Renee and Alex. Somehow Alex had my macaroni-and-cheese container in his hand. I couldn't even remember how that happened. They looked stun-gunned, like somebody had given them an electric shock. From Ali's reaction, I could feel in my bones that it was true. It seemed incredible at first. My friends' dad, chief of police, fooling around on his wife. I didn't think after hearing about Ali's mom and that perv that anything could shock me. But this did a little. I remembered Chief Bowen's face from the other night at the station, when he was trying to get Ali and me to lie. He had a heartless streak. I had just never seen it so clearly before. Maybe I couldn't have handled it before, so I didn't let myself see it.

I moved a step closer to Renee, enough to make sure she heard me but not close enough so she could get a swing at me. I was worried about her revenge system and what it could do to Ali.

"Renee, whatever you do with that piece of information is your business. But remember this. Ali held on to that for a year so she wouldn't hurt you. Remember that when you get real tempted to open that big unending mouth of yours in school tomorrow."

Her neck snapped a little, and she stood there swaying, like maybe I'd given her a different way to think of things. For a few seconds.

"She's *lying* . . ." She got tears in her eyes and her voice cracked. "My dad wouldn't *touch* that turbo slut-bag—"

She took off down the road without finishing, and Alex followed after her. I could tell she was really upset, and I wondered if it was because she felt in her heart that her dad was capable of it. I didn't know what to think. I ran over to Bo and Ali.

160

"I just couldn't help it," he spewed out. "Where does she get off passing her stupid judgment on everybody around here? She's calling *your* mom a slut while *her* dad was slutting, too? How can you just lie down for that, Ali?"

"Because! She is the daughter of the police chief who would love to put you away right now! All she has to do is walk into her house and announce what you just told on him. He will find some way to get back at you! It could break up his marriage."

"Ali, would you get the weight of the goddamn world off your shoulders, please!" He shook her. "You're not everybody's doormat! You don't have to protect guilty people! You don't have to make everybody love you! You don't have to do every guy just because he's there! The whole world is *not* your problem!"

"You're going to get arrested!" she hollered back.

"That's not your problem, either!" He pushed her aside and stalked off toward the woods.

"Where are you going?" she cried.

"I'm thinking I should disappear until Chief Bowen cools off. That girl could have her dad all over me before dawn—" He came back around to us and grabbed me by both shoulders. He muttered, "Listen. Look after her, but don't let her help anybody. Don't let her protect anybody. Don't let her carry the weight of the world on her shoulders." Then he kissed her really big and ran off into the woods.

As we walked home, Ali was calm, almost cold. I figured there was no more crying left in her. I wondered where Bo would go. I really hoped he wouldn't drop into the black hole next to Creed. Ali went to sleep when we got home, or at least she pretended to. I wasn't tired anymore, and I remembered what I'd totally forgotten down at the Wawa. The last phone number.

I looked it up again in our phone book, then sat up in my bedroom, just staring at the phone. Truth was, I wanted something to distract myself from the idea of Bo out in those woods. I finally picked up the phone and dialed. I got an answering machine. It sounded like a businessman's voice. "You have reached the Karzden residence. To leave a message for Doug, Athena, or Isabella, please wait for—"

My heart jumped. *Bull's-eye.* I was so wound up I didn't know quite what to say. The beep made me try to find my voice.

"This message is for Isabella. I'm . . . *uhm* . . . I'm a friend of Chris Creed's. We're . . . *uhm* . . . sort of looking for him? If you could, please call me back." I left my phone number and hung up.

I lay on my bed, trying to clear my mind of so many things, but little images kept passing in front of my eyes. Bo sleeping out in the woods . . . Creed's body lying dead in the woods . . . Creed at a psychic's, hearing of his own death . . . Creed and some sweet, innocent Margate girl down on the beach, doing whatever. I tried to dredge up some image of what she might tell me. But I couldn't get any. If I ever fell asleep, I don't remember doing it.

Seventeen

I tried to ignore everything and everyone in school the next morning, but I managed to catch an earful of a few things the first three periods. First, Bo had come to school. Second, Ali was walking around with him between first and second periods, talking to him and all the boons like it was nothing. And everybody was yakking about that, though I was pretending I didn't hear. After her blowout with Renee the night before, I decided, she'd probably just reached her limit and didn't care anymore what anyone thought or said. I couldn't forget her looking so zombified as we walked back to my house from the Wawa.

Third, I heard that the cops were coming for Bo. Again. I got the word from Ali—in a note she passed me during second period—who'd heard it from a couple of teachers proctoring near the bathroom, when she took the hall pass. She didn't know what he had supposedly done now, or if the cops just wanted to question him. I prayed Renee hadn't blabbed that thing about Chief Bowen and Mrs. McDermott around her house and set her dad looking for revenge. I also hoped that computer disk was still lying dormant and no wide-awake cop had decided to stick it in a hard drive.

As the bell rang, Ali and I nearly flew out of class, then found Bo in the cafeteria, sitting down with Shawn Mathers where they usually sat.

He shrugged like it was no big deal. "Look, whatever Chief Bowen or Mrs. Creed are up to now, I made up my mind. I ain't running and hiding from that snake of a woman, and I ain't afraid of no Renee Bowen, Queen of the Mouth Patrol." He laughed. "Hey, I been arrested before. Besides, this time I got your old lady. She'll keep me out of the can, whatever it is."

I was scared he thought my mom was God or something. I heard enough talk about my mom's work, and I wasn't sure she could keep Bo out of juvenile if Chief Bowen wanted him there.

I plopped into a chair beside Shawn Mathers without really thinking, and Ali plopped down on Bo's lap. She was sitting on the edge of his leg, trying to look nonchalant, but I could see she was pretty pleased with herself.

Shawn said, "Hey. Anybody want half an egg salad? Damn, I hate when my mom makes me egg salad."

"So, what's your mother doing making your lunch?" Bo snapped at him. "You ought to be making your own lunch. How old are you, anyway?"

"Fifteen." Mathers shrugged.

"Think I bother my mom to make my lunch?" Bo went on. "I not only got to make my lunch, I got to make the little kids' lunches or they don't eat."

"So, what do you want? A medal?" Mathers asked him. "My mom *likes* making my lunch."

"Give half to Adams. He's losing weight." Bo held on to Ali with one arm, while reaching over for half of Mathers's egg salad, then dumping it in front of me. "Eat that sandwich, Adams. You look like shit."

"He thinks he's everyone's mother." Shawn nudged me, like it was some big secret. I watched him, feeling surprised at how quiet his voice was. I had never heard Mathers's voice before. He had these fierce eyebrows and that face full of zits. I always thought if I heard his voice it would sound like a barking dog or something. He had almost a sweet voice, like a little kid's. He sounded a little slow maybe. But definitely not scary or loud.

My eyes moved off him and looked around the cafeteria. I caught at least twenty sets of eyes on me and probably fifty on Ali. I picked up the sandwich and said, "Thanks," and took a major, dramatic bite out of it.

"And don't be leaving no crusts," Bo went on. "Yo, Mathers. Give him one of them Tastykakes. They got eggs and milk in them."

Mathers grabbed his lunchbag. "What am I, the good fairy Give-it-all-away?"

Bo reached around Ali and snapped the bag from him. "Yeah. His mom works, and she expects him to buy the shit around here and actually eat it. Your mom wouldn't know no job if she fell over it. Now give him one, fool."

"Where's your lunch?" Mathers asked Bo, dropping a chocolate Tastykake in front of me.

"I slept in the woods last night." He shrugged like it was nothing. "Think my old lady missed me? Not until she had to start making lunches, which she probably didn't do, anyway. Hopefully Darla did, if she managed to find her way off Billy Everett's garage couch. You hungry, Ali?"

"No," she said. But he was reaching in his pocket and pulling out a dollar.

"Go buy us french fries, huh? Maybe french fries won't kill us." Ali took the dollar and walked to the front of the cafeteria, and we watched her all the way. Everyone else was watching her, too, just about.

"Shit, man, you're inspiring me." Mathers grinned at Bo. "If this goes good for you, maybe I'll ask out Jaleigh Overton."

My eyes wandered toward some action at the door. Mrs. Creed was coming in, followed by Chief Bowen and the officer they called Tiny. Mr. Ames was with them, too, trying to grab Mrs. Creed's arm. She didn't seem to notice him. I couldn't remember the police showing up in our cafeteria, ever. Sometimes they came to the school, but always to the office.

Bo laughed a little and said, "*Ooo,* here it comes, brothers and sisters. Now just be cool. They're going for the Academy Award—"

Shawn said, "Bo, are they coming after you?"

"None other."

"What'd you do now?"

"I don't know yet. Guess we're about to find out."

I watched his eyes stick on this crowd like he was trying too hard to be fearless, but I know he was petrified under it all. He had to be. I was.

He leaned back in his seat, so when Chief Bowen came up to him, he was looking at Bo upside down.

"What am I arrested for now?" Bo asked.

"You are wanted for questioning in the alleged murder of Christopher Creed." Chief Bowen's voice echoed through the air. "We have reason to believe you are involved, responsible, or had prior knowledge—"

Murder of Christopher Creed. Murder. My eyes shot up and caught a thousand eyes staring at us in this suddenly quiet cafeteria. Some kids far away were standing on chairs. The word *murder* kept banging through my head.

Bo was laughing, but I could hear an edge in his voice. "Oh. I murdered him. Okay." He laughed. "And how did I do that?"

"Get up, Richardson," Chief Bowen said. It didn't seem like he was going to elaborate right there.

"Does this have to do with a computer disk?" Bo asked casually.

Chief Bowen kind of froze for a second. I could tell by his expression the computer disk was big on his mind.

"If this is about that computer disk, you're about to make a fool out of yourself." Bo jerked his eyes on me, then turned around in his seat. "Ali, where'd the computer disk come from?"

Ali had come tiptoeing up from behind with the french fries. Her hand was shaking as she spat out the story about going to the library on Friday and moving it out of the library's files because they were curious about what Mr. Ames had said about a possible suicide.

If the cops' wanting Bo had nothing to do with the disk, they would have cut Ali off or asked what-the-hell disk was she talking about. Someone had actually discovered what was on it, I gathered. My mom had called it a sleeping dog that could look very incriminating. I guessed her sleeping dog had woken up. Mrs. Creed had actually been quiet through Ali's two-minute explanation, but then she came to life in her loud way.

"No, no, no!" she blasted, making Ali jump. "Christopher did not write that note! My son had a happy life. There is no reason why he would—"

"Your son was a social retard!" Bo blasted. "Ask Ames, if you're too blind to see the truth!"

"Richardson, get up, before I cuff you and drag you out of here," Chief Bowen said.

Bo stood but kept up his tirade to Mrs. Creed. "You *know* your son was losing it. With a psycho for a mother and—"

"You're a fine person to be calling anybody names!" She turned to Chief Bowen, pointing a finger at Bo. "He already confessed to the phone call—"

That was the end of my silent act. I jumped up and grabbed Chief Bowen by the arm. "He didn't make the phone call. *I* made the phone call."

Chief Bowen stared at me for a moment, and there was anger in his face. He looked angry that I was messing up this whole thing. He tore his eyes away to Ali, who, good as her word, was trying to tell him, "Chief Bowen, *I* made the phone call."

Fortunately, she spoke too quietly, and I don't think he understood her. He was pushing past me, with Bo beside him, and I had to grab on to the table to keep from falling backward.

He said over his shoulder, "There's already a confession on the books. If you'd care to argue with Mr. Richardson about it, you're welcome to do that later."

I watched in stunned silence as he and Tiny started off with Bo. I could not believe I had just stood there and told every inch of the truth about the phone call, and Ali told the truth about the disk before that, and Bo was still walking off in between two cops—one cop who was a wife cheat—with a sociopathic mother bringing up the rear. I think I was still more scared than mad. I was scared that these allegedly respectable people let this thing get so bad. I guess I thought seeing a situation clearly was just part of being a grown-up.

I let fly at the backs of their heads, "You stupid people, you *know* he didn't kill anybody! You just have to find some way to keep your own screwed-up version of reality going—"

A hand slapped over my mouth, and I felt a massive arm pulling me backward. I watched Chief Bowen turn and give me some don't-tangle-with-me stare, and it's good Mr. Ames had his hand over my mouth because I was running through every curse word I knew. Bo was laughing at the top of his lungs, though I couldn't figure out what was funny.

Chief Bowen hollered to Mr. Ames, "Get him out of here."

I saw Chief Bowen turn to Mrs. Creed and bark, "Sylvia, you're not invited."

She stopped in her tracks, and that's all I remember until I was in Mr. Ames's office and he was pushing me into a chair. I fell into it hard. I didn't know he had grabbed Ali, too, and he flung her by the arm, but not as hard. She dropped into a chair, and I could hear Mrs. Creed's hagging voice from somewhere nearby.

It got drowned out a little by Mr. Ames's voice, which was right in my face. "If you want to win people over, you need to work on your tact. You're taking lessons from Bo Richardson—"

"... going to lie for that boy, you two will suffer very, *very* serious consequences!" Mrs. Creed's voice blasted.

I turned to see Mr. Ames grab the door handle. She was standing in his doorway. I thought he was going to slam the door in her face. He got it about halfway shut, then stopped. They stared at each other. He looked like he couldn't take much more of her constant badgering, but it was his job to be polite to parents, and he was having a real inner battle here. She looked defiant, and my stomach was twisting.

After a moment he cleared his throat and said softly, "You may come in. I think Torey and Ali and I would like to have a talk with you. We want to tell you about Chris."

Eighteen

Mrs. Creed sat down slowly on a couch under the window as Mr. Ames shut the door. Her eyes shifted to him, then back to us. She firmly stuck out her chin, high, but her voice was shaking. "Fine. I'm here to listen."

She looked like listening was some sort of military pain-test that she was being subjected to, and she would endure it because she was a great American. Mr. Ames sat behind his desk and said, "Torey, you've known Chris since you were born, practically. I would like you to . . . share any thoughts that come to you. Sylvia, I want you to hear this. From another student."

That wasn't exactly what I was expecting.

"Well . . ." I hunted in my brain for something not too awful. "He was a good kid. I mean, he would never have thought to do drugs or cut school or curse somebody out—"

"He better not have," Mrs. Creed said, with a grin that died as fast as it came. She had her legs crossed, arms folded across her chest, and she wouldn't look at me. It's like these loudmouthed remarks were always on the tip of her tongue and she was just trying extra hard right now to hold them back. I wished she had tried harder with Chris.

"But he made it difficult to be a friend of his." I leaned forward. "I feel that—I think that . . . he never had a chance to learn how to be a friend."

She swallowed. "I always encouraged my children to be kind."

"Oh, he was," I said quickly. "But not hurting people and knowing how to get along with people . . . they're different. He was . . . different."

She stared at her corner of the couch like a robot and spat out robot words. "I wanted him to be different. I did not get into the Naval Academy by being like everybody else."

I blurted out, "I can see why you wouldn't want him to be like some kids. But what's the matter with me? Or Alex?"

Her face flushed like maybe she knew for once that she'd put her foot in her mouth. "I didn't want my son doing drugs or staying out late or hanging out or making other bad choices he would pay for later."

"Well . . ." I stayed out until, like, three sometimes, but only at Alex's or Ryan's. I had been drunk a few times, yeah. But I didn't feel like a future convict. "Isn't there some way you could have thought of so he could have friends but not make bad choices?"

She just stared at this corner, all totally proud. Mr. Ames had been rocking in his chair. He stopped midrock and said, "Sylvia, I would not be putting you through this if I thought the Richardson boy killed your son."

He twisted around in his swivel chair when she didn't respond, and he laughed awkwardly. "I wouldn't put you through this if I thought Christopher was . . . no longer with us."

A tear fell over her eyelashes, but she wiped it away almost as soon as it dropped. She glared at Mr. Ames. "I know what you think. You think this is another Digger Haines reenactment," she said. "You think my son, like Digger, is out there. And you're afraid if I don't stop pointing the finger that I'm going to end up suicidal like Bob Haines."

"No one has ever proven that Bob Haines committed suicide," Mr. Ames said quickly. "No one knows where he is today. But, yes, Sylvia, I think that . . ." He trailed off and stared at his desk clock like he was agonizing inside.

I realized this was only the second time I'd heard anything about Digger Haines, yet Mrs. Creed knew about it, and as soon as she mentioned it to Mr. Ames, he knew it right away, too. It was like this big secret story all the grown-ups seemed to know about, but no one talked about it. Mrs. Creed squirmed uncomfortably.

"I don't plan on winding up dead, Glen. I have better ways to cope," she said quickly. "I would love to think my son is *out there*. Do I look like the morbid type who would prefer to think the worst in an awful case like this? Not at all, Glen. There's only one problem with your theory. My son could *not* have written that note!"

"What makes you so sure?" he asked.

"I know my son. My son was happy. My son had a very good life. And he was happy." She said that part twice, like, for emphasis. "And if he *didn't* write that note, what's the *conclusion*, Glen? Somebody *else* wrote the note!"

I shuddered, reminded of some ancient schoolteacher cackling at a kid in class. Mr. Ames cleared his throat, but before he could think of something to say, Ali piped up.

"I don't . . . I just don't think he could be so happy watching everyone in his class go to dances and parties, and he wasn't allowed."

Mrs. Creed stared at Ali like she was crazy. "Chris was allowed to go out! We offered to *drive* him to the dances! I even signed up to *chaperone* the dances, before he said he wasn't really into them. How could I object to the very dances I offered to chaperone?"

This woman was an enormous stone wall. I wondered what she would make of it if one of us shared a bright question like, *Do you think your offering to chaperone had anything to do with Chris not being into it?* or, *Hey, great! What's better than driving to a dance with your mom, going in with your mom, and leaving with your mom?*

"My dad chaperoned a couple of dances," Ali started out casually, "in, like . . . sixth grade."

If Mrs. Creed got it, she didn't keep it. "I know my son! I also know that quintessential powder keg some people lovingly call the boondocks! I was raised down there, don't forget. I was a boon once."

I remembered hearing a few times over the years that Mrs. Creed was raised in the boondocks and that she'd had a hard life. But it never struck me as anything important. This time my eyes stuck on her as I watched her mouth move.

"They're not the victimized, misunderstood little darlings you make them out to be sometimes, Glen. My father was a drunkard. He used to tie me up with ropes and hang me upside down from the tree outside my bedroom window. After all the beatings I took as a kid, don't try and talk to me about any boon being incapable of murder."

"Don't you think you're generalizing a bit?" Mr. Ames asked quietly.

"Not about Bo Richardson. Are you forgetting what Mr. Richardson did to my Christopher last year?"

Mr. Ames sighed. I shifted around some more, and Ali was sucking air in and out like there was no tomorrow. This felt all wrong, but there didn't seem to be too much to say. I didn't need the graphic detail about Mrs. Creed being hung out with ropes to dry. It gave her some unfair advantage, in my mind.

"Pushing him over the bleachers is bad, Sylvia, but it doesn't amount to plotting a murder and covering it up," Mr. Ames said. "I've had problems with Bo Richardson, but he takes care of a lot of younger children at home, and he's got a good and responsible side as well. Don't forget, I've had problems with Chris, too, Sylvia. And I've also given him every possible break."

In other words, Mrs. Creed should lighten up on Bo due to the fact that so many teachers and principals had to break up fights, thanks to Chris's obnoxious streak.

"Well, it's not my fault that other children saw my son as an easy mark." She shrugged it off. "And need I remind you . . . there is a boon, sitting in the Steepleton lockup, who confessed to extortion in my son's disappearance."

I blocked all bad thoughts out of my mind and repeated what I had said in the cafeteria. "I made the phone call, Mrs. Creed. That's the truth."

"Oh no, it's not." She stared at me, so sure, so unshakingly confident. She even broke into a snotty laugh like I was oh-so-stupid and didn't get anything over on her for a minute.

I went on in frustration. "Mrs. Creed! Bo knew you were mad because he pushed Chris off the bleachers last year. He was afraid you were going to accuse him of this, just because of the bleachers thing. He wanted to go into your house to see if he could find evidence of what really happened. I made the phone call so that he could get the evidence, so he wouldn't go to jail, and so everybody who counts on him could have a chance at not going down the tubes with him. It was me. I did it. That's the truth."

She stared at me like a corpse. I could not read her thoughts to save my life.

Ali cleared her throat. Her voice still shook, and I wanted to throttle her for her voice shaking, because we needed some strength to fight this woman's unblinking sureness. "And Mrs. Creed . . . I was with Bo when we moved that file onto the computer disk. We got it from the library. It was already in the library's files. All we did was move it. I swear to—"

"Now, you listen to me!" Mrs. Creed was up and hovering over Ali's face so fast it looked like a military maneuver. Mr. Ames stood up, but she kept right on, almost nose to nose with Ali. "You people can sit here and tell your lies until hell freezes over. I do not care what you say, or what your agenda is. I care about one thing: taking that boondock kid who destroyed my life and making sure his life gets destroyed next."

She draped her handbag over her arm and straightened up stiffly. "Thank you for this most enlightening conversation, Glen. About chaperoning dances and curfews."

This sucks! my brain screamed.

But her exit line to us was, "Bo Richardson is going to *hang.*"

It took a minute for her choice of words to sink in. My Psych teacher would definitely have called that a Freudian slip. A fire lit in my ribs, and I jumped up. I went to shout at her that hanging an innocent kid wouldn't erase her own childhood hangings. But by the time I found my voice, she was already gone.

"She's the criminal, Mr. Ames," I blasted. "She doesn't break into houses, she just breaks into lives! And steals them! Between her and the cops . . ."

I trailed off because of how he was staring into space. I noticed for the first time how tired he looked.

"Digger Haines was my friend," he said, so softly you would have thought he was talking to the wall and not to us. "Digger was my friend, and I guess I should have know[n] that at some point it would happen again; it *had* to happe[n] again."

"What do you mean?" I asked.

He sighed. "Only that nobody learned a lesson. Nobody stopped believing that other people were more guilty than they were. Why do people have so much trouble seeing their own faults but such an easy time seeing everyone else's?"

I didn't answer because I knew he wasn't really asking me. It was just a question that he put out there. But a truth struck me. *Mrs. Creed would rather believe her own son is dead than believe she is at fault.* I would never have imagined that a human being was capable of so much denial. By the tired look on Mr. Ames's face and his last comment, I figured he must feel that she's not the only person out there capable of that. He was thinking of a few others, maybe Digger's dad, Bob Haines, and maybe even our own chief of police.

Nineteen

My mom was trying to cheer us up as she made dinner. She said the DA's office was having the computer disk shipped to a company in Silicon Valley, in California. The company had special technology that could determine what activity actually happened on the disk. They could determine if Chris's note on the disk was either a "save" or a "move," and on what day that activity took place. If the activity was a "save," that meant Bo had something to do with creating or editing the note. We knew that wasn't true. If they could prove the activity was nothing more than a "move," then it would support Bo's story, she said.

"The problem is, we can't get the DA's signature until tomorrow. The shipping alone will take twenty-four hours, which will put us into the weekend. And they don't do analysis on the weekends," Mom said. "They won't have a diagnosis until Monday, at the earliest. Tomorrow they're sending Bo to the juvenile-detention facility in Egg Harbor, just for safekeeping."

That set Ali into one of her messes. My mom was rambling something about Bo being a juvenile, that they could keep him like that without actually charging him—something. I was trying to keep a long fuse, but Ali's crying all the time was getting me a little crazy.

"Mrs. Adams, I'm afraid of him being near Chief Bowen." Ali told how Bo blurted out Chief Bowen's affair with Mrs. McDermott to Renee. "I'm afraid Chief Bowen will do mean things to Bo for telling his kids. Things that have nothing to do with Chris Creed being gone."

I didn't know what to say. I was way lost on this business of Mrs. Creed taking her life out on an innocent kid.

After dinner I went up to my room and just lay there vegging. The whole thing was reminding me of this Bible story Leandra told me one day. The Bible stories she learned in her childhood were scarier than the ones they taught in my church. Ours were about Jesus loving all races and kids, and nice stuff like that. In her church, they told kids what could happen to you if you died a heartless snob. This rich guy had died, and gone to hell because he had been all heartless to the beggars and poor people. When he got there he pleaded to God that he wanted to appear as a ghost and tell his relatives to clean up their act. God said to him, "Even if you went back as a ghost and told the truth to their faces, they would not believe you."

I had thought that was a far-fetched story, until now.

There were blank spots where I must have dropped off to sleep that night without realizing it. But I would come out of them and look at the clock when I did. No more than half an hour ever passed.

Friday I never set foot in the cafeteria. And Leandra never came up to my locker or stuck her head in any of my classes before the bell. I guessed she knew it was over, and I just couldn't get up enough feelings to care. Somehow I got through classes and football practice. I got tackled a lot.

I was definitely ready for some decent news, something to pick me up, when I got home. I noticed that there was a message on my answering machine and wondered if it was from Leandra—or Alex, who hadn't called me since our fight with Renee in front of the Wawa. The phone call I made two nights earlier had been completely forgotten.

I pushed the button. "Hi, I'm Isabella. You forgot to leave your name, so this message is for whoever called me. Yeah, you can come over anytime. I'm here this weekend, except Saturday day . . . My mom's taking me to the mall."

My mom's taking me to the mall. I remembered seeing Chris at the mall with his mom a few times, despite how the rest of us went with our friends. Sounded like Isabella and Chris were two of a kind. I stared at the answering machine and listened to the message a couple more times. Something about the sound of her voice made me curious. I guess I had expected her to sound really shy and hesitating. Creed had written shyness around her every move. She just sounded like a friendly person who was nice.

And she had misunderstood me. I had said I just wanted her to call, not that I wanted to come over. But all of a sudden that sounded like a really good idea. I needed to get out of this town.

I told my dad Ali and I wanted a change of scene, and we wanted to go eat and walk on the boardwalk. He dropped us off in front of Chris's uncle's restaurant around dinnertime. I watched his car drive away, before steering Ali up to the boardwalk. Neither of us was very hungry.

"This was a great idea," I said. It felt awesome to get out of the woods for a while.

"You look better." She grinned at me. "Past couple nights, I thought you were getting suicidal yourself. Did anyone ever tell you that you get too emotionally involved in things?"

"No," I said. I didn't think I'd ever had anything to become emotionally involved in before.

She was laughing. "Remember the time in third grade when we had that field trip to the wax museum?"

"Yes, and shut up," I said, remembering. They had this one exhibit called the Chamber of Horrors, and it had these wax guys in various torture maneuvers that had gone on throughout history.

"Some of us kept going back and going through again and again, but you refused to go after the first time." She giggled.

I shuddered. "I don't actually see the thrill of staring at a guy draped over a giant meat hook. Or a bloody, decapitated body hanging off a guillotine."

"We thought it was funny." She laughed again. "You wrote a poem for class the next day called . . . some big word."

"'Inhumane,'" I mumbled. "Seemed like a big word back then."

I didn't feel like telling her the whole truth, because she was laughing already. But my mom had picked me up from school because the trip made us miss the school bus. I couldn't stop thinking of those torture victims, and by the time we were halfway home, my stomach had had enough. My mom had just gotten a new car, and I remember her reaching into the backseat, all frantic, and dumping out this pair of shoes she had just bought so I could have something to heave in. I heaved into a shoe box.

"I always wondered what they did with all those bloody wax figures when they closed that place," I muttered to Ali. "I wonder if that wax guy is still hanging over a meat hook in some other wax museum . . ."

"At any rate, I liked your poem." She smiled. "It was sweet."

I couldn't remember the poem, but it was good to see her smiling. It gave me hopeful thoughts, like maybe Isabella would know where Chris was, and that he was alive and okay.

We walked about six blocks, then turned. The houses on the beach block in Margate were pretty huge. They were even older and even bigger than the homes in Steepleton, but the yards were really small.

I had heard stories that the girls in Margate could generally be a good time. There was lots of money floating around, but the parents weren't all glued to one another like they were in Steepleton. It was more of a city than our little historic "towne," and supposedly there were more drugs running around, more parents taking more vacations without their kids, more divorces. That made for good parties. When juniors and seniors at Steepleton got their driver's licenses, they started going to parties in Margate on the weekends. But I supposed there were a number of families like mine, and that this Isabella was from one of them or she wouldn't have been like Creed described her.

We started up the walk, and I looked at the house number I'd scribbled down to make sure it was right. The lawn was small, and the hedges needed cutting really bad. The doorbell was hanging by a wire. I looked in one window and saw kind of a laundry mountain on the dining room table, with folding chairs all scattered around but no real chairs. It didn't look much like my house. It looked kind of bare and undecorated inside. I knocked on the door. After a few moments I heard footsteps and saw a pile of laundry with legs in jeans coming toward us.

"Hi!" the voice behind the mountain said. "Back door! Front door's broken."

We went around to the back door and waited. About a minute later a girl in baggy jeans came to the door. She wore one of those tops that came just below her boobs, so her whole stomach showed. She had about a hundred long braids in her hair, with beads and feathers and all sorts of stuff on the ends. She pushed open the door, blowing smoke over our heads, from a cigarette in the hand she pushed with. She was cute, despite the hair, but looked old—about nineteen. Isabella's weird big sister that Creed described in his diary, I decided.

"Hi, I'm Torey. This is Ali."

"Come on in," she said, without even asking what we wanted. Very friendly family.

I walked past her into the living room. It looked real lived in, and the furniture was kind of falling down.

"We're looking for Isabella Karzden," I said.

"I'm Isabella." She looked from Ali to me, huffing on that cigarette. It stopped me cold.

"You're Isabella?" I said. This girl was smoking. She was so unshy and so artsy looking. I could not imagine what in the hell attracted this girl to Creed. Ali rescued me.

"Torey called a couple nights ago. We know Chris Creed."

"Oh, that's you guys!" She laughed. "Sit down. Here."

She pushed a bunch of clothes and coats off the couch with her arm, and they landed in a pile on the floor. "Sorry about the mess. My dad refuses to hire a housekeeper, and my mom lives in Philadelphia now. He pays her a *huge* alimony, which is why we're minus a housekeeper, probably. I don't ask questions, I'm just the token offspring. My mom shows up on Saturdays to take me to the mall. I wonder if you can buy a housekeeper at Macy's."

I remembered her mall statement on the answering machine and shook my head in dizzy disbelief. It's amazing how things can be so different from how they sound.

"You guys want a beer? Bunch of kids are coming over later. We can have the party before the party if you want."

"Sure." Ali smiled, rescuing me again.

Isabella disappeared into the kitchen, and I just knew something was horribly wrong here. I thought maybe we had the wrong Isabella Karzden. Ali was laughing.

"What's so funny?" I asked.

"Oh my god" was all she said, but she looked like she was putting something together.

Isabella plopped a green bottle down on the coffee table in front of me, and I stared at it. Beer never came to us this easy. We normally had to con Ryan's older brother, Earl, into running into Absecon, and it was a big, sneaky thing. This was like playing grown-up.

"Yeah, Roger told me about Chris disappearing," she said, dropping into a chair and pulling her legs up in a pretzel. "I was sorry to hear about that. He was sweet."

Roger was Chris's uncle who owned the restaurant where Chris met this girl. I asked, "So . . . you don't know where he is?"

She shook her head in confusion. "Why would I know?"

My jaw bobbed around, then I asked, "Didn't you go out with him last summer?"

"You mean . . . as in a boyfriend-girlfriend thing?" She laughed. "No."

I watched in amazement as she hunted for words. "Chris . . . was . . . how can I say it? He could latch on to you and just refuse to let go. I never wanted to hurt him. But he never gives up until you say, *Listen, kiddo. Reality check. I do not like you, I will never like you.*"

Ali covered her face and laughed. "Oh my god, I feel like such a bonehead. Torey, he made the whole thing up! We all knew he never had a grip on reality . . . I guess we should have figured he would make you up, too."

"So . . . you're not really his friends, either." The girl was smiling and all. She added enthusiastically, "Because when

185

you called and said you were his friends, I thought, Hmm . . . wonder what these dudes are like?"

I could see she wasn't the judgmental sort. I decided to tell her the truth. "He had this diary, and we got ahold of it. You're all over the place in it. That's why I thought you might know where he is."

"Oh Jesus," she muttered. "What did he say in this diary?"

Ali told her about the walks down the boardwalk, the thing on the beach, and this one outrageous sex scene that she must have read when I wasn't around and hadn't told me about. Isabella just kept shaking her head, and every once in a while she would nod.

"That is, like, ninety-percent fiction," she said. "Here's the real story. One day, on my lunch break, he asked me to go for a walk on the boards with him. I thought, *Why not?* That part is true. I could see he was having trouble getting along with the other busboys, and I felt a little sorry for him. He was shaking in his shoes when he asked me. I thought it was cute. So we went walking, and when we came back, it was like he was glued to my side for the rest of the summer. He was really, *really* hard to shake."

"So, you never actually went out with him?" I asked.

"Well, I did it with him once," she said with a shrug. My neck snapped a little to hear how she said that so casually. She went on, "I couldn't shake him, and after a while I thought, Maybe he just needs to hook up with somebody. So, why not? But it just made him ten times worse. I wish I hadn't now. Doing a virgin is not all it's cracked up to be."

I watched this girl, trying to imagine what it would feel like to have a runaway life like this. Just parties and having sex with people at random. And I couldn't get over that Creed spent his summer writing in great detail about something that never happened at all. It was nuts.

"And this one time, he told me he wanted to visit my aunt who's a psychic. I felt that he was trying to find yet another excuse to be with me. But I took him because I figured I could give my aunt the high sign or something. There have been times before when I was trying to ditch some guy, and my aunt would pretend to give him a reading and say that he shouldn't be with me. 'The woman of your dreams is waiting if you will let go of this wrong relationship.' It worked a couple of times. So, I let her tell his fortune with the tarot deck. I figured halfway through I would kick her under the table and give her the eye. She just started reading the tarot cards, and before I knew it, she said, 'I see death in the woods.' She read 'death in the woods' about three times and finally scared him so bad, he wanted to leave." She laughed pretty hard.

"Really?" I asked. "Was your aunt faking?"

"I don't think so." The girl shrugged. "I never gave her a sign. I've been meaning to ask her. But it's not like the kid was a big part of my life or anything."

She stopped herself from giggling, remembering the situation. "He did start to leave me alone more after that. In fact, he got kind of serious toward the end of summer. Serious and quiet. You know how he was always laughing and grinning and trying to get attention?"

"Yes," we both chimed.

"Who knows. Maybe he started to think about suicide at that point. I hope not, but . . ." She shrugged. "Pretty weird, huh?"

We both nodded. It was weirder if the aunt hadn't been faking. "Can we ask your aunt if she was being serious?" I asked.

"Sure." She stood up, with another shrug, and I thought she was going to the phone. "Bring your brew. She lives over the garage."

The garage was no neater than the house. It wasn't completely gross, but as we came up the stairs, I saw the type of mess that looked like nobody ever bothered to pick up anything. And the furniture was more used than the stuff in the house.

"Aunt Vera? These are friends of Chris Creed's."

The aunt was sitting in a big armchair, staring at *Wheel of Fortune*. She looked about forty, maybe, and was pretty heavyset. She was eating corn chips out of the bag and had an ashtray beside her with at least fifty butts in it. She didn't look at us.

"Remember Chris Creed, Aunt Vera? That blond kid I had in here in July? You kept reading something about death in the woods."

With that she looked at us. Looked me up and down, and then Ali up and down. She was chewing a big mouthful of corn chips. She nodded.

"Aunt Vera, this is really important. You know how sometimes you're really seeing, and then sometimes I bring a guy in here that you know I don't like? And you'll ... you know. Mess with him?"

The aunt started to smile but turned her eyes back to *Wheel of Fortune*.

Isabella laughed. "Come on, Aunt Vera. Tell us the truth. That kid is missing, you know. He's missing, and he lives near a whole lot of woods."

With that, the aunt stopped chewing. She blinked a few times. She had this knowing look on her face, and I didn't think she seemed that surprised.

"So ... you were being serious, right?" Isabella asked. "You weren't just fooling around with the men in my—"

"No. I was not fooling around." She shook her head. Then she looked at me. She said, "I saw death in the woods. And you will find death in the woods."

She kept looking straight at me. She had this raspy voice that sounded like a mixture of corn chips and too many cigarettes.

"What do you mean, I will find death in the woods?"

"You. Not anybody else. When you are alone, you will find him. In the woods."

I watched her, trying to decide what was going on here. I wasn't so naive as to think I would come in here and find a bunch of lit candles surrounding a woman with a bone through her nose. But she's telling me, around a mouthful of corn chips, with *Wheel of Fortune* going on in the background, that I'm going to find Creed. An image was coming into my head of me walking through the woods and coming across a half-decayed body. I laughed nervously, but the picture made my heart beat hard.

"What do you mean, *alone*?" I demanded. "Why do I have to be *alone*?"

The woman shook her head with a shrug and said, "I just see you finding him when you are alone. Nobody is with you."

"Can she really do that?" My head snapped toward Isabella. This just felt all weird, all wrong.

"Yes, she can do that." Isabella nodded hard. "She can meet somebody on the street, or in a restaurant, and just see things about them. Sometimes a lot of things. Sometimes just a few things. But yeah. She's doing it to you right now."

I looked back down at the woman, trying to get these flashes out of my head of a dead, unrecognizable body lying in front of me. The woman hadn't taken her eyes off me, hadn't even blinked. It made me want to run. Somehow I didn't.

"Are you saying that . . . he's really and truly dead?" I asked.

This time, she actually closed her eyes. She took in a long breath of air and let it out slowly. Then she nodded. "I see him. He is dead."

"But . . ." This was crazy. "But I don't *want* to find him dead in the woods while I'm alone. That's gross." It was terrifying. Ali and I had just been talking about that Chamber of Horrors making me puke once. And those guys were made of wax. If I came across a bloody body of somebody I knew—I could not imagine it. Maybe I would never go into the woods again, and that would be the end of that.

I guessed she didn't understand my meaning, because she said, "Oh, it's not all woods. It's . . . a primitive cemetery. Something like that."

"A burial ground?" Ali asked.

She nodded. "You will find him shot through the head on a primitive grave. There are other graves around, but this one is marked with three large rocks."

My chest turned to fire because I could picture right where she was talking about. There was a clearing inside the Indian burial ground. Legend had it that the Indians cleared it to bury their dead, and the pine trees never grew back. That's where Alex and I had played King of the Hill. Right there on those three rocks . . .

"Chris Creed is dead," I mumbled. "You're saying that Chris Creed is definitely dead."

I got hot and dizzy. I had said many times myself he might be dead, but you're never prepared to hear something like that. It was like when Chief Bowen had said the word *murder* the day before. Only this was worse. She was telling me I was going to find him.

"Oh, I rarely say specifics as definite fact," the woman said quickly. I turned to see her eyes staring back at mine like she was trying to cover herself somehow. "I'm saying I see death in the woods. I'm saying it has to do with this boy."

You just told me he was shot through the head, you stupid witch, my brain was heaving.

"Look, don't play with me," I muttered to her. "This isn't funny."

"I'm dead serious!" she said defensively. "I can't help what I see."

Whatever. I was thinking how many times Alex and I jumped and played on those rocks, never thinking, *doyee,* that they marked an Indian grave. Probably fifty times in our childhood we had jumped off those rocks.

She was sitting there with corn-chip pieces dribbling down onto her huge chest. I couldn't believe this woman with manners like a pig could just blow out something psychic. I don't know what manners had to do with it, but I was hypnotized, watching her.

Ali cleared her throat shyly and said, "Can you see . . . how he died? Did . . . somebody kill him, or did he kill himself?"

The aunt looked down, blinking into her lap until she swallowed more corn chips. Then she nodded. "Suicide. He killed himself."

"I mean, will the police be able to see that it was suicide?" Ali reworded it. She was thinking about Bo, I realized.

"If that's what they want to see," she said with a shrug. Not very encouraging.

"Well . . ." My brain was screaming with questions, and I just threw one out. "They already searched the Indian burial ground last Saturday. Nobody saw anything. How could all those searchers have missed a dead body in the middle of a clearing?"

She did that thing where she shut her eyes, took in a deep breath, and let it out. She said, "The dead didn't want to be seen. They can do that. Hide until they get what they want."

I wanted to say, *This is bull, the dead don't play hide-and-seek, and you're insane.* She spoke up before I had the chance.

"Be very careful about your actions. A person's liberty is at stake here."

Bo's liberty. I stared back and tried to think of ways she might be playing with me. She was definitely covering herself with that "I rarely say anything as definite fact." It made me mad, because I figured she was BS-ing me.

But how could she make up those rocks or that clearing that I knew so well? I wanted to ask her where Creed got the gun, but every time she had opened her mouth it just got worse and worse. I didn't want to hear any more.

I handed back the almost-full beer bottle to Isabella. "Thanks for your time."

"Oh, god, I'm sorry!" She came barreling down the stairs behind me and Ali. "I should have told her not to . . . not to startle you. Discretion is not her strong suit. That's why she's not in business. Like, who would invest in her?"

I stalked off toward the street, with Ali following me and Isabella apologizing behind us.

Isabella finally went back in her house, to party some more and forget this whole schmear, I guessed.

"That girl was too weird for me, Ali. And the aunt? You want to know what I think? Here's what I think! I think Creed was a very, *very* impressionable person. If she said she saw death in the woods, she could have put the idea in his stressed-out head. He might never have done it except for her big mouth. Psychic, my ass. I think she should be arrested."

"It's not her fault that Chris was messed up," Ali said quietly, but I wasn't in the mood to be sweet.

"And that girl? Oh my god. Let's just get laid with a sheltered kid because we're bored or something—"

"The girl is messed up, that's all. But she's no more messed up than Chris was. She's just cooler about it."

I glanced at her, irritated, wondering how she could make the girl so fast and so sure. I guessed that, somehow, going through family junk can have its flip side, like it can make you more insightful. And more generous, maybe. Ali was making me feel guilty on top of my heart attack.

"Are you going to go look in the woods?" she asked.

I realized that was the answer. "No. I'm not. Not to-night, not tomorrow, not ten years from now. If I ever get the chance, I will tell Mrs. Creed, and she can haul her sorry ass in there and look. I'll never go in the woods alone again."

Ali nodded and just walked along beside me like she didn't want to tangle with my foul mood. That was a good idea, because she would have lost.

Twenty

My mom was sitting at her desk in her study when we got home. I noticed her ink pen wasn't flying. She was just staring into space.

"What's up?" I asked. She shut her eyes and pinched the bridge of her nose with her fingers in a way I didn't like.

"Sit down," she told us. We sat, watching her rock and sigh.

"It seems that Bo announced to Chief Bowen that the man's children know about his affair last year."

"He's so stupid sometimes!" Ali cringed. "It was bad enough he said it to Renee!"

"Well, he told me that he thought Renee Bowen had run home and told her father as soon as she and Alex heard it. He thought he was telling Chief Bowen something he already knew. Let's say he was half stupid."

"So, what did Chief Bowen do?" Ali demanded.

As my mom told it, Chief Bowen's life went down the drain when Bo said that to him. He had been trying for years to keep his troubles under his hat, but now he felt like the town would know tomorrow. Bo said it so heartlessly, and he had already repeated it that way to one of Chief Bowen's own kids.

"Daryl lost his temper and hit Bo about six times," my mom said, rubbing the bridge of her nose in that tired way. "There were two other officers present and they saw the whole thing. I'm sure they would have kept the dirty little secret, but despite what you may think of him, Chief Bowen is not all bad. He resigned at six o'clock."

Ali and I sat there frozen. Chief Bowen had been chief of police since I could remember. I tried not to think about that. No point to it, except that it would make me crazy. Bo was really bad with authority figures, that much we knew. But he only brought up to Chief Bowen what he thought the man already knew.

"Did he break any bones? Did he really hurt Bo?" Ali asked.

"Bo's got a couple of black eyes, but nothing is broken. He'll be okay. But he's not helping his image at all. Even police are human. They really ... hate him. They would love to find evidence to convict him on this charge and send him off to someplace worse than Egg Harbor, never have to deal with him again."

I thought about this Egg Harbor place. There were mean kids in there. Ryan used to pass on stories to me from his dad about the kids up there. There was a kid in there for raping his own sister. There were violent schizophrenics, drug addicts, juvenile sex offenders, along with a general population of lawbreaking teenagers. I was glad Bo was pretty big. But I was scared a bunch of messed-up kids could get at him if they wanted to. I thought of Bo saving Ali from her mother's weird boyfriend. Now he had his back to the wall with people even crazier.

"I'll get him out on Monday." Mom said it almost in a whisper. "I'm still pretty confident that he will never be charged concerning Chris."

"How do you know?" Ali asked with a shaking voice.

"Because I think Chris Creed is alive." She leaned forward, took hold of that pen of hers, and brushed the feather under her nose. She looked off into space in a way that made me curious. And confused.

I muttered, "We saw a psychic tonight."

She shut her eyes slowly, and when she reopened them, they were glaring right at me with what my friends always called *the look*. It could boil you. She always told me that you made your own future, and that psychics could make you "fatalistic." Not only that, but a fake could really mess you up.

"We didn't mean to see her, we just sort of fell into it," I blabbered under her gaze. "We went to visit this girl Chris used to know. She took us. At any rate, the psychic said Chris is dead in the woods. She says he shot himself."

She rolled her eyes off to the side in a way that read complete disgust. Finally, she sighed. "Well, I'm not psychic, but I'm your mother. Do I rank in there somehow?"

"Yeah," I said.

"Chris Creed is not dead in the woods. I can take my paycheck to the bank on that one."

I stared at her tired face. "What makes you so sure?"

"Because I've lived here my whole life, and I know the people here pretty well. Glen Ames told me you had a conversation with Sylvia Creed yesterday. She may have been relentless, Torey, but what that boils down to is survival. People will do and think whatever it is they have to in order to survive. I feel that Chris probably learned his bad social skills from Sylvia. But he also learned from her to be a survivor," she muttered in a soft but firm way. "When he disappeared, I just knew in my gut, like I know this town, like I know the Creeds. Sylvia Creed is far from perfect, but her life didn't kill her. Digger Haines's life didn't kill him. I'm not a psychic, but I know people pretty well. And my feeling is, Chris Creed is alive."

"I sure hope you're right," Ali said.

"He could still show up tomorrow," my mom put in, though it seemed not likely to me. Creed was becoming like a vapor. A myth or a legend or something.

I kept waking up all night over these weird dreams. I think the psychic caused it all. I kept seeing myself walking up on those three rocks in the Indian burial ground and seeing Creed's dead body. I must have dreamed it six times. Each time something different was gross about the body. Once his eyeballs were missing. Once his feet were missing. Once, I turned the body over and it wasn't Creed—it was Alex. Around five o'clock I just decided that being asleep was too much of a pain in the ass, and I sat up and watched some infomercial for slimming down your buns.

By the time Ali got up, I had a headache and thought my eyelids weighed five pounds each. I was trying to eat oatmeal at the table, but it tasted like paste.

Ali said to me, "You're having a normal response. I would have dreamed the same kinds of things if the psychic told me I would find him when I was alone. But don't forget, your mom says he's alive." She smiled.

"I'd like to believe that. I think my mom can be totally smart about people. It's just hard when she's giving me her gut feeling and that stupid psychic is giving me everything but the weather."

"You will find him shot through the head on a primitive grave. There are other graves around, but this one is marked with three large rocks." The psychic's voice shot through my head. I'd been hearing it all night long.

"Maybe we should just go down and look," I told her. Her eyebrows arched up, and I guess she was remembering how stubborn I had been the night before about *not* going. "I don't feel like I have much choice, Ali. Not if I ever want to sleep again. I can just see myself having these dreams over and over until I see with my own eyes."

"I'll go with you. You know that." She squirmed. "But, *um* . . ."

I finished for her. "What about the part where I would be alone when I found him?"

"Yeah." She gazed at me uncomfortably.

I knew I wasn't going down there by myself. "Dead bodies don't get up and walk, I don't care what she says. Didn't she say she never claims to be . . . what? A hundred-percent accurate?"

Ali nodded. "Something like that. I'll go. Maybe when you see there's nothing there, you can come home and take a nice, long nap."

That sounded like reason enough to go.

The path to the burial ground had tall trees on either side that threw shadows, despite the sun. I wasn't nervous. I think I was too exhausted.

The clearing was up ahead. I slowed down. About twenty feet from the edge of the path, I stopped entirely. Something came over me. A bad feeling, almost like a wave.

"Let's not," I whispered.

Ali just stood there, staring straight into the clearing. The rocks were off to the left, where you couldn't see them.

"D'you ever hear about this place, Ali? You know how the pine trees grow like wildfire? Well, they don't grow in that clearing. Nobody's ever been able to figure out why not."

"I see little pine trees in there," she whispered back.

"Baby ones. But they all seem to keel over and die when they hit, like, two feet high." The Indians used to consider babies next to sacred. One rumor had it their ghosts wouldn't breathe death on the trees until they were no longer baby trees.

"You want me to go by myself?" Her voice shook.

"No." I tried to tell myself I was being superstitious. I took a few more steps, just enough so that I could crane my neck to see the first rock. It leaned against the second two, but I only had a clear view of the first. It gleamed in the sun in the dead silence of the morning.

"Ali, don't leave me, okay?"

"Why would I leave you?"

"I don't know. I don't want to be alone, and then, *boom,* the body drops out of a tree or something."

"There're no trees in there," she reminded me. "But, yeah, I understand."

I still didn't move. I was trying to get up my nerve, but she took a breath and said, "This is for Bo."

She stepped forward, and I was right on her heels, terrified of being left alone. We moved into the clearing and saw all three rocks. They were smooth on top and met in the center. There was no body on top. Slowly we circled around, looking on the sides, looking all around the clearing. The clearing was filled with white sand, almost like beach sand, with little pine trees and clumps of grass. Nothing to hide a body. One rock had a lip, so there was a space under it. It was big enough that a body could fit under it. I squatted down slowly and looked under the lip, then let out a breath as I saw straight through to the back of the rock.

I stood up, looked at Ali, and she looked at me.

I laughed. "That psychic can bite me."

"She did say you would be alone," Ali muttered, but I laughed again.

Some of my brain cells were starting to function for the first time that day. "She was wrong. Come on, think about it. Dead bodies don't move around. If he's not here today, he's not going to be here tomorrow."

"What if . . . he's been alive in the woods, and just hasn't died yet?" she mumbled.

I hunted around through my tired brain for reality. "I think we already established that Chris wouldn't know how to survive out here, and he had no friends who would hide him from his own parents. Besides, when I asked that psychic why nobody found him last Saturday, she didn't say he wasn't dead then. She said almost the opposite. She said . . ." It was something eerie, but I couldn't remember.

"She said, 'The dead didn't want to be seen,'" Ali finished for me. "She said the dead can hide until they are ready to be seen—"

"Yo, reality check," I muttered. "She's full of it. I don't even know what I'm doing here."

To keep up my pretend courage, I jumped on top of the rocks and gazed all around the clearing.

"You could be standing on a grave marker," Ali said, watching me with wide eyes. "Didn't that woman say the rocks marked an Indian grave?"

"Don't be superstitious. If it is a grave, then the occupants are dead." I looked down and lost my grin some. The three rocks met together, but there was a little hole in the center where they didn't fit just right. I watched it wearily and finally got down on my knees slowly. I was afraid to stick my eye right up to it. Something could reach out and fling itself at me. A hand, a finger bone.

"Ali, check this out," I whispered. When she didn't answer, I looked around. She wasn't anywhere in the clearing. My eyes scanned the woods as my heart banged, and I glanced up at the sky for a falling body.

"Ali!" I screamed and shot straight up. "Ali, don't leave!"

I stepped onto the rock with the lip to jump down. I stepped on the lip too hard and the rock faltered, tipping forward. I must have weighed more than when I was a kid. I heard Ali scream. I jumped to the ground and saw her lying under the lip.

"You don't have to squash me," she said. The rock dropped back down to its original place with a thud that gave me its weight to be almost a couple hundred pounds. I could have broken her rib cage.

"Oh my god, are you all right?" I dropped down to my knees, hauling her out from under. "I thought you left me."

"No. I just wanted to . . . I don't know, see if I could see anything from under—"

"Don't!" I snapped. "Alex and I never got under there. You know what lives under these rocks? Those giant sandworms you dissect in biology. Look, just . . . stand here and don't move."

Now that I knew she hadn't left, my nerve came back again. "There's a hole between the three rocks. I want to look down it."

She crinkled up her face. "There's no way for him to crawl in between these rocks. They fit together almost perfectly."

"Almost," I said. "I just want to do the . . . whole thing."

Whatever I meant by that. I jumped back up on the rocks, and without giving myself time to think about it, I knelt and looked down. The hole was pitch-black. Ali put her hand on my ankle, and it made me less scared of being dragged under by ye olde hand bone. I reached in.

I could feel the floor of the clearing with the tips of my fingers. It was flat and smooth, like nothing could grow on top of the sand in the darkness there. I felt something rough, about the size of a baseball. I tried telling myself it wasn't a hand bone and got my fingers around it. I pulled it out. Pinecone. I tossed it aside with a sigh and reached back in. I had to reach in up to my shoulder, and I could feel the hole was about two feet wide at the bottom, just big enough to fit my arm in at the top.

"Too small for a body," I told her, to make myself feel better, and then my fingers touched something smooth. It felt like a thin piece of plastic. I pulled, but it seemed to be stuck between the rocks. I pulled some more.

"There's something else," I said, gritting my teeth. "Just this one thing . . ."

It finally gave way, and I pulled it out. I sat there huffing, wiping the dirt off this piece of paper that had a plasticy feel to it. I saw some scribbling around a bunch of cartoon-type pictures. "It looks like a map, and the handwriting on it seems familiar."

"Yeah, it's familiar," Ali agreed right away. "Like Creed's diary."

I stood there frozen. Seeing this map was like hearing a voice from beyond the grave. It had to be the map Alex tried to tear that time he saw Chris coming out of here back when we were twelve. "You mean he *laminated* his treasure map?" I remembered laughing so hard when I said that. But holding this dirty old thing, it didn't seem so funny. It was a thin sort of lamination, so it still looked like paper. Chris must have shoved it down between the rocks four years ago, so his mother wouldn't find it, and forgot about it or something.

It was too eerie, too odd. We come here looking for the kid's dead body. We don't find a dead body, and yet something that once belonged to him shows up.

The woods had been perfectly silent all morning, but out of nowhere the trees started to rustle. I looked up, and a strong breeze came along that took the map right out of my shaking fingers. It sailed out of my hand, hit the ground, then blew up and around and fell against a pine tree. I dropped down off the rocks and ran to retrieve it. When I got about two feet away, another gust came and whirled it into the forest. I could see it rolling from corner to corner on the forest floor as little gusts took it. I started after it, then stopped. Something was making me scared, something about Indian ghosts. I could feel them. I stood there frozen, scanning the forest, knowing that Indian with the bow and arrow was out there, about to materialize right in my face again. I watched and waited until the breeze died away. I shut my eyes.

You're just tired, I tried telling myself, but nothing could convince my feet to chase after that map into the forest.

I turned and looked at Ali, and she looked at me.

"Let's get out of here," she said. She must have sensed something unusual, too, because she spun, then we hightailed it back through the shadowy trail so fast that an Indian ghost would have had to run us down to scare us.

I did actually fall asleep when we got home. In the family room, my dad had put on a Notre Dame game, and I saw the opening kickoff. It was daytime, plus a normal thing like a football game was on, and between that and my relief at not finding Creed's body, I just crashed out. Next thing I knew, my mom was shaking me, and it was late afternoon. I sat up and took the cordless she held out to me.

"It's Alex," she said.

I felt all funky—like you feel when you fall dead asleep in the middle of the day and you wake up and don't even know if it's day or night. I took the phone in a daze.

"Hello."

"Hey. You sound like you've been cutting logs."

"Yeah, major," I told him, stretching some. "What time's it?"

"About four-thirty. Torey, listen up. Can you meet me somewhere tonight? And don't bring Ali, okay?"

204

At that point, I remembered he was supposed to be mad at me. "Fine. But are you going to have Renee with you? I just can't cope with her right now, Alex."

He sighed. "Yeah, she's been a piece of work lately. No, I won't bring her. I just need to talk."

"Yeah, I understand." At least I thought I did. I thought he wanted to patch things up with me and not be so one-sided toward his girlfriend. "Where?"

"Well, definitely not my house, because Renee will be showing up here. And definitely not your house, because I don't want people hanging all over us." He sounded upset. "Just meet me in the woods behind your house. We'll go walking."

"Fine," I said, stretching and yawning. "But forget the old burial ground where we used to play as kids. We're not walking in there, okay?"

"Whatever. What's up with the burial ground?"

I hesitated for a minute, then figured he needed some comic relief from whatever was bugging him. "Some psychic told me last night that I would find Creed's body in there. I already looked. It's not in there. But hey, guess what I did find? Remember that time you punched him out over that stupid treasure map? I think I found the treasure map."

"You looked in there for Creed's body?" he asked in amazement. It didn't sound like he was the least bit interested in the old map.

"Yeah. It's not in there."

I could hear him breathing, and he finally said, "You goddamn well better hope you looked hard enough."

"What are you talking about?" I asked.

"Just meet me at seven. Behind your house. I have to go, Renee's coming."

I could hear him say, "Hey, babe," just before the phone clicked. I stared at the receiver, feeling disgusted enough to let my head fall back down on the couch. He was just as scared of her as all the people she mouthed off to. What a wuss. He was afraid to let Renee know he was talking to me. I figured I'd straighten him out at seven.

I met him back behind the fence, and he said, "Bring a flashlight. It's getting dark. I don't want to stumble into that burial ground with you and discover Creed's body."

I went in the garage and brought out a flashlight, getting irritated.

"Jesus, Alex," I said as we took off on a trail in the opposite direction from the burial ground. "I thought you'd be all, 'Oh my god, let's go find the body!'"

"Well, maybe I was, but now I'm not. I'm with you. It's not funny anymore."

"Yeah, I guess you heard about Chief Bowen."

"Renee says he told her mom the whole truth, like, the *whole* truth. He really had been with Mrs. McDermott, and a few other ladies, and it had been going on a long time. And he's moving out. He resigned after beating up Bo. But especially after beating him up, I guess he was even more afraid Bo would spew it all over town. He wanted Mrs. Bowen to hear the truth from him, and not from somebody else."

"'He's moving out'?" I repeated, trying to get a sense of reality about this. Mr. McDermott had moved out on Mrs. McDermott last year, and it had hardly been more than a shrug to me. This was personal. It was hard to think that me and Bo and Ali had the power to erase a twenty-year marriage.

"Oh my god," I muttered.

"Yeah, it's ugly—" A cell phone went off in his pocket and he sighed, pulling it out and staring at it. "Renee's all a basket case. She wanted to be with me, and I could see that, but I just had to talk to you. The only way I could get away to talk to you was to promise I would take her cell phone, so she could call me anytime."

"Does she know you're with me?" I asked, as he stared at the ringing phone.

"No way. Hello?"

He started jogging in place. Lifting his legs so high that you could hear sticks cracking when his feet crunched the earth. He was breathing like he had been running. "In about an hour. I want to do five miles, okay? I gotta get in shape. Basketball practice starts in two—"

He rolled his eyes. "Okay, half an hour . . . I know. I'm sorry . . . Well, you can wig out on me at my house when I get there, okay?"

He was actually managing to get himself a little out of breath. He hung up.

"Alex, do you have to lie about being with me?" I asked. "Are you that scared of her?"

"Right now? She could scare Frankenstein," he said. "She is far scarier than normal."

"I thought you really liked her."

"Well, put it this way. I like her when she's not being maniacal. I like her fun side. Which is more and more sporadic these days, and that's actually why I'm bothering you," he rambled. "I mean, I'm still really pissed at you. Dissing your friends and girlfriend for Ali McDermott and Bo Richardson is totally weird, bro. But Renee's got it in for you. You are in deep shit. I might be pissed, but that doesn't mean I want to see you go to jail."

My head jerked around so fast it hurt my neck. "What are you talking about?"

"Remember our fight in front of Wawa three nights back?"

I nodded.

"Do you remember Bo Richardson saying he shot Chris Creed in the woods?"

I stood there confused. At first I muttered, "He never said that."

Then I vaguely remembered Bo making a joke. Right before he spilled the beans about Chief Bowen.

"How did we do it, Adams?"

"We took a gun and shot him?"

"Oh, that's right! I forgot! I took a gun and shot him and left him for dead in the woods."

"He was joking," I muttered, but Alex was blabbering nervously.

"Bo asked you how *'we'* did it, to which *you* responded something like, 'We *shot him.*' Meaning, the two of you shot Chris Creed in the woods."

I shook my head like a dog, trying to get a straight thought.

"He . . . was joking," I stammered.

"Well, we don't think he was."

I watched him, watched his eyes, waiting for them to laugh. They didn't. "You think . . . Bo Richardson and I . . . shot Creed in the woods . . ."

I sounded like I was down a tunnel, trying to shout but didn't have the air.

"No. *I* don't think that. Renee thinks that. *I* think Richardson *told* you that *he* shot Creed in the woods. And that you just knew about it. After the fact—"

I got a fire in my gut that I thought would explode. I shoved him totally hard. I watched in awe as he stumbled backwards. "It was a joke, Alex! I thought it up out of my own head! I was thinking of the Digger Haines thing, where his dad supposedly took a gun into the woods . . . something . . . I don't know! Bo jokingly asked me how we did it, and I just spewed out the first thought that came into my head!"

Alex looked totally confused, like he'd had this pat little theory going and I had foiled it, but he still didn't want to give it up. His mouth was moving in a panic, and his lips were all shaky.

"Well, Renee was right there in front of him, and she thinks he was dead serious. I'm just concerned about you. I need to know. Did he tell you this beforehand? And did you think he was joking? Because if you thought he was joking, then you're not an accessory to—"

I hauled off and slapped him, sending him flying into a tree. "You guys are not stupid! You *know* that was a joke! What the hell are you guys trying to pull?"

Alex screamed in my face, "Richardson wasn't joking about the second thing he popped out with—about Chief Bowen and Mrs. McDermott! So we don't think he was joking about the first thing, either! I'm just trying to save your ass! You've got to tell me that Richardson merely told you, and you thought he was joking—"

That stupid cell phone went off again. I stared at it, in awe of this girl's superhuman nerve. I tried to talk louder than it.

"Damn it, Alex! I'm telling you, I thought of the thing about shooting Creed off the top of my head!"

"No, no, no," he muttered around that ringing. I thought of Mrs. Creed in the cafeteria. "No, no, no . . . Christopher did not write that note . . ." He stared at the ground. He couldn't look at me. I wanted to put his head through a tree.

"Why can't you believe me?" I shoved him again. "What, does it destroy your whole version of reality, Alex? Let me tell you reality! Renee is pissed that Bo spewed about her dad's sex life! She's pissed at me for standing up for him! Maybe she can't admit the truth to herself, but she just wants revenge! She knows a goddamn joke when she hears one!"

"No, no, no," he just kept saying.

"Well, guess what? You're in as big a state of denial as Creed ever was!"

"I'm just trying to help you!" he hollered back. "Renee just told the cops that Bo confessed to her. She told them I heard it, too! I'm just trying to save you from—"

I thought if that phone rang one more time I would go insane.

"Goddamn it!" Alex yelled. He punched the line all wide-eyed and confused, and said, "Hello?"

"Give me that thing!" I snatched it from him, despite him hollering, "No—"

"Renee, what the hell are you trying to pull? You are so goddamn selfish, why don't you wake up?"

"What are you doing there?" She recognized my voice somehow, though I don't think I ever screamed at her before.

"I'm here. Why don't you drag your ass over here and say your stupid lies to my face? You know that was a joke, that thing Bo said!"

"It was not a joke." Her voice cracked, and for once she didn't have any attacks. She just let the silence hang, and I could hear sniffing and crying.

I was glad. "Go ahead and cry. It's your guilt making you cry, you lying sack of—"

She blasted out a string of what I could do to myself. "You can go to hell! I'm telling the cops you knew! I'm telling them Richardson confessed to us, and Alex heard it, and we both heard you, too! Now get out of my life!"

"You—" I was going to tell her she would never pass off a lie like that, but she had hung up. I watched Alex stare at me all terrified, and it struck me like an oncoming train that maybe she could pull off a lie like that. If she could confuse Alex, who had known me since forever, she could confuse other people.

"I don't know what to believe," he said. His voice was cracking like he might cry. "I almost believe you, okay? But what are you doing now, talking about some psychic saying Creed is buried in the woods? It sounds really fishy, Torey."

"What do you mean?"

"It sounds to me like you're warming up some cock-and-bull story so you can get the body found. Maybe because you know where the body is, and it's bothering your conscience too bad, and you want to get it found without it looking bad for you and Richardson."

"Oh, go to hell!" I screamed. "You're insane!"

He stormed off down the trail, leaving me heaving rocks and sticks after him until a fire lit up in my shoulder socket. I flung myself down on the ground and bawled my eyes out.

I wondered if I could go to jail. Even if I didn't, I knew I might live with that question mark hanging over my head in other people's eyes forever. *Was Adams involved? Since there's no body, no evidence, how will we ever know for sure he wasn't?* I stood up. I didn't even realize where I was going until I looked down at the flashlight in my hand and saw that I had turned it on.

I think half of it was a rational thought. If Chris Creed's body was found, just maybe there would be a huge suicide note in his pocket in his own handwriting. Or maybe whatever he used to kill himself had his fingerprints all over it. Or maybe a time of death could be determined, and if Bo and I were both covered at that time . . . maybe, maybe, maybe. The psychic said I would be alone. Well, I was alone.

Twenty-one

I didn't understand how a dead body could appear at a spot where it had not been earlier. I don't think I understood anything, except that I was more scared of living people than dead people. I needed dead people to help me fight living people.

The back of my house shone in front of me, almost like a cartoon drawing, something that wasn't real. It's like the whole world wasn't real, except those three rocks. I cut across a few yards of woods until I was running up the trail to the burial ground. The psychic's voice was banging in my head like some tape I couldn't stop . . . *"You will find him shot through the head on a primitive grave . . . marked with three large rocks . . . He's ready. He will be seen now. Just remember . . . Be very careful about your actions. A person's liberty is at stake . . ."*

I stopped.

The same trail that Ali and I took so easily in daylight lay in front of me, dense with shadows, nearly black. I stood huffing. *Not Bo's liberty. It was* my *liberty she was talking about . . .*

"Oh my god," I muttered, and new questions choked me up. *How will it look if I find the body after everything Alex just said? He thinks I know where the body is. How will it look if I say, "A psychic led me to this place"? People will think I'm lying. I'll wind up in jail if I find that body . . .*

I mushed tears off my eyes so I could see my way home. I turned slowly around to go back. The eyes that met mine sucked me into a hypnotic return stare. Brown eyes that burned some fire of emotions while not being threatening . . . begging me for something. I watched in stunned fascination as the Indian moved past me down the trail, then stopped and stared at me again. He carried the same bow and wore the same feathers in his Mohawk as when I'd seen him when I was seven. But he wasn't aiming at me with that bow . . . he was beckoning me with it.

I shut my eyes. *Torey, you are messed up; you're losing it; you know it because you're seeing things again like a seven-year-old.* When I opened my eyes they were so filled up I could see only a blur ahead, but a black silhouette seemed to disappear into the burial ground. *Oh Christ, you really are losing it . . .* I wiped my eyes and could hear a bunch of gasps and chokes, and I realized it was me, choking on hypocrites and selfish people and lies.

I kept moving toward that burial ground because it was the only real place in the world. Everything else was a vapor. I turned off the path in a trance, half expecting to see the Indian on the rocks. I saw only darkness and the outline of the rocks in black. I could hardly feel my legs moving. It seemed more like the rocks were floating toward me. The sad sound of crickets rose to a moan as those rocks got closer and closer.

Three huge rocks floated up to me. When they were so close I could have kicked one, I raised the flashlight with a wrist that shook like it was broken.

The light beamed slowly across the rocks in shaky flashes. Shaky but sure. Flat, smooth, shining. There was nothing to break the air except an orange beam across flat, smooth rock. I stood there, shining the beam, waiting for I-don't-know-what—a ghost to appear, Creed to fall from the sky. The longer I waited the more tense I got, the more irritating those crickets sounded.

I finally sprang up on top of the rocks and shined the flashlight all around the clearing. Grass, sand, pinecones, trees, branches—all in shaky jerks—sky. My legs were rubbery from this combination of anger and relief. I didn't want to see a dead body, but I needed to find Creed with a definite suicide note, a definite cause of death, a definite time of death. He was not here.

But instead of leaving, I felt the strong need to stay and think about all this. I had seen something that could not have been real. An Indian ghost. When I was seven years old, I could shrug it off after a day or two. *You're not a little kid now, and you're seeing things, Torey. Which means you're some sort of nuts. Are you totally crazy or just in shock over being knifed in the back by your friends?* I hated Alex all of a sudden.

I looked around the clearing with the flashlight one more time. As the beam turned up more branches and grass and normal stuff, I felt very close to Creed. I could feel all his confusion over what was real and what was made up in his own head. I felt his wish for make-believe to come alive, for some sort of control over the universe so that if life started to suck, you could just imagine something else into existence. The air buzzed all around my head like it had in my basement that night. Like bunches of eyes burned behind me, burning a hole through me, begging me for something. Maybe there were a thousand Creeds out there. Begging for hope, for understanding, maybe.

I figured I could understand someone wanting to take his own life. If the world stopped making sense. If people became convinced that lies were true. This was the most dangerous kind of lying, it struck me, the kind that was happening to me now—where people need the lie so badly they become convinced the lie is true. It's dangerous because they can tell the lie with so much belief that it sounds like the truth, and they can make other people believe it.

Creed had lied, too—he had made me believe his diary. Renee's type of lying was different from Creed's diary, though. Renee's was meant to do harm, and Creed's was only meant to save himself from a life that seemed unfair and didn't make sense. I figured I knew why I didn't find him here. My mother's words echoed through the darkness. *I knew that Chris was leaving to survive, not leaving to die.* All that grinning he had done his whole life—it was like the diary. He might have believed he was superpopular every day. But he only did what he had to do in order to keep going. To be normal and be popular and have fun and have a girlfriend. He made real life mere shadows in comparison. When his make-believe world finally caved in last week—God only knows which twig finally broke the camel's back—he saw reality clearly. But he didn't survive years of abuse from other kids and lack of understanding from his parents so he could go die in the woods. I believed it totally at that moment. Creed was alive.

I felt some deep canyon of regret that I had sat ten feet from him through most of our years in grade school and could never see that he was a tortured person. I was so alone here, and maybe it was because I alone was meant to know. I could have screamed the truth to Alex—I could have breathed fire and burned down a couple trees—and Alex wouldn't have believed me. *People only see as far as they are able, and the rest of the truth is lost on them. A kid*

216

in the midst of us led a tortured existence. Bo Richardson wants to be everyone's mother. Christ died naked.

I had some sort of peace. There's something peaceful about what you know to be the truth. I had it, so much that I would rather be in jail with the truth than living a lie in the historic Towne of Steepleton. I stood up to leave.

"He's alive," I muttered to myself, to the dead Indians, to the choir of crickets. "He's alive, and someday I will find him."

I stepped to the edge of the rock with the lip that hung over. As soon as the rock faltered, I remembered the space underneath it and, too late, realized I was now heavy enough to tip it over if nothing was underneath that lip.

I flew headfirst onto the ground, flipped around, and stared wide-eyed as the huge rock met air underneath it, then came over on top of me. I clambered backward, which kept it from hitting me square in the chest, but it slammed down on my leg. I heard a crack.

I don't think I even yelled out at that point. I was shocked and messed up and couldn't feel anything. A slight burning hit the center of my calf as I tried to work my leg out from under the rock, but nothing more. The rock must have weighed a couple hundred pounds. The thought of Digger Haines losing his leg flitted through my mind, and reminded me of benching a couple hundred during football seasons. But benching, and sitting straight up and pushing a rock straight forward are two different things.

I felt my first jolts of pain as I rocked the thing across my bones a couple of times before heaving it on a roll to the side. I sat there huffing, shining my flashlight on this gash in my jeans. I could see blood and torn skin and a white, shiny thing poking through. *Bone fragment.* I stared in shock at this mess, wondering why a broken leg burned but didn't really hurt. It should hurt more than it did, I realized, and that scared me.

I tried slowly to get my good foot under me, and when I leaned forward, the beam of the flashlight from the other hand fell on a black hole.

I gazed at this black circle that the rock had covered, no bigger than a garbage can lid. Slowly I brought the flashlight closer and closer. I eased myself up on my good knee, gazing at this hole like my eyes were glued to it. I was hypnotized almost, feeling myself being sucked into it. I bent down very slowly but without hesitating, beyond being scared. My head penetrated the edge of the hole, and I brought the flashlight slowly in, so I could see a dirt floor maybe four feet below. Dirt and something shiny beneath it. Rock. Old Indian cave.

I moved the beam across the smooth wall that was maybe thirty feet away. The beam moved down to the floor, to some sort of long bundle wrapped in a reddish blanket. There was another bundle a few feet closer, and another about ten feet from me. I froze, realizing what was in those blankets. They were wrapped with some sort of leather crisscross ties and covered with specks of gold, like jewelry or charms. I wished I had paid more attention to Lenape history in school.

If you entered a grave, you might feel that you were insulting the dead and making them not rest in peace. I had none of that feeling. I would have sworn there was a feeling of relief in there. I couldn't explain it, but even when a little breeze swooped down, I felt a sense of peace and only a mild ache in my leg. The breeze made a terrible groaning sound against that smooth wall, like it had not entered here in years. Before my eyes, one of those red blankets turned colors. I wondered if I was imagining it, or if the light beam from the flashlight was faulty. The blanket seemed to be turning slowly from red to brown.

My heart started to bang a little, and this weird feeling began to raise the hair on my arms. I moved the light beam off the blanket to keep myself calm. And that's when I spotted a body that was not wrapped neatly in blankets or even covered with one. It looked out of place in this shrine. There was nothing sacred about this body: *sneakers . . . blue jeans . . . T-shirt . . . blond hair . . . face turned into the rock wall . . . gun pointing straight up the wall . . .*

"Oh Jesus Christ . . ." I breathed.

My worst fear. Somehow I pulled myself into the hole and slithered to the ground, staring hard through the shaky beam of the flashlight. It was not like a horror movie, where the body might spring out at you or come back to life. This body was dead, and it was going to stay dead and never move a muscle again. That's what horrified me the most, the finality, the stiff hardness, the unmoving whiteness of those fingertips. The look of no return. I eased over to it slowly, wondering why there was no smell of death in here. I had never smelled death, but I knew instinctively that death should smell bad. It was hard to breathe, and there didn't seem to be any smells except a slight mustiness that was making me dizzy. I shined the flashlight on the side of his face. He had on a mask, I thought at first. What looked like black tar covered everything from his ear forward so you couldn't even see his expression. It got very thick around a black hole above the ear. Blood. Blood turned black.

I could feel my stomach heaving, and I shut my eyes.

"Chris, why?" I moaned, and it sounded like a thousand voices in that cave. "I would have helped you, I would have, I'm sorry . . ."

The air rushed through again in a way that reminded me of the barbecue gas grill lighting, that *FFFFFFFF-FOOOOOM!*, and I actually thought I smelled a barbecue gas grill all of a sudden. My heart banged wildly, and all at once, my broken bone started to burn like someone had stuck it on a spit.

I started to holler in pain, but the yell stuck in my throat. Another sound, almost like crackling, made me stay quiet and listen. It sounded like the place was on fire. A scorchy smell wafted up my nostrils. I beamed the flashlight around, but the other bodies lay calm and peaceful in their brown blankets. I tried to figure out where that crackling sound was coming from, but my own pain was deadening my thoughts. I beamed the light on the wall and down, until it crossed the gun and rested on Creed's hand. Before my eyes, the skin turned from white to brown to black and started to peel back, like layers of burning paper. It peeled from the ends of his fingers, flipping back almost like curling ribbon, revealing red layers that turned black, then more layers, and then specks of white. His bones. The gun finally dropped and lay pointed straight at me, in a pile of bones, with the black flesh still sizzling and shrinking.

I screamed at the top of my lungs. This body was burning right in front of me, only with no flames. It was like an invisible fire was eating Creed away to nothing and eating my leg away, too.

All I know is I screamed and screamed until I couldn't scream anymore. And somehow I had gotten outside into the blackness again, though the scorchy stench had followed me out and my leg still felt on fire. Red lights were flashing in my eyes and people were running all around me, screaming, too. I heard Renee Bowen's voice, I thought, but Ali's face was staring at me in front of a huge flashlight.

"Your mom's here," she said. "Your dad, too. We're getting you help, okay? Torey, what happened? What is that terrible smell?"

I just gripped her around the neck, saying, "I've just been in hell . . ."

Twenty-two

Yellow fuzz glitters dropped down the backs of my
eyelids, following a bezillion yellow fuzz glitters. Boring.
But opening my eyes would be a bad thing. They would
know I was awake. Time to torture the kid again. . . . *Son!
Are you in pain? Do you remember? . . .*

Decision made: Nameless. Legless. Clueless. Ageless.
Me. Like when I used to sit with my big-buttoned tape deck
between my Velcro Keds. Four years old, and there was
nothing except the music. The brown warthog song.

Four brown warthogs sleeping in the wood.
One heard buzzing . . . and up he stood.

A tread got near, and a mild crash. Dishes, followed by
the voice of authority. "Mr. Adams, we know you're awake.
You have to eat this time."

Caught himself a dragonfly. . . . MMmmMM good.

Nurse Ratched. The carnivore. The suppository rapist.
She had wanted me to choose between food and a feeding
tube for our next bout with reality.

"Mr. Adams, I can see your eyelids moving."

She didn't like me. Thought maybe I committed a murder, something like that. Something like, I went back to get a body found and broke my leg so people would feel sympathy for me instead of revulsion. Some people were thinking that. Sometimes I could hear voices echoing out in the hall. I opened one eye a slit to see if my mother was in the room with that George friend of hers. George was supposed to be my attorney. He had on an olive green suit last time he was in here. Olive green was the hot new color for suits. *I'm glad I'm not a grown-up.*

The only one in slit range was Nurse Omnipresent. She was like God. Knew your thoughts by the slit in your eye.

"You're not allowed any visitors. Not until you eat something, drink something, and say something to Dr. Fahdi. He's a very expensive psychotherapist, and your parents are not paying him to watch your eyelids dance. And your leg will not heal on mere inhalation. Do you understand?"

The bed was moving. The top of it, at least. I was bending at the waist, coming up to meet a bowl of off-white barf. The nurse grabbed my arm and forced it toward the spoon. It made me think she was planning to push my face into this oatmeal, and I had other ideas.

"Before you get violent, think of who my mother is," I muttered, swallowing the razor blades in my throat. I could feel her glaring like four brown warthogs. She thought I committed a murder, something like that.

"Your mother is not here. Nor will she be here until you eat. So, you can rot here alone, or—"

"Fuck off."

I shut my eyes again, wondering if she planned to dump my head in this bowl. I heard her pick up the phone and punch in numbers. They told me I hadn't eaten in five days, but I knew they were lying. Five days, I would be completely and totally starving and not able to resist. She could bite me.

"Dr. Fahdi? It's Carol Flannery. He just spoke . . . Yes, I'm quite certain . . . 'Fuck off.'"

Three brown warthogs sleeping in the wood.
One heard buzzing . . . and up he stood.
Caught himself a dragonfly. . . . MMmmMM good!

"Oh, and before that he threatened me. No, not my life, my bank account."

Two brown warthogs sleeping in the wood. . . .

"He still won't eat, and I think he knows I'm ready to drop the diplomacy tactics. Sure. Whatever you say."

She hung up. "He's coming right down. And if you're eating when he comes in, you'll probably see your family. If you give the profanity a rest."

She left, and I sat staring at this bowl of mush until it became two bowls. All food smelled burny, like burning flesh. There was a lemon slice beside the iced tea. I picked it up and brought it dangerously close to my nose. *Deep-fried, barbecued lemon. I am not dreaming this, I am not.*

I flung the lemon, and it landed on my cast and stuck there. I stared, feeling the hot juices eat away at my cast, right through to eating my ankle out from underneath it.

Dr. Fahdi came through the door, and I pointed. "Get it off! Hurry!"

He took his time, studied it like it was oh-so-interesting. "It's just a lemon."

"It's burning my skin. Get it off!"

He picked it up and laid it on the table next to where my mother used to sit. I heaved in breaths, trying to decide if the burning had stopped. I decided it had. I looked at him suspiciously, wondering why he looked so pleased.

Oh yeah. I had planned on never talking again. The doctor had screwed me over, sent that acid-infested lemon in here on purpose. Now he could gloat.

He pulled the chair up close to my bed and sat in it. I could feel him staring at me. I just couldn't get focused on anything but this burnt, scorchy food. It was alive.

"Your mother spoke to me," he said quietly. "There's been an autopsy. Finally."

I couldn't remember what an autopsy was. Had something to do with my mom's tax returns.

"But I'll let your mother tell you about that." He was watching me. Watching and watching, so much so that I was expecting him to bring a bag of popcorn out from under his seat and start munching. *Yo, a movie costs seven bucks. Cough it up, Dr. Make-me-puke.* I didn't like the look about him. His expression showed too much concern. Pity. Deep, deep, terrible pity.

"There must be something you'd like to talk about," he said.

Not with this mountain of barbecued, smoked oatmeal winking at me.

"Get the food away... It smells." I tried not to breathe until after he moved the tray. He put it on the floor, but I knew it was down there.

"What does it smell like, Torey?"

Gobs and gobs of greasy, grimy gopher guts
Concentrated monkey meat, tantalizing birdies' feet

"Like ... stuff."

All in jars of pinkish purple porpoise pus—

"What kind of stuff?"

224

I would hurl, I knew, if I talked about this smell. It doesn't make much sense that I wouldn't care if I died but I would care if I hurled. So much for logic. Well, everyone's screwing logic these days, logic and Mrs. McDermott.

"Where's Ali?" I asked suddenly. I couldn't believe I had forgotten about Ali.

"She's outside," he said, and I heaved a sigh of relief. Something had made me think maybe Ali was gone to a spa in Florida.

"I want to see her."

"She's with your family. They're waiting for you to eat."

Well, Ali was okay. Then I was okay. I cast a sideways glance at this shrink, wondering in a haze what sort of bargaining power I could come up with. My head got flooded with thoughts. I spat them out.

"Did you know that Christ died naked?"

"Yes. I've heard that."

"So, how come he's always wearing a loincloth?"

"You mean . . . in the artistic renderings?"

I nodded, wondering why this shrink dude didn't look confused by the idea. Fahdi. Maybe he was Muslim or something. He spoke with an accent. *Yeah, well, ain't his religion, why should he care?*

"Do they bother you, the artistic renderings?"

"Yeah."

"Why?"

Why? Did your mother die in a blond wig? "Because it's not the truth."

"Would you prefer to see the truth?"

He had his legs crossed like a girl. Guys my age didn't sit like that unless they were secretly itching. I wondered if something happened to guys, maybe when they graduate from college. If they decide to go on to medical school or grad school or law school, they also decide it's okay to sit like a girl. Something like that. If you're a construction worker in the end you never sit like a girl.

"What, you think I'm some sort of a pervert?"

"No," he said too calmly. "I'm trying to figure out where you're going with your thought."

Better you than me, Dr. Zen Buddhism. "I don't know."

"But it bothers you."

I cast a suspicious glance over the bed bars and noticed that no green steam came rising off the tray. Dead hand bone kicked over and evaporated.

"Jesus was supposed to be an innocent dude. You see all these pictures. And he's, all, got his hands nailed down by the palms. And there's this crown of thorns on his head. And there's all blood running down all over the place in some of those pictures."

"Yes."

"I even saw one where his eyes are rolled up backwards. I mean, I just don't understand how people can show all the violence. But they single out the nudity. Nudity is a problem, but all the violence isn't. I don't understand people."

He nodded, biting his pencil. I couldn't see any teeth marks. He'd been biting this pencil on and off since he came in here, but there were no teeth marks. The man had disgusting self-control.

"We live in a culture that has definite quirks about both sex and violence," he told me.

Maybe. Except this has been going on for centuries. It's not cultural, it's universal. This picking of truths, like you're picking melons at Superfresh.

"Have I been hit in the head?" I asked him.

He just blinked at me. "Not to our knowledge. Your leg was broken and . . . you've had emotional trauma."

"Yeah. Well . . ." I wondered if emotional trauma can change the way your brain works. I wondered if it can make

226

you a mean person instead of a nice person. I felt like I had been a nice person, once.

"I want to see Ali," I told him.

He looked down at his feet, and I knew he was looking at the food tray. He was playing games with me. They all were.

"Torey"—he sat forward—"we need you to eat. You can see your friends and family. All you have to do is eat. That's the plan for the moment. I agree with it."

"You don't understand," I muttered.

He looked like he thought he did understand. He sat there staring at me with this I-know-something-you-don't-know *ha-ha* look that I couldn't tolerate. Whatever. He didn't understand what it was like to be so sure of something. So sure you would stand on a rock and tell yourself your hope was complete. *Chris Creed is alive. You can find him. You can help him, do something nice for him. He did not disappear to die; he disappeared to live.*

He didn't understand what it was like to have your truths turn to crispy critters in stinking, rotting laughing that smelled like something you could never, ever describe, yet never, ever forget. Flaming pickled cow's ass would not do that smell one-tenth of a hair of justice. You would smell it until you died.

"You don't understand," I told him. "You will never, ever, ever, ever, ever, ever understand. Do you understand me?"

He stayed quiet. He stared at me until I was gone again—daydreaming about warthogs, fighting actual sleep due to mortal fear of the sneak attack of the lemons.

When perfect lives come crashing down, some people say they come down with a vengeance. The more perfect the life, the more complete the destruction. I've heard that. I can't remember the few places I'd heard it before my ten days in the Atlantic City Medical Center, but one place I seem to remember that from is church. I seem to remember this theory that we're all dealt fifty-two cards by the end of our lives. If you get all aces in the beginning, you have a greater chance of getting your twos and threes in rapid succession later. And when we die (the dying part makes me think that the Church had something to do with this lesson), we stand up in front of God, sort of realizing that there are no greater lives, only greater beginnings, middles, or ends. And greater depths under lesser appearances.

For sixteen years I had a perfect life. I got my share of twos and threes in the weeks following the corpse. My head started to clear, and I kept waiting to get arrested. One of the threes was not getting to go home after being released from the hospital. I got transported to a mental health facility up near Camden, which specializes in several things, one of which is post-traumatic stress disorder. I was convinced, when I first found out, that it was some maneuver of my mom's to put off my getting arrested. I call it a three because a two would have been getting arrested in the hospital.

A two was that this mental health facility also specializes in eating disorders, and there were actually twin sisters from my high school admitted there for treatment. They were cheerleaders, Leeza and Arial Cortez, and I felt kind of surprised, because they were beautiful girls who weren't, like, skin and bones. I guess they recognized me, too.

You might think that people in mental health would be very sympathetic toward another person in mental health. I was in a haze the first three weeks but got the gist somehow. I think they were very embarrassed to see someone they knew, and they went to town making sure the other patients knew that my situation was a lot worse than theirs. They would whisper to other patients, and I had the pleasure of overhearing them a couple times. "... *helped kill that Chris*

Creed kid out in the woods, just hasn't gotten arrested yet ... did something with the body ... made him crazy ..."
A definite two, especially during those first three weeks, when the truth about what actually happened hadn't sunk in yet.

Probably the biggest ace I received is that particular truth. It's the hardest thing for me to talk about, even still. It takes me back to that ten-day stay in the medical center, which I have almost completely blocked out, except for me regressing to nursery rhymes. I don't like to think about it or tell it. But it's the tail end of my saga, so I'm letting fly.

My mom came in the same day I first talked to Dr. Fahdi, despite Nurse Flannery's bigmouthed threats.

My mom said, "There's been an autopsy. I'm going to tell you about it."

I couldn't remember what an autopsy was, and I don't think she really expected me to comprehend it all. I'd say she wanted to tell it, just so it would be out there and I could chew on it when I felt like it.

"The truth is what we suspected all along, but I didn't want to bring it up to you until we were sure. To backtrack, if we had been wrong somehow, would have been ..." She eased down in the chair beside me, so I could see only the top of her head. "I can't begin to imagine what you must have gone through in that cave. Torey, I've known you since before you were born. And you are the last person in the world who should have seen that ... well, the geologists from Stockton are calling it 'immaculate decomposition.' Not a legal term, so I'm not treading on familiar ground here."

She pulled her foot out from under her and replaced it with the other, so she bobbed up for a minute and I saw her face. She looked deathly tired. Her exhausted voice went on. "'Immaculate decomposition' is what happens when oxygen strikes a body that has been ... well, that has been, um, dead. For some time. The, um. The cave you entered was air sealed. First by the Lenape Indians. They considered those little caves sacred. Actually they're not even caves, did you know that? They're cavities in enormous chunks of limestone that lie buried about six to twenty feet under the ground along the coast here. Since there are no cracks per se, like in a regular cave, they can be airtight if a stone is rolled in front of them in just the right way. Generally the Lenapes buried their dead in the ground, just like we do. But if they found one of these limestone cavities, they would use them to bury Indian chiefs and their family members. I don't know who those particular Lenapes were, exactly, but we think they must be a chief and two other family members."

I saw her head bob up a little again, like she was shifting around in the chair. She wasn't looking at me. She didn't expect me to say anything, because she went right on.

"I've talked to the Stockton geologists. They were there for the next two days. They were very nice. Left me a number of messages on our answering machine. I think they heard what . . . happened to you. And it was important to them . . . that you understand. If you want to. If you can. When you moved the stone, a strong gust of wind must have sent a rush of oxygen into the cave. Apparently the, um, the body had been decaying without oxygen, which is a strange phenomenon. At first sight the body will appear to be almost warm to the touch. But if someone were to touch it, it would feel like . . . a bag of leaves. Something like that. With the first strikes of oxygen, the outer layers begin to, you know, peel away.

"Torey, the psychiatrist mentioned that you've been smelling burning smells and have a scorchy taste in your, um, your mouth. Something like that. I just want you to know that, well, the body never caught fire. There was no fire,

Torey. It just sounded like that, and maybe had given every impression. You were not in hell, Torey."

The silence was long, and I was staring at the ceiling trying to grip hold of some thought that would keep me from hearing this. I didn't want to hear it, not really. It was interesting; it was attracting me somehow. But it didn't change what really mattered.

"Chris . . ." I muttered. "Bo and I would never have hurt Chris like that. *The truth* . . . you need to make people believe *the truth*."

"Yes." She stood up, and I could see her face clearly and wished I couldn't. Her eyes looked like shattered glass with foaming rims. She had been crying a lot. But somehow she looked relieved. She had ahold of my hand, and I could feel it shaking.

"Bo is free. Mrs. Creed has quieted down these past few days. I'm not sure how long it will last, but this autopsy would silence anybody. You don't have to be worried about getting in any trouble over this. Torey, the body you found was not Chris Creed. The body belonged to Bob Haines."

It took me a minute to remember who Bob Haines was. That domineering father of Digger Haines's. My mother had said he was probably a businessman selling art in Los Angeles. I could feel the mattress, like, sinking into the floor. I could feel this enormous band around my chest loosen. My back loosened, my legs loosened, my cheeks loosened.

Seeing a body decompose right in front of you is not something you get over in an hour. And hearing that I hadn't seen Chris Creed was like hearing the sky was purple. It never, ever occurred to me that I wasn't looking at Chris Creed in the dim glow of my flashlight—Creed with a thick, black, bloody mask over his face. Half the reason I ended up in mental health was that it took me two or three weeks to believe that. I would think my mom was lying to make me

231

feel better, or she was trying to keep me sane so I would agree to eat food. I wanted to believe it. But I couldn't believe it.

My mother was mumbling something about Bob Haines being part Lenape and probably thinking that it was okay to share the grave. He must have known about it, somehow; managed to enter without bringing too much fresh oxygen onto the dead. Something about, he didn't want to bother people who disrespected him with the prospect of a funeral. I could hardly hear her.

I was confused, to say the least. In thinking she was either confused herself or lying to me, I blurted out the sacred question. I asked it in a whisper. "Mom. If I didn't see Chris in that cave, then where is he?"

She dropped my hand and reached up absently for my hair. She ran her fingers through it like she hadn't done since I was ten or eleven. She wasn't looking at me, though. She was looking out the window. And if I didn't know my own mother pretty well, I would have sworn there was some look of great victory in her face.

She only said, "I don't know."

Twenty-three

We tried to blow Leo's room full of shaving cream last night. That's a prank I caught wind of from some alumni who learned it at Purdue and came back this week for graduation ceremonies. Dorm pranks aren't real dramatic around here because you can get kicked out of school. But Cartright reasoned that we're graduating in two days, and we all have our letters of acceptance to our colleges, so there's not much the Gestapo could do to us.

Cartright and this enormous dude, Todd Melefanti, whom we fondly call the Melephant, took this huge envelope, filled it with shaving cream, and shoved the flap under Leo's door. The idea is to jump on the envelope, which would force the shaving cream in a thousand directions from under the door to permeate everything in Leo's room, including his tux for the graduation dinner tomorrow night, which we knew was hanging on the front of his closet.

It was probably my fault, because I'm the one who relayed this prank in detail to Cartright, though I never take credit for being the instigator in a prank—this one included. I can dream them up and design schemes to avoid detection, but I don't have the nerve to execute. Or maybe I just don't have the energy. That's where Cartright comes in. He calls me the brains of the operation when I tag along behind him, yawning.

Cartright and I backed away from the envelope to make way for the Melephant. Cartright figured Mel's extra hundred pounds from constant junk-food consumption could send a more powerful blast on the unsuspecting Leo. We were standing there on either side of the envelope, and I noticed Mel's fat feet were, like, glued to the floor behind it. He pointed, and I realized right away what his problem was. Cartright, the genius, had sealed the envelope. You're supposed to leave it open, so the shaving cream has an escape valve. No telling which direction the blast would travel. Mel started waving his hands like *don't*, but Cartright was wound up for the kill and wasn't seeing anything. When Mel moved backward against the wall instead of forward with a jump, Cartright jumped on the thing. The *BANG!* sounded like a cherry bomb. I closed my eyes for fear of getting hit in the face.

By the time I opened my eyes, Cartright and Mel were halfway down the hall, running backward, waving the envelope at me to haul my ass. I just stood there with my jaw dropped. Mel's front side was completely white, from head to toe. When Leo opened the door going, "What the hell gives?" he was faced only with me and the wall, which sported a perfectly shaped white outline of an enormous fat kid.

"What's up, Leo?" I said, for lack of something better.

"What the hell was that noise?"

Fortunately I didn't have to answer, because he was absorbed in the outline on the wall. He stuck one finger in it, put it to his nose, and sniffed. Then he stared, the corners of his mouth widening out.

"You know what?" he breathed. "I know this is crazy, but that shape looks exactly like Todd Melefanti."

"How about that." I pulled a laugh out of somewhere.

I'm still not a great liar but find I can ride out most situations by not offering any information at all. He didn't know we were pranking on him; the envelope was with Mel and Cartright. He admired the silhouette for a few moments more, then turned to me.

"So, what're you doing at my door? You come to hang out?"

"No," I said quickly, "I've got stuff to do. But . . ."

I kind of went through meltdown watching his face fall. I don't think anyone ever knocked on his door for any reason except to borrow something. *Poor Leo,* I thought. *Poor Creed.*

"Leo, about the other day, man, I'm sorry. I don't know what got into me."

He grinned in this combination of surprise and discomfort. "It's okay, man. I just figured you were wigging about something. Had nothing to do with me. That's what I thought."

"Yeah. Absolutely."

"So, you're okay now?"

"I'm fine."

"So . . . what was bugging you, man?"

I sighed, deciding on the honesty routine. Less energy involved. "I was just reading something I wrote last year. You know, something that I was tied up in. You know, something that was important to me."

"Yeah? Have anything to do with that guy you're looking for?"

I watched him, thinking the guy had no shame. "What did you do, click through my files while I was in class?"

"No way, man. You got that web site. I've seen your web site. It's interesting. Way interesting."

I don't know why that bowled me over. I mean, I know when you post a web site, everyone and their brother can see it. I just always had these thoughts that whoever looked at my web site was from France or Iowa or Toronto. Since I didn't talk about my web site to anyone around here except Cartright, it seemed totally weird that people I lived with could look at it. Having read all of Creed.doc, I felt less keyed up, less concerned that Leo could ruin my life at this point. Still, I was glad we were graduating soon.

"I saw it on your hard drive last week when you let me use your computer," he said. "I don't know why, I just called it up later on my terminal."

I nodded, polite as I could, thinking, *I never, ever said Leo could use my computer, but he made it sound like I did.* I turned to walk away. Because the next question would be, "Did you find the guy yet?" If I ever gave anyone an out-loud dissertation on the weirdness of my web site replies, it wasn't going to be Leo. I could feel him doing his usual stare routine on me as I left.

I didn't feel like hearing Cartright and Mel guffawing. I just went back up to my room and turned on my computer. I called up what I had written the night before. I wrote it just after I finished reading Creed.doc. The memories hadn't left me completely insane—just full of regrets, which I tried to get over by writing more. I didn't like my original final pages. I didn't have enough brainpower, back when I wrote the thing, to tell a whole lot about what came down in Steepleton after the body turned up. I wrote the new file to explain things that have happened since I came to Rothborne.

I watched my screen bring up the last thing I saved, which I called Creedmore.doc:

I didn't get out of mental health until Christmas, and had decided at that point not to go back to school. My parents, diplomatic sports that they are, let me finish on a home-study program and signed me up at Rothborne for my senior year. I spent most of my spring writing Creed.doc, but I tagged along with Bo and Ali sometimes when they were going to the mall or to the Wawa. It was hard being around anyone, but especially them in certain ways. People whispered a lot when I was with them but didn't recognize me quite as much when I was alone. I loved Bo and Ali but hated the idea that people could accept a lie without question—and being with them seemed to heap that situation on my ears like an air raid: "*. . . killed that kid in the woods . . . just never found the body . . . his mom's a lawyer, so . . .*"

Not everyone believed it. Alex actually came over a few times, like he wasn't sure he should have ever believed Renee, and he even apologized once. But that wasn't good enough. He seemed like a little kid all of a sudden, all immature, talking about how he hasn't gotten laid since Renee. Big deal, like he had to let me know that he wasn't a virgin anymore. He broke up with her the day after I got injured, and he couldn't get over the fact that she henceforth called him a socially inept retard. She continued to call Ali a slut, despite the fact that Renee sleeps with all her boyfriends and has a new one every three weeks.

Ali and Bo broke up at the end of the year, but only because Ali wanted to graduate early and go to college. She wanted to go far away, and settled on Boston U. Bo quit school when she did, figuring he had no reason to go anymore; he was almost eighteen, anyway. He took a job at a gas station. But he's still the only person I feel like seeing when I have to go home for a holiday, and I always stop at the station. He wants to go into the army, and I'm trying to talk him into it.

Renee Bowen stuck to her story—Bo and I had played slice-and-dice with Creed—long after it got out that the body found belonged to Bob Haines. She gathered a great following at first, and I decided people love to believe evil shit about other people. The new police chief, Chief Rye, addressed the student body, along with Mr. Ames, and they tried to counter Renee's story with their feeling that Chris had run away, because a body would have shown up, especially if two novice-killer teenagers had been the culprits. A lot of people dropped it at that point, at least dropped me from their suspect list, though it was harder to drop Bo.

He reveled in it, but not me. I stayed home, stayed out of harm's way until it was time to leave for Rothborne. I suppose I looked guiltier by having left. But screw 'em all, I figured. All I had wanted to do was help a few hurting people—Bo, Ali, and Creed himself. I didn't figure for my next trick that I'd lay myself wide open for the grand trophy of small-town scrutiny and humiliation, compliments of Renee Bowen.

She added to the mess by saying that her dad split from her mom because too many people were lying about him and he couldn't take the strain. Jesus and Mary.

I've stayed awake wondering what people think when they spit out some enormous lie, like, do they even stop to think, *Why am I saying this?* or do they just grab on to it like one of those folding deck chairs that floated off the *Titanic*? Is it a choice or a panic reaction to deep-brain freeze? Those types of questions have probably kept me awake at night—probably more often than questions about ghosts and psychics.

Which isn't to say I haven't done my pondering about all of that—ghosts, psychics, whatever is out there. Some people like to state their opinions as fact. I'm sort of the opposite. I'm afraid of believing some lie for the sake of convenience.

It would be very convenient for me to say that after what happened, I absolutely do believe in ghosts. On the one hand it makes sense that I saw one. There actually was a body in the Indian tomb that didn't belong there, and I had no way of knowing that. I was on my way home to spill my guts to my mom and would probably never have gone in there had I not seen what I saw. Or what I *thought* I saw.

There are a couple things that make me feel otherwise. A lot of mystery always surrounded the burial ground where the pine trees never grew. That fact was written off to the legend that Indian ghosts killed off the trees as a statement about the place being sacred. After I unearthed the grave and the Stockton professors came running, they discovered the cavity was in an enormous limestone slab that lies only about five feet under the earth there. Stockton proclaimed that no pine tree could take root there because when the roots got deep enough to hit the slab, they would die from self-strangulation.

Limestone. Not ghosts.

With that part of it solved, I had to take another look at what happened to me. Mysterious as it seemed, a possible ghost gets some of the life sucked out of it when its brother mystery proves to be nothing more than five feet of legend covering science. And this is the tough part. Believing I saw a ghost would be a lot more convenient than believing I might have the type of mind that could hallucinate under extreme provocation. I think that's where most people would fall off. I haven't yet. It's tough, but I'm generally not swearing to any ghosts—not unless I'm in an emotional mood.

Then, there's the psychic who told me I would find the body, and what do I believe about psychics? The fact that the psychic nailed certain things but screwed up whose body it was seems to work more against her than for her. That's a pretty major part to screw up.

However, Dr. Fahdi pointed out, for the sake of diplomacy, that the psychic never actually said she saw Creed.

One thing I remember about her speech was an implication that the dead want to be seen now, and that seems like another miss. There is no possible reason why Bob Haines would want to be seen. The fact that he crawled into a grave to kill himself indicates that that's where he wanted to stay. After the discovery my mom tried to contact Digger Haines to tell him. His former law office told my mother he had died in Detroit, a victim of a drive-by shooting—one of his former clients who had gotten a bad verdict. It was something else I didn't need to hear, another gory death, and it meant that finding Bob Haines wouldn't even mean anything to Digger. Maybe it did something good for the Lenapes, who some ghost-lovers might say did not share Bob's feelings about additions to their graves being welcome. But that gets back into whether I believe in ghosts killing off pine trees and all that stuff. I don't take truth from circular arguments, and I have no opinion about psychics.

I have wished I could have talked to Digger Haines, at least once. I would have liked to ask him what he had hoped to find when he left Steepleton. I'm sure it was some sort of search for truth, based on my mother's comments about him. I wondered if he found it stifling to live in a place where people didn't really care what a truth was.

Here's the mother of all lies.

After the autopsy, Mrs. Creed got back on her soapbox about Chris being dead in the woods somewhere. A few days later, Justin Creed paid a visit to the principal of his middle school. The principal picked up the phone and dialed the new chief of police before Justin even had a chance to spew the whole thing. Justin told them that the night before Chris disappeared, Chris and his mom had had an argument. It was over his privileges, or the lack of any. Mrs. Creed was saying *she* would decide what privileges her children had, and that was the end of the story.

Justin swore that he heard Chris threatening to send a derogatory e-mail about her to Mr. Ames the following day. Mrs. Creed solved that by removing all the cables to Chris's computer system. While she was disassembling, Chris read calmly over her shoulder the letter he planned to send. Justin said from what he heard, it sounded exactly like the e-mail that Mr. Ames had received from Chris, the one sent from the library.

Mrs. Creed had blown a lot of shit around—that Chris could not have written that letter—and yet, there's the truth: Chris read the thing to her before he ever disappeared, and before the cops ever got it and showed it to her.

The horror is that *I* was in mental health, and Mrs. Creed was still cooking dinners, chauffeuring kids to and from school, and making speeches in church. I've come to think that she wasn't going to any great effort to cover up the letter when she gave her little "Why Would My Son Run Away?" spiel that Sunday. Maybe as far as she was concerned, she had never heard the letter. It didn't exist.

There is justice in an insanely cruel world. Despite the twos and threes I started getting after that night I discovered Bob Haines, I got one surefire ace. My fourth week in mental health, lyrics started passing through my head. First it happened in small breezes, then in waves, and tunes would roll right in underneath them. I'd spent years agonizing to make up even dumb songs, and all of a sudden, all I had to do was pick up a pen and kick back. Some were morbid:

> *Two torn aces on a stone,*
> *Two torn aces burn to stone,*
> *Two young men at the mill wheel grinding,*
> *One left standing and the other went flying,*
> *Gone, gone, gone, in the morning.*

So I'm not Eric Clapton, but it's a step up from "A Song to the Blues."

Some lyrics got insanely hopeful:

On a mountain, somewhere over there,
Broken bones grow straight like arrows.
Broken hearts unfold to care.
I am strong. I'm an answer to a prayer.
I am hope. I'm a fountain.
I am someone. I am someone, over there.

Considering I didn't drop any acid to get my lyrics, I'm okay with them. I'm very grateful, and I feel like I owe something to Creed. Yet I don't play my songs for anybody. They're private. And I can't find Creed to give him a tape. Nobody in Steepleton has ever found so much as a hair from his head.

It gets me with almost a crushing sadness sometimes, because to me, he has become a hero and a legend. He was an innocent kid, a victim, and I still have the same feeling I had when I first saw my name in his note. Like I could have shared some part of myself with him—whatever part he was thinking of when he saw fit to put my name in his e-mail. So I feel like there's a part of me rotting on the vine sometimes, no matter how many songs I write and what other things I do.

I did get obsessed for a while with finding things to do. I was watching TV one night when I was still in the psychiatric hospital. I saw a documentary on these guys in Belfast who refused to cut their hair until some IRA guy got released from prison, and there were IRA sympathizers walking around all over Belfast with hair to their asses. I liked that story and decided I would not cut my hair until someone turned up information on Creed. By the start of senior year, I had a ponytail about six inches long, and fortunately they don't care much about hair length at Rothborne. I never told anyone in Steepleton why I was doing it, except Ali, because I was afraid some Renee Bowen sympathizer would accuse me of trying to prove my innocence.

My dad promised me a Dodge Durango for graduation if I did cut it. I refused on that count, too, but eventually decided that hair was a nonfunctional protest and I could probably find other ways to help my own cause.

The functional thing, which I've kept up until this day, is trying to find Creed through the Internet. I got the idea last summer, the last time I saw Dr. Fahdi. He mentioned Chris's love of the Internet.

"His very last words to the town were via e-mail. You should try to find him and send him your story," Dr. Fahdi suggested.

Dr. Fahdi had known me for a number of months at that point, and he knew I had not been part of any murder. And he also agreed with my stance that Creed was probably alive. I had returned to the same conclusion I had reached that night I stood on top of the three stones, before the one fell over on me. I had walked in Creed's shoes that night. The week previously, I had walked in little Greg's shoes, I had walked in Lyle Corsica's shoes, Ali's shoes. I still feel like I can walk in other people's shoes, and as for Creed, I decided that maybe he had "died" in the figurative sense. Maybe the psychic was right when she related him to death in the woods. Maybe I found death when I found that stupid treasure map, which stood as some sort of symbolic memorial to him. Maybe just after he sent his good-bye e-mail to Mr. Ames, he visited the woods, and there made the decision that Chris Creed—or at least those parts of himself that he wrote that he hated—would die.

The e-mail he sent said, *I wish that I was born somebody else.* I am convinced he actually left Steepleton, and his intention was to become somebody else. Not just anybody else, but a person with the traits he admired in each of the people he mentioned in his note. I don't know what all those traits are, but I know who those people are. And since I feel like I connected so well with Creed that night on the rocks, I'm banking on my own intuition.

I found a web site that you can join for a monthly fee, and it will look up any name you submit and send you the e-mail addresses that correspond with that name. I've looked up Torey Arrington. I tried Alex Healy. I tried Mike Adams. There were ten names in Creed's e-mail, and there's a hundred ways to mix them up before you start spelling them funky and stuff like that. It's like pulling needles out of a haystack. But I still send out one or two copies of this story a week. I'll pull some name combination like that out of my hat, check that name-search web site, and send the story to any e-mail address that corresponds with the name I dug up.

I have gotten a lot of replies. None of the signees ever claims to be Creed or to know Creed. It amazes me that some people actually read through the whole thing. I keep up my hope, though some weeks it feels like a habit.

I do get my up weeks. Then, if I'm not convinced I'll ever find him, I am convinced that the search is fun. During those weeks I'll even post some awards to my web site, which I call "In Search of Christopher Creed." I even scanned in his picture from the freshman high school yearbook, with mine alongside it.

Here are some of my awards:

1.—Most Flattering Reply to My Story about Chris Creed
Dear Torey,

Your writing is very sensuous and tenderly glazed with the passion of ocean breezes. If I had a candle and you, I would dance naked to "Titanic" while you read passages of this poetic journey from sweet youth to robust manhood. Open your sweet arms to me, my poet.

Love,
Torey J. Healy
(J. stands for Jane)

2.—Most Insulting Reply to My Story about Chris Creed

Dear Mr. Adams,

I am not the person for whom you are searching. You are not a man yet, though you may think you are by virtue of the fact that you actually wrote down a couple hundred pages of magnificent twaddle. The fact you failed to capture was the pain of the Creed mother and father, but being that you're just a boy, you could not understand the agony of parents who lose a child. Parents are not perfect, and perhaps when you mature, you will rewrite your piece to the effect that you understand the Creed family's grief. I, too, came from a poor background. I, too, was in the military. The military provided the first secure situation in my life. I, too, raise my children with structure and discipline and the spirit of the military. My children are very well adjusted and don't wear long hair, unlike you.

Signed,
Alex Healy

3.—Reply Most Likely to Be from Chris Creed in Disguise

Dear Torey:

While your story fairs somewhat intriguing, you have split over two hundred verbs from their modifiers and started as many sentences with a preposition. Use your spell-checker and/or stick to songwriting.

Michael Alex Adams

4.—Reply That Makes Me Believe Totally That Creed Is Alive

Dear Torey:

I must say you have not only chronicled a very honest account of an extremely painful issue but you have painted the details in such a way that I could not resist scrolling down, and I was utterly swept into the circumstances. I wish I could say I am the person for whom you search. But I can say that I, while not being a writer, am a great lover of mysteries. Also, I am studying to be a psychotherapist, and with this combination of analytical learning and love of the genre, I will take the liberty of making comment and perhaps helping you out on your search.

Your idea about Christopher Creed lying to himself about his life as a means to survive was very insightful. While seemingly very bizarre behavior, it actually prevents a child from having to cope with hopeless situations until such a time when he is old enough, or wise enough, to cope. Perhaps as your story makes its way around the world of the Internet, other youths will be touched by Chris. And when they cross paths with the child in school who seems different, who seems obnoxious and intolerable, perhaps they will remember Chris Creed and they will find their tolerance, their compassion.

You mentioned, but did not circle back to, your thought when you stood for the first time outside the school corridor with Ali McDermott, and the two of you were discussing Chris Creed. You said, "You're making it sound like it's more dangerous to have a slightly weird family than a totally weird family." Let me close upon that thought for you.

While radically negative families can, obviously, cause more overt trauma, a "slightly weird" family can have more lasting effects over a lifetime, effects that are harder to untangle because of their subtleties. A mother who beats her children can cause damage, but a mother who waltzes into her son's room while he's changing or chronically roots through his clothing can cause just as much damage. The difference is that it's much harder to prove this to the patient.

Enough said for psychology. I want to comment now on two points you failed to notice about your own story that may, eventually, lead you to Creed. I see very obviously that he is alive. You walk in people's shoes fairly well, Mr. Adams, but you're not as insightful with clues.

First, you never gave any credence to the treasure map found in the burial ground. Alex was very focused on Chris's choice of words, such as "I would venture to say" and "suffice it to say," and with Chris's seemingly inappropriate preservation of the map via lamination. Perhaps, had it not blown away from you so mysteriously (I don't even want to touch on your supernatural elements, for I'm not sure I believe), you would have had the visual aid to remind you later that the map is crucial.

Chris told Alex he had buried treasure there. The main thrust of his mother becoming convinced he hadn't run off was that none of the money in his bank account had been touched. Perhaps there was a treasure, perhaps it was replaced by the map from its many-year hiding place, and perhaps that treasure funded Chris's trip to places unknown. Perhaps it was nothing more than a hundred-dollar bill or some lost billfold.

But now, where did he go?

He was a sheltered boy and not capable of much on his own. You failed to notice the importance of Ali's statement to you concerning Mrs. Creed's family. The two of you were spying from her bedroom, and Ali said to you, "Mrs. Creed's two sisters hate her so much, they haven't spoken in years. If he turns up dead, she'll probably call them, but not before." Perhaps, if these women understood their sister's insanity so well, they would have sympathized with the boy. Perhaps he contacted them in another state, perhaps via the Internet. Perhaps their sympathy led them to agree to hide him, finish raising him. The fact that they were all once "boons" means his life would have been harder with them in some ways. But because of the strain under which he appeared to exist, I would say he probably would have found a life with them very accommodating.

However, I don't really think that tidbit will help you locate him tomorrow.

I would venture to say that the relatives are sworn to secrecy. You can hunt them down if you wish, but my feeling is that they will not talk until the young man gives the word. And psychologically speaking once again, I don't think that time is yet.

I would venture to say that Chris Creed does not want to be exposed, for fear of his parents.

I would venture to say that you should not bother him with urgings to come forth until he is, quite possibly, twenty-five.

I would venture to say that, while your earnest desire to uncover him is admirable, he wishes to remain undiscovered for the time being. Thank you for sharing your story.

And thank you for sharing your name . . .

Yours most truly,
Victor Adams

Reader Chat Page

1. When Torey hears that the Creeds believe their son Chris was "grounded" and "normal," he is amazed at how clueless these parents are about the way their kid really was. Do you think your parents know the real you? How might they describe your personality to others? How is it different from the way your friends might describe you?

2. This story explores the repercussions that one person or event can have on an entire community. Can you think of an example of this—either positive or negative—in your community, or in the news?

3. Chris Creed's disappearance brings up lots of questions for Torey, like these: "If Creed had written that note, we would have had to point the finger at ourselves, or at least take a good long look at our ways and agonize over questions. Like, could we have played it out differently? Could we have been nicer? Do we have a heartless streak, and can we be bastards?" What are your feelings on these issues? Have you ever wondered how the manner in which you treat people affects them? Do you think even good people are capable of being "heartless" at times?

4. This story demonstrates the sometimes devastating impact of rumors and gossip. Cite some examples of this in the story. Have you ever been affected by gossip?

5. Ali says, "People are blind . . . All they see is a person's reputation." This is certainly true of Bo, along with other characters in the story. What kinds of assumptions does Torey have about Bo before he gets to know him? What surprises him about the "real" Bo? What qualities does Bo possess that Torey admires?

6. If you had been in Torey's place, would you have let Bo take the blame for the phone call from the baseball field? Why or why not?

7. When the police come to school to take Bo away, Torey is stunned. He muses, "I was scared that these allegedly respectable people let this thing get so bad. I guess I thought seeing a situation clearly was just part of being a grown-up." How do the grown-ups in this story fail to see things clearly, in Torey's opinion? Was there ever a moment in your life when you realized that adults are capable of making mistakes, too? How did that make you feel?

8. How does Mrs. Creed's upbringing influence her opinion of Bo and her treatment of Chris? How might she have been different if she had not been raised a "boon"?

9. What do you think Mr. Ames wanted Mrs. Creed to understand about her son? Why did he request that Torey tell her?

10. What positive traits does Mrs. Creed believe she was passing to her son? Can you think of an example in real life of a person's best intentions hindering the progress of another person or situation?

11. Mr. Ames wonders, "Why do people have so much trouble seeing their own faults but such and easy time seeing everyone else's?" Why do you think this is so? Cite an example of someone in the story doing this.

12. Why does Torey stop associating with Leandra, Alex, Ryan, and Renee? How do they contribute to the madness surrounding Chris Creed's disappearance? Do you think Bo was right to reveal what he knew about Chief Bowen to Renee?

13. If Chris Creed is alive, what kind of changes do you think he would want to make in his life after leaving Steepleton?

Chatting with Carol Plum-Ucci

Question: How long have you been writing?
Carol Plum-Ucci: I wrote my first poem when I was eight. In fourth and fifth grades, I placed in (may have won) the city-wide essay contests. My kids are pretty jealous; I just never had any doubts about what I wanted to do, save that period most of us go through in seventh and eighth grade where we want to be either a veterinarian or a pediatrician. I went there, but bounced back after a couple months.

Q: What is your writing process? Do you work certain hours or days?
CP-U: I've been very prone to writer's block, so I write whenever I get the urge, and I stick with it until the block gets me again. I've written all of my published books that way. I do have to be somewhat scheduled, as I also teach college (English) and homeschool my daughter (she's eleven as I'm writing this). Duty is ever calling, but when you get the inspiration, nothing can really stop it. I don't worry about it anymore.

Q: Are your characters inspired by people you know?
CP-U: Lani Garver was inspired by a real friend of mine whom I call "my angel." He gave me a lot of fodder for Lani's past by telling me his past. But that's unusual, at least for me. Generally, characters are part of the author's psyche. To create characters, an author is actually paring off parts of his psyche and doling them out. Almost all my characters are like that.

Q: How do you come up with story ideas?

CP-U: Generally some issue charges me up, and that's the fodder. It's the type of issue that makes you think, "Wow, that is so unfair. Why is life like that? What can be done about it?" For example, *Streams of Babel* came from my reflections on how people of other nations can really dislike Americans. We're just people, trying to make life work well with what we're given, and it feels strange and uncomfortable to me, this being an object of disdain because of where I was born and raised. Hence, the book arose on what average, small town people would feel like if terrorists took a shot at them.

Q: What advice do you have for aspiring writers?

CP-U: My first bit of advice is to keep it fun. If an aspiring writer, still in high school, feels like he is forcing himself to do the daily discipline thing, forget about it for a while. For me personally, high school was a great input time. I barely wrote a short story. That came later, when I was older and my time was more my own.

My second bit of advice is to seek out a college major other than creative writing. Students are better off majoring in journalism or advertising or even something like psychology, where they're prepared to do 'real life' during the day and use that to fill their idea tanks. Novels get written, regardless, and you can either be fed or starving in the process.

Q: You often write about the strained relationship between teens and authority figures. Many of your stories expose the hypocrisy of parents, teachers, or the police. Do you think it is important for teens to question authority?

CP-U: I'm always surprised to hear that (though I hear it often), because extremely grounded adults are always in the forefront of my stories, and I feel great affection for them. Some great examples include Torey's parents and Principal Ames in *The Body of Christopher Creed*; Claire's father, all the doctors and medics, and all the guys in the band in *Lani Garver*; Evan's entire family, Principal Ashaad, and Edwin Church in *The She*; and Captain Lutz in *The Night My Sister Went Missing*. For some reason, the bad adults eclipse the good ones, and I'm not sure why that is, except that scandal tends to be more noticeable than stability.

I don't have personal issues with authority, though obviously, it is important for anyone of any age to question situations with which they're uncomfortable. I always tell my students, "Just because it appears in the pages of a book doesn't mean it's accurate."

Q: Many of your books feature characters who are missing, possibly dead. What do you hope readers will take away from your exploration of these ambiguous situations?
CP-U: I don't really know why I keep revisiting the theme of missing people. I have Chris Creed, of course, and Lani Garver, and Casey Carmody in *The Night My Sister Went Missing*. It could be something as simple as that I have a peaceful nature and just don't have what it would take to create a serial killer for intrigue. It could also have something to do with my fixation on spirituality. Missing people tend to take on a divine status. They become mythical and may personify my journey through the mysteries of life and death.

Q: The ocean is often a key element in your stories. What does the sea represent to you, and what draws you to write about it?
CP-U: When I first became a writer and it became obvious that I would have to do some public speaking, I started to

examine my normal life for interesting fodder and realized how extraordinary certain aspects were. For one, I was raised in a funeral home. I spent half of my nights awake, waiting for corpses to come up the stairs. As well, I was raised on a barrier island. The islands speak to me, as do the Pine Barrens, where *Creed* took place. I realized I didn't need to go anywhere to have the perfect settings. I'm drawn back to them again and again, and in fact, I've broken writer's block by moving the settings of novels out of some other place, like the mountains, and down to the shore, where I can smell the sea and taste the salt in the air. Good settings work like characters, and I know mine very well.

Q: Many of your stories feature characters who are trying desperately to get a grip on reality—but are unsure what *is* reality. Do you think this is something that teens struggle with?

CP-U: I use words in my stories like "convenient reality" and "his own version of reality," and heroes accuse antagonists of "picking their truths like melons at Superfresh." Much of this is lower language expressing my higher convictions about the supernatural.

What is truth? is a question most people struggle with, especially today, when it is considered very uncool to say something is ultimately true, unless it's that nothing is ultimately true. If you're one of these people who truly believes something is ultimately true—I'm talking here about spirituality and the nature of God—you'll experience some tension. Most people still believe in an intelligent God; most people still believe in God's willingness to reveal his nature to man. However, once a person claims to have been a recipient, he's crossed a line that most will find intolerable, unless it's to do with concepts very trendy, very vague, or very convenient. We believe universally what we can't endure personally, and it gets us stuck in neutral.

I'm mentioning this because I think many teens feel the tension surrounding the pursuit of higher belief today. But art has always been the great peacemaker, the great means for us all to say all that we desire, and I've enjoyed watching rich symbolism, bearing out my favorite truths, appearing endlessly in my stories.

Q: In *The Body of Christopher Creed,* many characters reputations belie their true selves. Do you think it is important to second-guess our perceptions and judgments of others? What do you think we learn from stepping outside of our comfort zones and rejecting assumptions?

CP-U: This gets back to one of my favorite themes: *Nothing is as it appears to be.* It's a good philosophy to hold to, I think, because it prevents people from passing judgment too quickly. I have a saying a girlfriend sent to me in an email that I posted by my terminal for a while: "Remember that everyone is fighting different battles." Hence, when somebody is mean or hurts my feelings or forgets to return my call when I really need them, I try to remember that they could have problems like Bo's or Ali's. It's more to do with them than with me. It helps.

A fun moment for me in *Creed* was writing about Torey bringing his guitar to school one time. Bo Richardson had been standing around and admiring Torey's spontaneous concert and asked if he could play the guitar sometime. Torey responded something like, "Do you know how to not drop it?" And Bo replied, "Do you know how not to be an asshole?"

It was one of those moments where Torey went from taking a remark at face value to understanding some of the anxiety that inspired it, and it was a turning point. I think Torey became less apt that day to blindly throw out remarks that could sound condescending and proud.

We are not soothsayers. We can't often know what battles people are fighting, but we can all assume that everyone is fighting them. So, let's turn the other cheek, not because it shows some sort of remarkable charity, but because it shows that we're seeing life how it really is. And mercy tends to come back to us when we need it the most.

Q: The mystery in your stories is often deepened by a touch of the supernatural. What draws you to write about the unknown?
CP-U: I think I'm drawn to answering the big questions: What are we doing here, and what does it all mean? Certainly, the things we can see, smell, touch, taste, and hear leave clues to the meaning of life, but they are far from sufficient to answer these big questions. I'm kind of obsessed with the afterlife, which started in the funeral home when I was about eleven years old. One job of mine was to sweep up flower petals dropped by the flower shops delivering funeral arrangements before a viewing. I had to do this before the family came in, and it was a dreaded job. (Never turn your back on a corpse. Why not? I don't know. Just don't.)

One time I had one eye on the petals, one eye on the gentleman in the casket, and I realized that, for the first time, I was seeing someone whom I had known when he was alive. It took me a minute to recognize him, because people do look different when they're dead. My dad was a master craftsman at making death look dignified, but you can't put that spark of life back, no matter how good you are. So, I stood there and stared, remembering this man, the many things I had seen him doing.

Some people think that a dead body is horrifying because it could jump up. At that moment, I was seeing a different facet. Death was horrifying because the person *wasn't* going to move, not this day, not next week, not in this body. That got me thinking of what happens after death, and I have spent a lifetime with that in the back of my mind, my thoughts, my motivations. I guess that's logical. Whatever happens when we die, eternity is a lot longer than this life, so let's find out how we're supposed to play this one out. If this world, cranky and stubborn as it can be, is supposed to be approached like an investment, let's invest. If it's supposed to be joyful, let's find our joy.

Life is a journey, and I may not have always lived up to my ability, but I have always lived purposefully, and I guess readers get caught up with me, raising the questions, looking for the answers, looking to be a little more understanding, a little less judgmental, a little more merciful. I hope so.